"Well, now that you've found me, what do you want?"

"To find out how you are," he said, "and what made you leave."

"I'm fine. And I left because I wanted to."

If Shahna hadn't known him so well, she might have missed the flexing of a muscle in his cheek as he clenched his teeth. Kier had a formidable temper that he usually kept rigidly in check. "That's no answer," he rasped. "Why don't you tell me the truth?"

The truth? Where would she start? "The truth is," she said, "I'd had enough—of everything. Sydney, the rat race." *Of living life on the surface, of a relationship that wasn't going anywhere, of hiding my real feelings because you didn't want to know about them, of being afraid that you'd find out and cut me from your life as ruthlessly as you had every other woman who shared it for a brief time.* "I needed… wanted something different."

Dear Reader,

It's August, and our books are as hot as the weather, so if it's romantic excitement you crave, look no further. Merline Lovelace is back with the newest CODE NAME: DANGER title, *Texas Hero*. Reunion romances are always compelling, because emotions run high. Add the spice of danger and you've got the perfection of the relationship between Omega agent Jack Carstairs and heroine-in-danger Ellie Alazar.

ROMANCING THE CROWN continues with Carla Cassidy's *Secrets of a Pregnant Princess*, a marriage-of-convenience story featuring Tamiri princess Samira Kamal and her mysterious bodyguard bridegroom. Marie Ferrarella brings us another of THE BACHELORS OF BLAIR MEMORIAL in *M.D. Most Wanted*, giving the phrase "doctor-patient confidentiality" a whole new meaning. Award-winning New Zealander Frances Housden makes her second appearance in the line with *Love Under Fire*, and her fellow Kiwi Laurey Bright checks in with *Shadowing Shahna*. Finally, wrap up the month with Jenna Mills and her latest, *When Night Falls*.

Next month, return to Intimate Moments for more fabulous reading—including the newest from bestselling author Sharon Sala, *The Way to Yesterday*. Until then…enjoy!

Yours,

[signature: Leslie Wainger]

Leslie J. Wainger
Executive Senior Editor

Please address questions and book requests to:
Silhouette Reader Service
U.S.: 3010 Walden Ave., P.O. Box 1325, Buffalo, NY 14269
Canadian: P.O. Box 609, Fort Erie, Ont. L2A 5X3

Shadowing
Shahna
LAUREY BRIGHT

INTIMATE MOMENTS™

Published by Silhouette Books

America's Publisher of Contemporary Romance

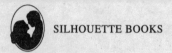

SILHOUETTE BOOKS

ISBN 0-373-27239-1

SHADOWING SHAHNA

Copyright © 2002 by Daphne Clair de Jong

This edition published by arrangement with Harlequin Books S.A.

Visit Silhouette at www.eHarlequin.com

Printed in U.S.A.

Books by Laurey Bright

Silhouette Intimate Moments

Summers Past #470
A Perfect Marriage #621
Shadowing Shahna #1169

Silhouette Special Edition

Deep Waters #62
When Morning Comes #143
Fetters of the Past #213
A Sudden Sunlight #516
Games of Chance #564
A Guilty Passion #586
The Older Man #761
The Kindness of Strangers #820
An Interrupted Marriage #916

Silhouette Romance

Tears of Morning #107
Sweet Vengeance #125
Long Way from Home #356
The Rainbow Way #525
Jacinth #568
The Mother of His Child #918
Marrying Marcus #1558
The Heiress Bride #1578
Life with Riley #1617

LAUREY BRIGHT

has held a number of different jobs but has never wanted to be anything but a writer. She lives in New Zealand, where she creates the stories of contemporary people in love that have won her a following all over the world. Visit her at her Web site, http://www.laureybright.com.

Chapter 1

He came out of the mist.

Morning cloud lay softly in the hollows of the blue hills embracing the Hokianga Harbour, and drifted across its glassy waters.

Shahna Reeves, about to enter her cottage, paused at the steady put-putter of an engine. A small basket of fresh, warm brown eggs held between her hands, she watched the white hull of a motor launch emerge from the curling wisps of vapor.

The boat turned and slowed until it was nudged expertly alongside the weathered and worn jetty. There were two men aboard—the boat's chunky, brown-skinned owner-driver, Timoti Huria, and...

Already on her way down the grassy slope, Shahna abruptly paused, her heart jumping erratically, her breath snagged in her throat.

The taller man leaped onto the jetty and took a backpack from Timoti's big hands. A gray T-shirt stretched across taut muscles as he swung the pack to the worn, uneven boards, and designer jeans molded a trim male behind and long legs.

Timoti called to Shahna, "Brought you a visitor, Shahna. Okay?"

The newcomer, hoisting the pack onto one shoulder, turned and lifted his dark head, fixing her with a challenging ocean-blue stare.

Shahna swallowed. It wasn't okay. Far from it. But if Kier Remington had come this far to find her he wasn't going to go away just on her say-so. And she didn't want to involve Timoti in a physical confrontation. Jerkily she nodded, then found her voice. "It's okay. Thanks, Timoti."

Satisfied, he revved the engine, and the launch backed and proceeded along the harbor, stirring a white-edged trail in the water.

His passenger started up the hill, coming to a halt in front of Shahna, their eyes level because the sloping ground negated the six inches' difference in their height.

He subjected her to a leisurely inspection, from the dark brown hair curling gently about her ears, the loose T-shirt and unfashionable denim cutoffs, and down lightly tanned bare legs to the disreputable sneakers that she had thrust on her feet to go feed the hens.

Traveling upward again, his scrutiny halted on the basket of eggs.

A slight, disbelieving smile curved the explicitly masculine mouth. Shahna remembered how that mouth had felt on hers, firm and sure, warm and hungry. Shockingly she remembered too her own hunger for him, for his kiss, his touch, his arms around her, his male scent in her nostrils, his skin sliding against hers, hot and slick and exciting.

A familiar, long-denied longing assailed her body and made her legs weak. "What are you doing here?" she demanded.

The last thing she had expected was that Kier would come looking for her. Dismay warred with exhilaration at the thought that he might have cared enough to do that.

He lifted his eyes to hers. "More to the point, what are *you* doing here?"

His gaze went beyond her to the cottage. Despite the white paint she'd lavished on the worn boards, the fresh green trim on the windowsills, and the new corrugated iron roof, she knew the sagging front steps and big up-and-down windows betrayed its colonial-era beginnings.

Shahna said, "The Hokianga is one of the most beautiful places in the world." Dodging the real question.

He half turned to survey the harbor that thrust deep into New Zealand's North Island, its myriad inlets and tributaries snaking through bush and farmland.

The sun was slowly bringing it to life, glinting on lazy ripples chasing each other across the surface as the mist melted away and crept up the hillsides, lingering on the bush-covered curves.

"It's very pretty," he agreed politely, and turned his attention to the immediate environs.

Around the cottage the grass was kept short by sheep that had fled at the sound of the approaching boat. A stand of dark-leaved trees, relieved by nikau palms and lacy tree-ferns, protectively embraced the small clearing.

His deep-blue gaze came back to her, and a lean, strong hand reached out to touch a tiny curled feather adhering to one of the eggs. "Very earth mother."

Shahna stiffened, something uncomfortably like fear cooling her heated skin, and he said, "Are you going to invite me in?"

Panic nearly sent her running into the cottage, to slam the door behind her. Childish, and almost certainly futile.

She didn't really have a choice. "All right. Come on in."

Reluctantly Shahna led him inside.

Kier dropped the backpack on the old hinged-seat settle near the door and followed her across the polished kauri boards and colorful scatter rugs.

The kitchen, separated from the cosy main room only by cupboards beneath a waist-high wooden counter, was small and narrow. Shahna had placed the round dining table and four wooden chairs on the living room side of the counter after her landlord knocked out the partition between the rooms.

Ignoring the chairs, Kier propped himself against the wall between the two areas and resumed his study of her, his relentless gaze intensifying the jittering of her nerves.

He seemed alien here, out of his normal city environment. Even away from his own country. Shahna could almost believe she was dreaming, had conjured him from her subconscious as she too often did in sleep. Except that he was too real, too solid, too altogether male—dangerously so. There was nothing dreamlike about this.

She put the eggs down without looking at him. If she did, she might not be able to prevent herself from staring back, drinking in the sight of him, absorbed in the sheer seductive pleasure of his sudden appearance from the blue.

Trying for normality, she asked in a voice that seemed unreal, "Do you want some tea, or coffee?"

"Coffee would be good." Watching her fill an electric kettle, he remarked, "You do have electricity, then."

A wood-burner warmed the cottage in the winter and heated her water, but it was too hot for that now. "All mod cons." She gave him a straight look, deliberately tamping down her wayward emotions—the fluttery fear, the guilty excitement, the sheer wonder at his presence. "All those I need, anyway."

His eyes lit on the telephone sitting on the counter. "Your number's not listed."

"It's under the landlord's name. I lease this place from the farmer next door—it was the original homestead in the days when the main transport was by water."

"The sheep aren't yours?"

Shahna laughed. "The McKenzies run a few sheep on their farm along with dairy cattle."

She took sugar and pottery mugs from a cupboard, busying herself to keep in check a foolish desire to fling herself into his arms and seize the moment that, with a sick dread in her heart, she knew couldn't possibly last.

Glancing at him while she fixed the coffee, she saw that Kier was looking around now with assessing, perhaps disparaging eyes.

The furniture wasn't new, not because she couldn't afford it but because it would have seemed inappropriate in the mellow old building.

She'd chosen mellow colors too for walls and upholstery and the grooved decorative frames around the uncovered windows. Soft blues melded into grays and greens, with touches of old-rose and lavender and an occasional splash of deep crimson.

Colors that echoed the hazy bloom that blurred the distant hills, the ever-changing mirror of the harbor, the dark green leaves of the native trees with their paler undersides, and the starry bursts of pohutukawa flowers at Christmas.

Kier's coolly critical appraisal helped to steady her unruly emotions.

He had given her no clue that this was anything more

than a casual visit. With a bit of luck and a lot of self-control, she'd survive it with her hard-won serenity intact, her self-respect preserved and her secrets safe. "You're out early," she said, her hand on the coffee plunger. It was barely eight o'clock.

Kier returned his gaze to her. "Timoti had to catch the tide. He was going to pick up his wife's sister and I caught a ride."

"Have you had breakfast?"

"Timoti's wife gave me bacon, sausages and eggs." The couple ran a bed-and-breakfast in the waterside village of Rawene and took tourists on fishing or sight-seeing trips. "What about you?" he queried.

"I'm okay." She put a plate of coconut cookies on the table, poured the coffee and sat down. "Help yourself."

She lifted her mug, using both hands because they were shaking a little and she was afraid of spilling her coffee. The bitter liquid scorched her tongue.

Questions raced through her mind but caution urged her not to ask them.

Kier looked around again at the old kauri dresser holding plates and cups, the pots of herbs on the kitchen windowsill, the sparse furniture. "Doesn't seem like you, Shahna."

Shahna shrugged, a good stab at seeming indifference. "Maybe you didn't know me as well as you thought."

His voice turned brusque. "What does that mean?"

She lifted her head from her contemplation of the coffee in her mug, making her eyes blank, her face expressionless. "Just what I said." He had never known how deeply she had allowed her emotions to become engaged in their relationship. Thank heaven.

He had never cared enough to find out, she reminded

herself acridly. But, to be fair, she had guarded her secret well.

Kier kept looking at her, as though expecting more. But she certainly wasn't going to divulge to him here what she had kept hidden for so long and at such cost. Even if he'd had an unlikely change of heart, too much lay between them now. There was no going back.

When she didn't offer anything further he said, ''After three years, I'd have said you owed me more than three lines of farewell.''

Shahna's hands tightened about the warmed curve of the mug. ''I don't *owe* you anything, Kier. That was part of our…arrangement. No strings, remember? The way you wanted it.''

A faint flicker of straight black lashes was the only sign that she'd disconcerted him. ''What you wanted too, as I recall.''

Oh, she'd fooled herself for a short while that it was enough. She'd gone into their relationship with her eyes wide open, knowing the terms, and agreed to everything, imagining she was getting the best of all worlds. Good worlds. Plenty of people would have said she was mad to give that up. Sometimes she thought so herself. Although in the end the choice had been out of her hands. ''That isn't what I want anymore,'' she said.

''And this is?'' Kier's unsparing glance swept again around the confined space. He shook his head. ''I don't believe it,'' he said flatly.

She hadn't cluttered the small rooms with furniture and decorations but she thought the cottage looked fine. ''How did you find me?'' she asked, deflecting him.

''I saw some of your jewelry at the airport when I flew into Auckland for a business meeting, and…when that was over I had some time to spare.'' His face, his voice, were studied, and lowered lids almost hid his eyes as he ran a thumb over the rim of his cup.

So it had been a fluke, a casual happenstance followed up on a whim.

Kier hadn't been searching for her all this time. A small, futile spark of wild hope died, leaving the taste of ashes in her mouth.

"They surely didn't give you my address?" The airport's high-priced souvenir shops were a logical target market for her handmade jewelry, ticketed with her name and logo. She hadn't thought of Kier flying in from Sydney someday and seeing it for sale.

"It wasn't as easy as that. But it gave me a starting point."

Whatever had led him to do it—curiosity? a sense of unfinished business?—he wouldn't have given up once he'd decided to explore the chance discovery. Determination and acuity, plus an instinct for sound investment, had brought Kier Remington success, respect, wealth. And a lot more besides. "Well, now you've found me," Shahna said. "What do you want?"

"To find out how you are," he said, "and what made you leave."

"I'm fine. And I left because I wanted to."

If she hadn't known him so well she might have missed the flexing of a muscle in his cheek as he clenched his teeth. Kier had a formidable temper that he usually kept rigidly in check. "That's no answer," he rasped. "Why don't you tell me the truth?"

The truth? Where would she start? "The truth is," she said, "I'd had enough, of everything. Sydney, the rat race." *Of living life on the surface, of a relationship that wasn't going anywhere, of hiding my feelings because you didn't want to know about them, of being afraid that you'd*

*find out and end it, cut me from your life as ruthlessly as
you had every other woman who shared it for a brief time.*
''I needed...wanted something different.'' She wouldn't
go into detail about how the realization had been forced
upon her.

''You've certainly got that.''

She had, by removing herself not only from Kier's by-
ronic spell, but from the world of corporate images and
office politics, and a social life that involved too many
overcrowded occasions where the wine flowed freely and
the object was not so much enjoyment as the all-important
exercise of *networking,* everyone with an eye to the next
useful contact.

Creating nature-inspired jewelry in a rural backwater
was about as far from that world as one could get.

''How long,'' Kier asked, ''will it last?''

His cynicism raised the fine hairs on her arms in hostile
reaction. ''As long as I want it to,'' she answered, deliberately calm. ''I love this place.''

His eyes lingered a moment on a wall-hanging she'd
made just for fun, driftwood and shells knotted into faded
green twine hung from a discarded, moss-covered fence-
post. ''You live here alone?''

Shahna's heart gave a brief lurch. Timoti and Meri
hadn't told him...?

Silently she blessed their discretion. The locals were
protective of one another's privacy. They wouldn't have
volunteered any information he hadn't specifically asked
for. ''You mean, do I share it with a man?'' Of course
that was what he meant. ''I don't need to.''

''Taking the feminist high ground? The sisters would
be proud of you,'' he commented. ''You never did need
a man, did you, Shahna? You only let me share your bed
on occasion because it was convenient.''

Her fingers closed hard around her cup as she curbed the temptation to throw it. How dare he accuse her, in that stinging tone? When he'd made it plain from the start just how he viewed their relationship.

To be fair, at that stage she had been relieved that he didn't want to delve into her inner self, seeming content with the outer shell that was all she exposed to the world, especially to the male half of it. It was only later that she'd become greedy—needy. A dangerous state to be in, inviting heartbreak.

"Calling the kettle black?" she taunted, allowing her anger a brief release. "You didn't need me, either. Any personable woman would have…fulfilled your needs quite adequately."

His hand was lying on the table by his cup. She saw it curl into a fist, then relax before he answered her. "You underrate yourself," he drawled. "You were much better than adequate."

To her chagrin, Shahna's cheeks burned. "Thank you," she said, her voice brittle.

Perhaps he had actually missed her for a time. Missed the passion she'd given him, the delight he'd found in her body. As she had fiercely, dismayingly, missed his love-making—sometimes tender, sometimes playful, more often colored by the same driving intensity he gave to his work and to his other recreational pursuits—tennis, squash, rock climbing.

Kier had never been a team player. Even in bed his competitive spirit had surfaced, along with his desire for perfection. He had always seen to her needs before his own, and if he thought he'd failed to satisfy her completely he would make sure of it before he left her bed, or sleep overtook them both. When she took the initiative and gifted him with pleasure he would reciprocate with interest, guiding her to greater heights of physical sensation than she'd ever believed possible and leaving her sated, exhausted into a dreamy, euphoric lethargy.

Memories set her skin on fire. Hastily she lifted her cup and buried her nose in it.

She wondered whose bed Kier shared now, and suppressed a pang of jealousy. It was none of her business. And jealousy wasn't appropriate. It never had been. They had agreed to be faithful to each other for as long their affair lasted, but she had ended it and Kier was now free to sleep with whomever he wished.

So was she, of course. And had been since she'd left him a brief note along with the key he'd given her to his Sydney apartment, and hours later boarded a flight to New Zealand.

Even if the opportunity arose again she couldn't imagine wanting another man for a long, long time, no matter what logic told her about the normal physiology of a healthy twenty-eight-year-old woman.

Kier had carved a place in her heart despite never wanting or intending to. She had to face the fact that she'd made no such lasting mark on his. "I'm sure there was no shortage of candidates to take my place," she said, putting down the mug.

Kier's eyelids flickered, then shuttered his eyes so that she couldn't read his emotions. "I'm choosy," he told her shortly.

And cautious. After they'd met it was weeks before he asked Shahna out, months before their first night together in her apartment.

Kier Remington, self-made millionaire, head of his own private company and key player in Australia's business and financial world, was known for quick decision-making, his keen brain working lightning-fast to weigh

the possible consequences of a potential move. But he was
equally capable of a ruthless patience. Less alert companies had been caught napping by a takeover bid from
Remington Finance and Industries, the groundwork having been laid months before.

In his private life, Shahna had discovered, he was
equally astute and equally focused. They had been sleeping together for almost a year before he told her he had
decided at their first meeting that he was going to make
her his lover. He'd taken the time to get to know her
because he wasn't interested in a short-term affair and had
soon deduced that she wasn't, either.

But he had also ensured that she knew he wasn't offering permanence. The only promise he was willing to
give, or that he wanted from her, was that as long as they
were lovers there would be no one else. When either of
them wanted out they would say so without fear of re-
crimination.

She couldn't help a bitter surprise now at the subtle
signs that he'd been annoyed when three years later she
took him at his word and walked away.

Maybe it was because the decision had been hers. He
had never taken kindly to having control removed from
his own hands.

Shahna had been forced to take that action, but he could
have no notion of how she had agonized over it before,
after and since. And what unexpected complications had
followed, although for those she could blame no one but
herself.

And the last thing she wanted was to involve him in
them, now or ever. She glanced anxiously at the clock on
the kitchen wall.

"Going somewhere?" Kier asked. The clear implication of the slight sneer in his voice was, where was there to go around here?

"I have things to do." She hoped he'd take the hint. "Timoti should be back this way with Meri's sister in about fifteen minutes. If you wait on the jetty he'll pick you up."

"Keen to get rid of me, are you?" She knew that stubborn look—the determined thrust of his jaw, the swift drawing together of his brows.

"We have nothing more to say to each other, do we?" Shahna tried to sound indifferent, growing increasingly anxious. "It was good of you to drop by, Kier, but as you see you've no need to be concerned about me."

"I have a lot more to say," he said forcefully. "And I still want to know what went so wrong that you had to hide away in another country."

"I'm not hiding away. I just wanted to come home."

"You told me you had no people in New Zealand anymore, no ties. You haven't lived here since...when? You were twenty or so?"

"Eighteen." She didn't recall ever telling him exactly, perhaps a measure of how superficial their knowledge of each other had really been. Not entirely his fault, she acknowledged. Reticence about her family had become a habit long before she met him. "It's not a matter of family ties. There are other things I missed. Things I didn't realize I was missing until..."

Kier leaned forward. "Until what?" he pressed. "Was it something I did?"

Shahna smiled thinly, mustering some kind of defense. "Everything doesn't revolve around you," she said. "I just decided I didn't like the life I was living. So I changed it."

He stared at her, patently unable to comprehend her

decision. "What was wrong with it?" he demanded. "You had a successful, interesting career, your own home, friends—and, I thought, a satisfying love life."

All true. Shahna had been earning a very good salary in a large PR and advertising firm. She had started in their art department and discovered she had a gift for both imaginative innovation and organization that led to a move sideways and then her rapid promotion through the system.

She had bought her own apartment, close to the firm's city offices and with an expensive glimpse of Sydney Harbour.

Her friends were dedicated high-flyers who worked hard and played equally hard when they got the chance, and it had been fun, stimulating—living in a heady, fast-moving world that left little time for introspection or deep reflection.

Kier Remington had been part of that world.

Her boss at the agency had called her to his office to introduce her as one of their brightest young stars, to whom he proposed handing the Remington publicity portfolio.

When she entered, Kier had stood up to shake her hand, folding his strong fingers around it, and his eyes, the fathomless, intense blue of summer seas, found hers and sent an astonishing spiral of heat down her spine.

All she'd heard about Kier Remington had led her to expect a cold, emotionless man with a ruthless streak. He hadn't got where he was at the age of twenty-nine by being softhearted.

A recent shake-up in one of his high-profile companies had made headlines. Top managers had abruptly lost their jobs among rumors that they had engaged in murky insider trading. Financial commentators were having a field day and a tight-lipped Kier Remington was shown on the TV news, brushing off reporters' questions with a curt "No comment."

It was understandable that he wanted a vibrant new PR campaign to repair the damage to his firm's reputation. Shahna knew she was up to the job and would enjoy it, but had given very little thought to actually working with Kier Remington.

She hadn't expected his smile to make her heart flutter like a schoolgirl's, so that she had to assume a brisk efficiency to hide the effect he had on her.

Nor had she expected the glint of humor mixed with sexual challenge that lit his eyes, as if he knew exactly how she was feeling and was giving her fair warning. He didn't bother to hide his attraction to her, and at the end of the meeting, with another brief handclasp he'd left her fighting a dangerous excitement that tightened her chest and made her entire body seem to consist of melting marshmallow.

As the door closed behind him she had been torn between relief and a sudden feeling of letdown.

Of course it was flattering that a man as good-looking and spectacularly successful as Kier Remington was interested in her, but she mustn't get carried away.

Bracing herself for an aggressive pursuit, she had made a decision to resist. The Remington campaign was a giant step upward in her career and she didn't want to jeopardize her future prospects by mixing sex with business. Too many people had crashed and burned trying to achieve that impossible balance.

But there had been no next-day phone call, no contact at all until she had studied the portfolio as she'd promised, and then phoned him with a list of suggestions.

He listened, then said briskly, "We need to discuss

these ideas of yours. Lunch? How are you placed tomorrow?''

So businesslike that she had no excuse to refuse.

On her arrival at the restaurant he'd skimmed her with
a look and accepted her handshake and deliberately cool
smile with knowing amusement in his eyes, making her
straighten her shoulders and tighten her hold on her
leather briefcase as she returned him a blank, frosty stare.
He'd given her a longer look then, a keenly observant
look, as if sizing her up, coming to some conclusion.

But from then on his manner had matched hers, and
she'd been impressed by his quick mind, his consideration
of another viewpoint before putting forth his own, and not
least by his willingness to accept that she knew her job.

He had made no suggestion of seeing Shahna socially,
sticking strictly to business and making her feel foolish
about the stern reminder she'd given herself to be thoroughly professional.

When she walked away from him after thanking him
for the lunch, she wondered if it was her own imagination
persuading her that she could feel his gaze as a prickling
sensation between her shoulder blades.

Oh, Kier had been clever. Clever and calculating. When
she discovered just how carefully he had played her, with
a campaign as subtle as it was dead on target, she had
been faintly chilled. But by then it was too late.

Sitting across the scrubbed wooden table from him, she
felt an echo of that chill. Once Kier made up his mind to
do something, nothing would deter him. Any setback to
his plans was merely a goad to achieve his object another
way, coming at it from some unexpected direction.

Her mug in her hand, she stood up, hoping this time
he'd take the hint. But although his own cup was empty

he kept it cradled in one hand. "So what do you do all day?" he asked.

Shahna couldn't stop herself from casting a hunted glance at the clock. "I have a studio outside." She indicated the visible corner of a small building just a few feet away. "A converted washhouse, actually where I work."

"Nine-to-five?" Kier queried. He too glanced at the clock.

"Not exactly. Whenever I...well, whatever hours I please." Shahna placed her mug in the sink. She was *not* going to offer him a refill. "If you want to catch Timoti..." she started to say in desperation.

"I told him I wasn't going back to Rawene today."

"Oh?" She looked at the backpack on the settle. "You're taking a holiday?" Not his usual kind for sure, although she remembered him telling her he'd backpacked through Asia when he was nineteen. "What are your plans?"

It was a moment before he answered. "I haven't made any definite plans." Another pause. "Except to see you, talk with you, catch up on what you've been doing. Why are you so anxious for me to leave?"

As if he'd given the cue, from the next room came a tiny whimper, another louder one, and then a series of babbling sounds and a childish call of "Mum-mum!"

Kier went very still, his body immobile and his face a study in stone. Shahna too felt momentarily paralyzed. A sickening sensation made her stomach drop, and her temples throbbed.

Then Kier spoke, hoarsely, his knuckles going white as his hold on the cup in his hand tightened. "That's a baby!"

Chapter 2

Shahna unglued her tongue from the top of her mouth. "Yes."

She could claim she was baby-sitting, fob him off somehow. But Kier, she knew, wouldn't be fobbed. And what was the point of lying? He'd find out sooner or later if he wanted to.

"Mum-mum!" More peremptory this time. She heard the rattle of the cot side as the baby hoisted himself up and clung, waiting for her to come to him.

"You'd better go," she told Kier. "I have to pick him up."

Kier rose from his chair, rocking it back so that it teetered. Automatically he steadied it and shoved it under the table, using both hands. His voice grated. "I'm not going anywhere!"

"Mum-mum..." Forlorn now, followed by a short silence and then a loud wail.

"I have to pick him up," Shahna repeated distractedly and headed for the bedroom.

* * *

A baby. Kier's hand clutched the back of the wooden chair so hard the edges cut into his palm. He felt as though someone had punched him in the gut.

Shahna had a baby. He couldn't get his head around the idea. In all the time they'd been together she'd never said anything about wanting children. After they'd both obtained medical certificates, she had relieved him of the responsibility for contraception and he'd been glad of that. He'd trusted her not to slip up on taking her pills, just as she'd trusted him to keep to his word on the exclusive nature of their relationship.

Minutes ago she'd told him she wasn't living with a man.

That didn't necessarily mean she was celibate—after all, she had never lived with Kier, either, only slept with him on a regular basis, and kept a few clothes and toiletries at his place, as he did at hers.

A convenient arrangement, she'd reminded him.

And it had suited him, as she'd said. At first.

He wasn't sure when he'd begun to find it less than satisfactory, when he'd started toying with the idea of asking her to move in with him—and put it off because Shahna seemed quite content as they were. And because he needed to be sure of her before he risked rocking the boat. Risked, perhaps, losing her—a prospect that had roused sensations he hadn't felt in years, uncomfortably close to fear and a sense of powerlessness; a prospect that made him hesitate to endanger the status quo.

Despite three years of great sex and equally enjoyable companionship, he still felt he'd hardly peeked beneath the smooth, unruffled and intriguingly impenetrable surface she'd presented to him at their first meeting. He hadn't been sure how she would react to his surprising desire for a greater intimacy.

Somehow Shahna had got under his skin as none of his previous lovers had. There was something different about her, something that had him hankering for more...not just of her beautiful body and her quick mind with its unusual blend of practical and imaginative that made her so good at her job, but the essential Shahna inside, of which she allowed only tantalizing glimpses.

And while he had been considering and strategizing how to persuade her to live with him, she'd left—vanished without warning, without explanation. Nothing but a three-line note thanking him for the good times and wishing him well.

He had never been so angry in his life. No use telling himself she had every right, that he had asked for no more, promised no more. Or that he'd probably had a narrow escape from making perhaps the biggest blunder of his life, allowing a woman to breach the barriers he'd carefully preserved for years. The suddenness of her departure, the lack of any discernible reason, had outraged him.

Today all the anger and outrage had come flooding back.

She looked different, a little more rounded than he remembered, softer. Her hair was shorter, the slight natural curl unconfined, and with no makeup she presented an intriguingly scrubbed look that he'd previously seen only rarely.

But she was as desirable as ever. Without his even touching her, his body responded the same way it always had since the first time he'd taken her hand and looked into her clear, momentarily startled and then wary hazelgreen eyes. Responded in a way it had failed to do to any woman since she left.

It wasn't that she was any more beautiful than numerous other women who entered his orbit. Or even that she was smarter. He knew plenty of highly intelligent, talented, beautiful females. In the last eighteen—no, twenty—months, far too long to brood over losing a lover, he'd deliberately cultivated a few of those other women. Had even vowed that he would take one of them to bed. But before it came to that he had lost interest. None of them were Shahna.

It was Shahna who inconveniently haunted his dreams. Shahna he reached for in the mornings before he was fully awake, only to encounter a cold, untouched pillow beside his own. Shahna whose body fitted so well with his, whose mouth was a miracle of softness and passion, whose lightest touch could bring him to instant responsiveness, whose subtle woman-scent had lingered in his apartment, catching him unawares when he opened his wardrobe long after she'd removed the clothing once stored there, or the drawer from which she'd forgotten to take several lace-and-silk scraps of underwear, or the bathroom cupboard that still held a perfumed body spray. Perhaps she'd left it on purpose because he had given it to her. Just as she'd scrupulously left the several pieces of jewelry that had been his gifts on her birthday or at Christmas, the only times she'd been willing to take anything expensive. Her rejection of the fruits of his wealth had maddened him, but he recognized and respected the integrity behind it.

Removing his hands from the chair back, he studied the red marks on his palms. He could hear the baby cooing, and Shahna murmuring words he couldn't catch. An unpleasant, peculiar dread churned his stomach.

Then she appeared in the doorway, carrying the child.

Kier didn't know much about babies, but this one wasn't newly born. Its sturdy little legs splayed as Shahna held it firmly on her hip with one arm, the other hand supporting a plump bottom encased in some kind of red-and-white-checked overall worn with a tiny yellow T-shirt.

It struck Kier immediately, with a sense of unreality, how competent she looked, how—motherly. He had never seen Shahna with a child in her arms before.

The baby turned a round head capped with dark, loose curls, stared at him for a second with big deep-blue eyes, and then buried its face in Shahna's shoulder.

"This is Samuel," she told Kier. "Commonly known as Scamp."

Shahna made herself meet Kier's eyes squarely. There was no getting out of this now.

Kier looked poleaxed. He was still standing where she had left him, and he stared as though he'd never seen a baby before.

Samuel turned his head for another peek. But when she would have put him down he clung to her, nervous of the stranger. She walked across the small living area to the settle and sat with him in her lap, letting him inspect their visitor from a safe distance.

She saw Kier pull air into his lungs, and then he said raggedly, "You should have told me."

Maybe she should have, instead of hoping he would be long gone before Samuel woke, avoiding any need for explanation. Now Kier was bound to ask questions—questions she didn't want to answer.

Samuel looked up at her inquiringly and she smiled at him, reassuring him that everything was all right, that she wouldn't let the big, angry man hurt him.

Because Kier was angry. She could see it in the telltale jut of his jaw, the blue fire burning in his eyes, the tight-drawn contour of his mouth. His voice when he spoke was raw and iron-hard. "You buried yourself in this place because of him? A bit extreme, isn't it?"

She said, stung to defiance, "I'm not ashamed of him, if that's what you mean. Lots of people know I'm a solo mother. Everyone around here."

But no one from her old life. Shahna knew she was begging the question.

Kier seemingly made an effort to calm himself, but his mouth remained tight and his eyes were storm clouds. "*I* didn't," he bit out.

Samuel looked at Shahna again, puzzled. She took his hand. "It's all right, Scamp. We have a visitor." She looked up at Kier and the baby followed her gaze.

Apparently deciding there was no danger, Samuel wriggled, indicating he wanted to get down, and Shahna lowered him to the floor. Immediately he turned over on all fours and took off with remarkable speed toward Kier, bent on a closer investigation.

Kier watched his approach with something like trepidation, until Samuel's head almost butted against his jeans. The baby's fingers found the laces of the expensive walking boots temptingly in front of his nose, and tugged, freeing one end that promptly went into his mouth as he sat back with a grunt.

"Should he do that?" Kier asked Shahna, but didn't wait for her answer. Obeying some instinct, he stooped to pick up the child, holding the small body awkwardly between his hands before he hooked out the chair again with a foot and sat down.

Instead of subsiding on his knees, Samuel straightened

his legs and waved his arms, making encouraging noises. He wanted to bounce.

Fumbling a little, Kier soon got the idea, and Samuel giggled, enjoying the game.

Kier's rigid expression gradually relaxed. He looked bemused and almost startled. Shahna very nearly giggled herself.

"He's strong," Kier said, surprised, as Samuel pushed off once more against his thighs, waving his arms enthusiastically.

Shahna smiled, proud of her son. There had been a few anxious weeks after his birth, but now he was full of energy and had even begun trying to walk around the furniture, looking terribly pleased every time he hauled himself to his feet. But he still found crawling a more efficient means of locomotion.

Tiring of the game, Samuel plumped down on his bottom and tipped his head back to study Kier's face, lifted a dimpled hand to pat the man's cheek, and said something incomprehensible in a satisfied tone. Then he took a fistful of Kier's T-shirt and began sucking on it.

"Hey!" Kier tried to gently disengage the death grip on his shirt. "That's not edible."

"Give him one of those," Shahna suggested, indicating the coconut cookies on the table.

Kier obliged, and Samuel grabbed the proffered treat, losing interest in the shirt. He bit a piece off the cookie, then offered the remainder to Kier. "Uh?"

"No, thanks." Kier shook his head. He was staring at Samuel as though the child were an alien species.

"Uh?" Samuel persisted, generously.

Shahna got up. "Here, I'll take him." She pulled a wheeled high chair from its corner by the fridge, where it had been hidden from Kier's view, and popped Samuel into it, fastening the tray.

Kier didn't seem able to take his eyes off the baby. The grim look had returned and his face was paler than normal.

Shahna picked up Kier's mug. "Do you want anything more?"

"I could use another coffee."

There was no point in refusing that now. She poured it and put it in front of him, then fed Samuel a bowl of cereal and some milk in a plastic baby cup.

By the time Samuel had finished and she'd wiped his mouth and hands and lifted him down, Kier was rinsing his coffee mug at the sink. Samuel crawled efficiently to the settle and pulled himself up, banging on the lift-up seat and saying, "Ta, ta."

"All right." Shahna moved Kier's backpack to the floor so that she could open up the storage compartment and extract a basket of toys. "There you are."

Samuel was easily bored, and after painfully twisting an ankle Shahna had realized the danger of having small objects scattered throughout the cottage's limited floor space. Now she restricted him to a few toys at a time, but choosing from the lot would keep him occupied.

Attracted by the novelty of the backpack, Samuel had discovered the plastic buckle on the end of a nylon strap and was chewing on it.

"Does he eat everything?" Kier asked, frowning.

"Pretty much. He's teething." She'd had to pick him up in the early hours this morning, in the end giving him a spoonful of prescription medicine. He would have been up for breakfast well before eight but the interrupted night had disrupted his sleep pattern.

She handed him a toy tractor from the basket to distract

him from the backpack, then made to heave the pack onto the settle again.

"I'll do that!" Swiftly Kier strode across the room and took it from her. His hand brushed hers and she quickly stepped back, a rush of sheer physical pleasure leaving her shaken and dismayed.

"What have you got in there?" she queried to distract herself. The pack was heavy.

"My laptop, among other things. And a mobile phone."

"That won't be much use around here."

"So I discovered last night. Then Timoti told me they don't work in the Hokianga." He directed a searching look at her. "If you're not hiding, why pick this godforsaken spot?"

Shahna kept her voice steady. "It's a good place to bring up a child. And I can live cheaply here."

"Are you short of money?" he enquired sharply.

"No, I have some savings and the money from the sale of my apartment. But I want to make it last while I build up my business."

"Your jewelry. Can you earn a living from that?"

"I hope to." Her work was becoming known to discerning buyers, and it didn't sell cheaply. It was intricate and time-consuming, each piece unique, and worth every cent.

"A good place to bring up a child?" Kier sounded skeptical. "The middle of nowhere?"

Shahna smiled inwardly. Naturally the remoteness of the area horrified him. He was totally out of his normal element. "There's a village a few miles away, with a store that sells milk and bread and groceries, even a daily paper."

"What happens if he's sick, or you are?"

"The hospital at Rawene runs a nurses' clinic over here, and a doctor comes across once a week. Or I can drive to Kaitaia hospital in about an hour."

"Drive?" Kier looked out the window where, beyond the neat A-frame henhouse, a couple of telephone and power wires ran alongside a barely discernible farm track, overhung by trees. "I don't see any car."

"I keep it next door at the farm."

He pulled his gaze from the crowded trees. Somewhere in the distance a bull roared. "This is a far cry from Sydney."

"Yes," Shahna agreed. "I don't expect you to understand." Born and bred in Sydney, Kier was a king of the concrete jungle.

His gaze went back to Samuel, who was lifting toys from the basket to discard them on the floor, occasionally pausing to try one for taste. "I don't understand any of this." Kier lifted hard eyes to hers. "You didn't deliberately get pregnant, did you?"

Shahna drew a deep breath. The question bought long-denied emotions to the forefront of her mind. Guilt, grief, shame and a tearing, exquisitely painful regret.

He had asked for the truth. She would give it to him. "Actually...yes." The bare truth with no excuses or explanations, unvarnished by the complexities surrounding her reckless decision.

In hindsight it hadn't been the wisest thing to do, but she couldn't find it in herself to regret giving birth to Samuel.

Again anger smoldered in the blue depths of Kier's eyes. "And planned to bring him up without a father?"

Planned? How could she reply to that? "Not...exactly," she hedged.

"Then why didn't you contact me? Don't you think I had a right to know?"

Shahna went cold, despite the summer-morning heat creeping into the cottage. Sun-wakened cicadas shrilled in the trees outside.

Her hands clenched, clammy with sudden sweat, and Kier's face seemed to recede and then swim into focus. She'd never thought she'd have to confront him with this. It was like a bad dream. "No," she said, looking at him steadily. "He's not yours, Kier."

Kier blinked, then seemed to brush her denial aside, making a scornful sound. "What sort of fool do you take me for?" he inquired with forceful sarcasm. "It was certainly no bloody virgin birth!"

Samuel, who had been looking from one to the other of them while clutching a small stuffed rabbit, suddenly burst into loud sobs.

Immediately Shahna's attention switched to him. "It's all right, Sam-sam!" She gathered him up into her arms and shushed him, gently swaying her body from side to side to soothe him. "He's not used to people quarreling," she told Kier quietly, her hand cradling the baby's head on her shoulder. "Shh, darling. No one's going to hurt you." She kissed a fat tear from a rounded, rose-petal cheek.

Samuel snuffled into gradual silence against her while she murmured comforting words and Kier stood by, black brows drawn together.

Shahna wiped the child's hot face with her fingers, and Samuel turned his head, stared at Kier and pointed, saying accusingly, "Ma'!"

"Yes." She had to laugh a little at his baby aggression. "Man. That's Kier. Mummy used to know him."

Ominously Kier's mouth tightened again.

"Kee?" Samuel queried, looking at her for confirmation.

"Kier. He won't hurt you," she assured him again. Though Kier's murderous expression indicated he would have liked to hurt someone, hit someone, she knew he wouldn't.

"Kee." Samuel gazed at Kier with solemn suspicion.

"Does he understand you?" Kier asked, the savage look consciously banished, although his face still looked tight and his voice was strained.

"Not every word. He understands tones of voice."

"I didn't mean to frighten him." Kier was looking back at Samuel, keeping his voice low. "I'm sorry."

"Kee," Samuel said again, and leaned away from Shahna's hold, stretching his arms toward the man.

Shahna smiled. "Apology accepted."

Kier instinctively held out his hands to take the baby reaching out to him. Two chubby arms came about his neck, and incredibly soft curls tickled his chin. He put one arm under the padded little behind while the other held the small, sturdy body close to his chest.

A weird mixture of emotions overtook him. A kind of awe at this tiny human being showing him forgiveness, at the trust being bestowed on him. And a strong urge to preserve that trustfulness, to protect the little guy from hurt.

And a sudden, totally unexpected fierce possessiveness.

Apparently a hug was enough for Samuel. He squirmed, giving a clear signal that he wanted to be put down, and Kier bent and let him go.

Samuel made straight back to the toy basket, and when Kier straightened, his arms felt oddly empty. The warmth of the baby's body still clung to his T-shirt.

"If you'd told me," he said, unable to keep a certain righteousness from his tone, "I would have helped. I would have looked after you."

"I didn't need anyone's help." Shahna seemed almost desperate as their eyes met over Samuel's head. "And certainly not yours."

As if he were the last person she would have turned to. Kier's temper nearly boiled over. He resented her assumption that he'd have reneged on his responsibility.

Her tongue momentarily flicked over pale lips. "I've already told you, Kier," she said with careful clarity, "you're not Samuel's father! Another man is."

Chapter 3

Another man?

Another man had made love to Shahna, had shared the intimate secrets of her body, had *made a baby* with her?

Inwardly Kier reeled, his mind in turmoil again. The only emotion he should be feeling was relief. Instead he felt cheated, and disappointed, and downright red-rag furious. He had to swallow hard and clamp his jaw firmly shut so as not to frighten the baby again.

"I didn't expect," Shahna said defensively, "that you'd jump to conclusions so fast."

"How old is he?"

Her eyes met his full on, her head held high. "Eleven months."

There was a short, prickly silence while he rapidly calculated. "You didn't waste any time."

He knew he sounded accusing. And that he had no right to accuse her of anything. But his bed must have hardly cooled from her leaving it before she'd been hopping into someone else's. All ready to have the someone else's baby.

His stomach plunged. "Were you sleeping with his father before you left me?" he asked.

Her eyes went glass-green with temper and color flared in her cheeks. "You know me better than that. At least, I thought you did."

"*I* thought I did too," he said. "But as you mentioned before, maybe I didn't know you so well after all. Are you sure you *know* who the father is?" If she was lying to him that should force the truth from her.

"Of course I'm sure! It wasn't you," she said. "There is no way it's possible."

She sounded quite definite, and he supposed she'd know. Assuming she was telling the truth. "So where is this guy?" he shot at her, still not wholly convinced. "In Sydney?"

He thought at first she wasn't going to answer. She looked away, then back at him. "Actually, in New Zealand."

"You came straight here when you left me?" No wonder his inquiries hadn't found her.

"Yes, I did. I mean, I was working in Auckland for a while before coming north."

"You met him there? How? When? How long had you known him?"

She blinked as if he'd shocked her, then said steadily, "None of that is any of your business."

She couldn't have known the man long. It had certainly taken him a hell of a lot less time to find his way to her bed than it had Kier.

Yet earlier she'd told him she *meant* to get pregnant! "If your biological clock was sending off alarm signals," he asked, "why didn't you talk to *me* about it?"

"You were very clear that babies didn't figure in your plans."

He'd never thought they figured in hers, either. She'd given him no reason to think it. "I don't recall that we ever discussed the possibility," he said. "Except in the context of making sure it didn't happen by accident."

He'd been just as much concerned for her and her career as for his own freedom. It was all very well for women to think they could have it all, and for men to promise they'd do their share, but he'd seen female colleagues and employees juggling work and family, seen them drive themselves to exhaustion and turn down promotions, miss out on the top jobs because their energies were divided.

Some of them maintained it was worth it, but dammit, Shahna had never said she wanted a baby.

Had she?

He couldn't recall the details of every conversation they'd ever had, but he was pretty sure he would have remembered that. "Why didn't you say you felt differently?" he said, trying not to sound affronted. "That isn't why you left?" Without even mentioning any desire for a child?

Shahna hesitated. "In a way...I suppose it was."

What the hell did that mean? She hadn't wanted *his* baby, but she'd been perfectly willing—*eager*—to have someone else's? "So what did you do?" he demanded, his anger spilling over. "Sleep with the first man who came along? Use a sperm donor?" It had never occurred to him before that she might be one of those women who wanted a child to fulfill their womanhood, without the bother of having to share its parenting with a man. But then it had never occurred, either, that she'd walk out of his life without a backward glance.

To his considerable surprise she looked stricken. "I...it wasn't like that," she said, leaving him none the wiser. "And anyway, it's *not* your business."

About to hotly dispute that, Kier clamped his teeth together. She was perfectly correct, of course. If Samuel wasn't his—he looked at the oblivious little boy, who had found a colored metal xylophone and was inexpertly banging on it with his hands—then he had no rights. And no obligations.

For some reason the thought didn't please him.

Shahna went down on her knees and fished in the basket, coming up with a wooden baton for the xylophone. She put it into Samuel's hand, and after gently removing it from his mouth, encouraged him to use it. Samuel grinned at her, attacked the keys with gusto, then looked back to his mother for approval.

Staring at her bent head as she folded her fingers around the pudgy baby hand and picked out the tune of "Twinkle, Twinkle, Little Star," Kier felt excluded. Restlessly, he shoved his thumbs into the pockets of his jeans, shuffled his feet.

Shahna got up from the floor. "Well," she said, obviously waiting for him to leave, "I'm sure you can get a ride to the ferry if you want to go back to Rawene the quickest way. Or on to another town if you intend to explore the Far North. The locals are good about picking up hitchhikers."

He'd promised himself that seeing her one more time would complete the sense of something unfinished that had haunted him since she left; rationalized that the occasional nightmares about Shahna caught in some terrible, dangerous situation and his futile efforts to rescue her would stop once he knew she was alive and well and didn't need him. That once he'd tied up the loose ends and found out the reason for her abrupt departure, he'd be able to heal the aching, gaping wound inside him that she'd inexplicably left, get on with his life and be happy.

So now that she'd made it clear she *was* alive and well and didn't need him, now that he knew she'd walked out on him apparently because of some biological imperative that, not being a woman, he didn't understand and probably never would, why couldn't he walk away as easily as she had? Why this feeling of massive reluctance at the thought of it?

Maybe because he'd found more questions than answers.

When Shahna looked up Kier was still standing stubbornly unmoving, looking down at her and Samuel. A new sound penetrated above the tinny tinkle of the xylophone. An engine sound—not from the water, but coming closer and then cutting off, outside of the house. A truck? "Sounds like you have another visitor," Kier said.

"My landlord is going to put up a fence for me today."

Morrie McKenzie had promised to build her a childproof fence. The small lawn at the back between the vegetable patch and her studio was already enclosed, but with the river so near the house, and sheep droppings dotting the grass, she had to keep the front door closed or put a wooden barrier across it in case Samuel escaped.

A brisk tap on the door sent her to open it to a burly, tanned young man, wearing only khaki shorts and sturdy boots.

He ran a hand over thick, blond-streaked hair and grinned at her. "Hi, Shahna. I've got your fencing here. The old man was gonna come too, but he's got a splinter in his hand and it's infected or something. Mum had to help out with milking this morning.'' He looked beyond her, curiosity in his bright blue eyes. ''Hi, there.''

Kier was standing at her shoulder. Shahna sensed him without looking around.

She had no choice but to introduce them. ''Kier's a friend of mine from Australia,'' she explained. ''Kier, this is Ace McKenzie, my landlord's son.''

Kier leaned past her to offer his hand. ''I can help with the fence.''

Ace looked at him appraisingly as he accepted the handshake.

Shahna objected, ''You don't have any experience.''

Kier shot her a look, his eyes glinting wickedly, then turned a bland one to the other man. ''I'm sure Ace can clue me in.''

''Sure thing,'' Ace agreed happily. ''Be glad of a hand.''

''You don't need to—'' Shahna began, but Kier was already moving her firmly aside and going down the steps to join Ace. ''Let's do it.''

They did it.

Kier helped Ace unload corner posts and supports and a posthole digger from the truck he'd parked near the house, and together they worked at digging in and leveling the posts.

Samuel, perched on Shahna's knee while she sat on the top step, watched the activity with total absorption at first, but when he showed signs of wanting to join the men she took him inside despite his noisy protest.

Kier looked up as she shut the door behind them, muffling Samuel's indignant wails. The sun was hot on his back, and his T-shirt clung sweatily to his body. He debated following Ace's example and dispensing with the shirt, but at this time of day he'd probably burn rather than brown, and risk future skin cancer to boot.

"Hold this?" Ace asked, and Kier turned to steadying a metal standard while Ace rammed it into the earth.

Despite the heat, he was enjoying the unaccustomed physical work. He didn't have the muscular bulk of Ace, but he'd always kept trim with his chosen sports and an occasional gym workout. Which wasn't the same as using his muscles to actually build something. It was a long time since he'd got his hands dirty.

After a while Shahna came out of the house, carrying an opened beer bottle and two glass lager handles.

Ace straightened, wiping the back of a large hand over his forehead, and grinned at her. "Good one, Shahna. Just what we need."

Not usually a beer drinker, Kier too was grateful for the cool, bitter draught. He drained his glass while Shahna stood by, and then handed it back to her. Somehow they fumbled the exchange and the glass dropped to the ground, which was fortunately soft enough not to break it. "Sorry," he said.

Shahna was already scooping it up. "My fault," she acknowledged, taking Ace's glass, too.

"Where's Samuel?" Kier asked.

"Playing in his room." She surveyed the work they had done and said, "Lunch in about an hour? I'll feed the Scamp first and put him down."

Ace said, "I can go home for lunch."

"No!" She paused. "It's no trouble, and seeing you're here you might as well eat with…us."

When the supports were in Ace surveyed them with an experienced eye and turned to Kier. "How about a dip before lunch?" He jerked his head toward water—gleaming and invitingly cool.

Kier looked down at the grubby jeans that clung to his legs. "I'm not dressed for swimming."

Ace grinned at him. "You don't get *dressed* for it," he said with exaggerated patience. "Just drop the jeans, mate." As Kier glanced toward the house, Ace added, "You've got something on under them, haven't you?" He bent and began unlacing his boots.

What the hell, Kier thought. Shahna had seen him often enough in less than the black briefs he wore under the jeans. He snapped open the fastener at his waist and lowered the zip, and within seconds he was following Ace and taking a shallow dive off the jetty.

When ten minutes later they pulled themselves onto the jetty again Shahna was there with two folded towels in her arms.

Ace's shorts were dripping and clinging to him. He shook his streaming head, and Shahna gave a startled exclamation as water sprayed, spotting her shirt in large, spreading blotches.

"Oops, sorry!" Ace reached for a towel. "Thanks." He began vigorously rubbing at his hair.

Shahna handed the other towel to Kier.

A silvery droplet ran from the curve of her jaw down into the neckline of her cotton shirt. Involuntarily following its progress, he saw that water had already darkened her shirt over one breast. He watched the center intriguingly peak beneath the fabric, and when his gaze jerked back to hers, saw the chagrin in her face, and recognized the helpless desire in her eyes.

The surge of his answering desire had him hastily allowing the towel to unfold while one fist held it loosely against his body. Triumph seemed to expand his chest, and blood drummed in his ears.

Shahna had inexplicably left him, but she still wanted him.

In that instant he made up his mind he wasn't going to tamely go away and leave her here in the weird, closed little world she'd made for herself. They had always had terrific, incredible sexual rapport, and more besides that he couldn't put into words. And there was that nagging, unsettling conviction that if only she would open up to him, he'd find something wonderful and precious, something he couldn't afford to miss.

She might have been able to walk away from it all, but he couldn't. And now he had found her again, he wouldn't.

Shahna turned away, almost suffocating with the effect Kier had on her. She knew he'd seen and responded to it, and a treacherous part of her reveled in that knowledge.

But she had Samuel to think of. No longer a free, single woman whose mistakes would rebound on her head alone, she had knowingly taken on the enormous responsibility of bringing a child into the world. And now all her actions had to be weighed against that.

Kier might have been willing to "do the right thing" when he believed she'd given birth to his baby. But she'd told him he wasn't Samuel's father, absolving him of any moral duty, so couldn't expect him to take into much account the needs of a child who wasn't his. Looking after Samuel's welfare was up to her.

Just as it had always been.

Kier changed in her bathroom. Ace, refusing to sit at the table in his wet shorts, parked himself in the doorway with a plate on which Shahna had piled cold meat, cheese and salad accompanied by wedges of crusty bread.

"Homemade?" Kier helped himself to a thick slice and looked at Shahna quizzically.

Shahna nodded. Although ready-sliced loaves were available at the garage-cum-mini-market a .few miles away, she liked watching the yeast swell the dough, liked taking fresh new loaves from the oven and cutting off a few slices to eat while they were still warm.

"Delicious," Kier decided after taking a bite. "There's no end to your talents, is there?"

She glanced at him sharply, but there was no sarcasm in his expression.

From the doorway, Ace said, "She makes great chocolate nut cake."

"Cake?" Kier queried.

She had sometimes whipped up a meal for the two of them, or made dinner for friends. But he didn't recall her ever baking cakes.

"Ace has a sweet tooth," Shahna said casually.

So she made cake for him? Regularly? Kier looked at the other man. His brawny, tanned shoulders and deep chest shone in the outdoor light, and surely the mop of sun-streaked hair, the candid blue eyes and the white-toothed, slightly cheeky grin would be attractive to women.

To Shahna? She'd sat watching the fence-building this morning, and whenever Kier looked up she certainly hadn't been concentrating on him. Had her gaze been drawn to Ace, shirtless and muscular, and working with a practiced competence that Kier was unable to match?

Kier wondered how often Ace came to the cottage. And what else he did besides erecting fences.

Samuel had obviously recognized Ace, pointing and calling "A'e…A'e!" as if pleased to see him, which Ace had acknowledged with a cheery wave and "Hi there, Scamp!"

Samuel's eyes were blue, too. Was it possible that Ace...?

He looked from the young man to Shahna.

She'd said she hadn't—*exactly*—intended to bring up Samuel without a father, but also that she wasn't living with a man. So how did those contradictory statements fit?

As Kier turned to stare at Ace with an oddly strained look on his face, Shahna studied him across the table. He was even better-looking than she remembered, and a little ache caught at her heart.

Leaving him was the hardest thing she'd ever done. And now, just when she thought she was finally getting over that and all the pain and anguish that had followed, he had to come sailing back into her life.

This morning she'd made the excuse that it wasn't fair to shut Samuel out of the excitement of watching the men work, but the truth was she hadn't been able to resist it herself.

Despite Ace's minimal clothing and well-developed muscles, it was Kier's lithe body and masculine grace that sent pleasurable goose bumps chasing over her skin when the close-fitting T-shirt stretched across his shoulders as he easily lifted a post, that made her heart pound as his jeans molded themselves to his haunches when he bent to drop the post into the ground. She'd watched him in covert fascination, plagued by memories that clogged her throat and made her blood run faster, only switching her attention whenever he glanced in her direction.

The men returned to the fencing while Shahna washed up, then she worked for half an hour in her studio before lifting a grouchy Samuel from his cot and placing the barrier across the doorway so he could see the men while she baked a cake.

By midafternoon a sturdy mesh fence, sporting barbed wire strung on angles at the farm side to discourage cattle from leaning on it, enclosed the front of the cottage.

"That'll keep the little fella out of mischief," Ace declared with satisfaction, "and the stock away from him."

A gate with a childproof catch was the finishing touch, and then they celebrated with more beer and slices of fresh chocolate nut cake before Ace threw his tools and the unused fencing materials onto the tray of his truck, called, "See ya!" and roared off along a rough roadway through the trees.

"Thank you for your help," Shahna said to Kier as she gathered up glasses. "Um...would you like a shower before you go?" His sweat-stained T-shirt and jeans would probably never be quite the same again.

"If you toss your clothes out the bathroom door," she said, "I'll wash them with a load I'm putting through." It would mean he'd have to stay a couple of hours at least while his things dried but that would hardly matter now and, as she said when Kier hesitated, "I owe you that much."

"You don't," he contradicted her, "but thanks."

By the time he came out of the bathroom wearing clean clothes she had the washing machine going in the enclosed porch off the kitchen. Samuel was walking around the living room furniture, making his precarious way from the settle to a chair, to the sofa, and then complaining that the nearest dining chair was just out of his reach.

When Kier entered, the little boy twisted to look at him, lost his balance and fell on his rear end, breaking into a roar.

"Is he hurt?" Kier asked as Shahna picked him up.

"No, he's just a bit niggly because his tooth's bothering him."

"Is that why he looks so flushed?" The rounded cheek that Kier could see was bright red.

"Mmm." Shahna patted Samuel's back and spoke to him. "You're not going to let me get any more work done today, are you, Scamp?"

"I'll watch him for you," Kier offered.

She looked surprised and suspicious. "I can't take advantage…"

"I wouldn't do it if I didn't want to."

Shahna couldn't recall when Kier ever had done anything he didn't want to. But why would he want to do this? "You're not used to babies," she reminded him, torn between a stupid desire to make the most of the short time he'd be here, and a fear that he might find out more than she wanted him to know about her feelings for him.

"You'll be here," he reminded her, "if we have any problems. Right, Sam?"

He held out his hands invitingly to Samuel, who regarded him with suspicion for a moment, then said in a tone of pleased discovery, "Kee!" And reached for him.

Doubtfully, Shahna relinquished the child into Kier's waiting arms. "I don't know…"

"He'll be fine. And if he's not I'll call you," Kier promised.

He wouldn't need to. She'd hear if Samuel were upset. "Your washing," she said. "I was going to hang it on the line outside."

"I'll do it."

Shahna hovered uncertainly, but Samuel was absorbed in a renewed inspection of Kier's face, his scrutiny just as fascinated and far less covert than her own earlier, and Kier seemed to be returning the compliment.

Samuel grunted, then pointed an imperious finger to the toy basket, now tidied and placed on top of the settle.

"You want to play?" Kier asked. "Okay."

Neither of them was taking the slightest notice of Shahna, so with faint trepidation she left them to it.

It was difficult to concentrate as she gently shaped lengths of delicate silver wire, to be set with pieces of polished amber-gold kauri gum.

Gradually she became absorbed in the work, clearing her mind of everything else. Hearing Kier's voice, she looked out of the open doorway and saw him dump a basket of washing on the ground, where Samuel sat under the single wire that had been strung between the trees and the house and was held up by an old-fashioned manuka-branch clothes prop. Kier had found the container of plastic clothes-pegs that had a hook for hanging it on the line, but when Samuel stretched out a hand he placed it in front of the baby.

"Mistake," Shahna murmured, and couldn't help smiling as Samuel promptly upended the pegs all over the ground.

Kier laughed, and laughed again when Samuel laboriously picked one up and offered it to him. She heard him say, "Thanks, pal," as he took the peg and fished a towel out of the basket of washing.

Shahna watched as he inexpertly hung up the towel and picked out another, before she turned back to what she was doing, smothering a nagging sadness that had settled around her heart and that mingled, confusingly, with an undeniable pleasure at just having him in sight.

Accustomed to keeping an ear cocked for the sound of Samuel waking from a nap in the room just a few yards from the studio, she heard him when he began to fuss, and was getting up from her workbench when Kier appeared in the doorway, holding the baby.

"I think he needs changing," he told her, and thankfully handed the wriggling, indignant little bundle over to her.

As she took Samuel from him, Kier looked beyond her and said, "Mind if I look around?"

"Go ahead," she invited after an infinitesimal hesitation, and bore her son off to the house.

Kier walked around the small room, where the long-nosed pliers Shahna had been using lay on a sturdy workbench under the single window. Tools hung on the walls, and a high padlocked cupboard occupied one corner.

A collection of photographs almost covered a large corkboard. Landscapes, pictures of rippling water and of wave patterns on sand, mixed with close-ups of ferns and moss, leaves and flowers. And display shots of necklaces, pendants, brooches and bangles, echoing the nature photos so closely he could clearly see where the inspiration for the jewelry came from.

He recognized the necklace that had caught his eye at the airport, rippled titanium and uneven pieces of green and white beach glass etched with abstract designs, distinctive in its unique, almost rugged beauty.

When he'd seen Shahna's label it felt as if fate had struck him a blow in the heart. For months he'd been trying to convince himself he didn't give a damn, that except for the worrying dreams and the residual baffled anger that occasionally attacked him, he was over her.

Until her name on a cardboard tag, catching his eye, squeezing a tight fist about his heart, had proved to him that he wasn't.

Chapter 4

He'd wanted to ditch his meetings and find Shahna. Instead he'd persuaded himself to be coolheaded, concluded his business in Auckland as speedily as possible and then hunted her down.

He picked up a glass jar full of small seashells—some white patterned with brown, others purple or brilliant orange.

There were more jars holding weathered bits of glass, lumps of golden kauri gum, colored stones, even fragments of old china. A magpie collection.

Kier smiled, remembering her fascination with junk shops and markets where she'd buy bits and pieces he could see no use for.

She'd turned old, ugly and broken costume jewelry into quirky earrings and bracelets, or decor accents, like the drift of colored glass cabuchons spilling from a conch shell on her bathroom windowsill, catching the sun in the mornings.

Once she'd fallen in love with a faded fringed silk shawl and hidden the tears in the delicate fabric by draping it in folds on the wall over her bed.

He wondered if she still had it, if it hung over her bed now.

Hearing her voice, he looked through the open window, directly into another a few yards off, glimpsing a corner of a child's cot. Shahna bent over it, and although Kier couldn't see Samuel, he heard the little boy chuckle as Shahna laughed.

Her head lifted and her eyes met Kier's. Feeling almost voyeuristic, he raised a hand to her. She lowered her eyes and turned away.

Minutes later she was back in the studio, Samuel in her arms. "Thanks for looking after him," she said, "but it's getting close to his tea time now. There's no need for you to stay any longer."

"It must be difficult," Kier said, "working around a baby."

"I do a lot while he's asleep. And as long as I'm not using acid or soldering, he can play here quite happily while I'm busy."

Kier looked about. "You've turned a hobby into an art."

"I took a six-month course with a good tutor," she said. "And I've had help from local artists here. They've been wonderfully supportive."

"Wouldn't it be easier to find markets in the city?"

"I made some contacts in Auckland before I left. Enough to start me off."

He indicated the corkboard. "Those are your work?"

"Yes. I photograph everything before it's sold. There's an album in the drawer, there."

He opened the drawer of a battered chest that supported

one end of the solid workbench, and took out a tooled leather volume. "This?"

She nodded.

"I'll leave you to it while I fix something for Samuel to eat."

"He can stay with me while you do that if you like."

She gave him a strange look, and shook her head. "We've imposed on you enough."

He felt as though she'd slapped him. As she went back to the house he had a strong urge to follow her and force some kind of confrontation. Instead he bent his attention to the pictures in front of him.

Shahna almost wished she hadn't invited Kier to look at the album, although she was proud of her work and wanted him to know it. Seeing him prowling 'round her studio, his keen gaze taking in everything before he looked back at her, had unsettled her.

When he rejoined them she was placing a peeled banana half in Samuel's outstretched hand and removing the empty bowl in front of him.

"I'm impressed," Kier said, making her feel ridiculously pleased and proud. She already knew she was good—people with much more knowledge than he had said so. Yet Kier's praise gave her greater pleasure than anyone's.

"Thank you." She tried to sound nonchalant.

"If you don't mind I'll leave my things to dry here and pick them up tomorrow."

"Tomorrow? I thought you'd be moving on today."

"No," he said. "I won't be." He was regarding her narrowly as though watching for her reaction. "I'm staying."

"Staying?" Shahna stared blankly at him, her heart doing a flip. "You can't! Not here."

Perhaps annoyed at her obvious dismay, he said shortly, "Ace offered me a bed at the farm. Hokianga hospitality, he said."

It was famous, but Shahna hadn't bargained on Ace being quite so ready to volunteer it, although she knew his parents would happily give Kier one of their spare rooms for the night.

"He said they'd expect me for dinner," Kier said. Unless he was intending to stay in the cottage, Ace had said, adding with a sidelong glance, "But Shahna's only got the two bedrooms, and there's plenty of room at our place."

Kier had wondered if the invitation was a means of discovering just how close he and Shahna were. Or even of ensuring that he didn't spend the night with her.

But Ace had quite cheerfully gone off and left Kier to find his own way later to the farmhouse. He didn't act like a jealous lover.

Shahna watched Kier walk away until he was out of sight among the trees. In the morning she would hand over his washing and make it clear she had no claim or interest in him before sending him on his way forever.

Never mind that the thought made her heart turn to lead and brought a lump into her throat that threatened to choke her.

And never mind that she dreamed of him all night—disturbingly erotic dreams that left her lethargic and yet dissatisfied.

In the morning Samuel was eager to explore his newly fenced domain.

First, though, Shahna wanted to get rid of the sheep

droppings. She was busy with a bamboo rake while Samuel watched her from behind the barrier across the doorway, occasionally complaining at his imprisonment, when Kier arrived.

She turned from her task to see him striding across the space between them, stunning in fresh jeans and a shirt a shade darker than his eyes. Before she'd had time to catch her breath and say good morning, he'd taken the rake from her. "Let me do that."

"I can manage."

But he was already getting on with the not-too-pleasant task, and Samuel chose that moment to protest in earnest about being left out of all the fun.

"Look after Sam," Kier said, as if she wasn't doing that, Shahna thought with mild annoyance as she went to quiet the baby, then carried him over to say hello.

"What do you want me to do with this stuff?" Kier asked.

"Bag it and add it to my compost. Now that we have a fence I plan to put in a flower garden along the front of the house."

"The ground's pretty hard," Kier said.

He would know, after digging holes for the fence yesterday. "It's fertile," she told him. "There's plenty of manure from the sheep and my hens, and Morrie promised to get me a load of untreated sawdust."

"Do you have a spade?"

She fetched it for him and held a bag while he emptied the sheep manure into it, then he hauled it around the back and forked it into her compost heap. After that the least she could do was offer him a cup of tea.

While Samuel chewed on a piece of toast in his high chair, she asked, "Do you know how Morrie's hand is?"

"It looks bad. Alison insisted on taking him to get it looked at this morning."

Shahna was fairly sure that Morrie wouldn't have let his wife persuade him if he hadn't been in considerable pain and probably more than a little worried. "Poor Morrie. I must phone Alison later."

"You're quite close to...the family?" Kier inquired.

"They've been good to me, and I try to repay them any way I can."

"You can't have many friends, out in the country like this."

"I know most of the locals, at least to say hello to. And there's a playgroup that I take Samuel to twice a week. All the mothers get a chance for some adult company."

Kier glanced at her shrewdly. "Do you miss that? Adult company?"

"Not much. But it's nice to talk to people with similar interests now and then."

"Similar interests?" Kier looked incredulous.

"We all have young children, for one thing," she reminded him rather tartly. "But we talk about a lot of other things too. Books, art, the education system, what's in the news, farming, TV—I don't have one, but the McKenzies ask me over sometimes when there's something special on... It isn't all knitting and cooking."

"I'm sure it's very stimulating."

She flashed him a look. "It may sound boring to you—"

"It just doesn't sound like you," he commented. "Unless you've changed a lot."

"A baby gives you a new perspective on life."

Kier scowled at her, perplexed. "It doesn't lead many people to alter their life so radically."

"I suppose not," Shahna acknowledged. "But it was the right thing for me…and the Scamp."

Hearing his nickname, Samuel began to bang on the tray of the high chair, making little crowing noises. Shahna offered him another piece of toast that he declined decisively by throwing it on the floor. Chiding him, she picked it up and popped it into the scrap bucket she kept for the hens before releasing him from the chair.

Kier stood up too. "I'll dig that garden for you."

"There's no need…"

But he didn't listen, merely casting her a withering look and going right ahead anyway.

He certainly got it done faster than she would have and with less effort. Shahna discouraged Samuel from helping and took him inside to distract him with toys, before returning alone to see Kier chopping up the last of the turned sods. "Thank you," she said sincerely. "I'm very grateful."

He plunged the spade upright in the soil. "No sweat." A lie; his face was glistening, but it only added to his attraction.

He swiped an arm across his forehead and grinned, as if realizing he'd used the wrong words. Shahna caught her breath, her heart tumbling. It was rare, that grin of pure enjoyment. Kier had always been sparing with his smiles, and often they hid less innocent emotions.

She couldn't help an answering smile, looking up at him as the sun lit his eyes, making them bluer than ever, and picked out glints in his dark hair.

"Of course, if you really want to thank me…" he said softly, and stepped toward her.

She should have protested, or at least turned away, made it clear his kiss was unwelcome. Instead she waited with a sense of expectation as he took her shoulders gently and bent his head until his mouth met hers.

She closed her eyes, and involuntarily her lips parted under his warm persuasion. She could feel the sun beating on her hair, and hear the water rippling along its bank, Samuel babbling a wordless little song in the background.

Everything faded as Kier's mouth worked a familiar magic, making her breath come unevenly and her skin tingle with anticipation when his hands slid down her arms and fastened on her waist to draw her closer.

She lifted her hands, momentarily resting them on his chest, fighting the urge to fling her arms around his neck. Instead, with a supreme effort, she pushed against him, and wrenched her mouth from its erotic enthrallment.

His hands tightened for a second on her waist, and then he let her go. They stared at each other, her cheeks hot, his eyes glittering with a fierce satisfaction.

Shahna swallowed hard, unable to tear her gaze away. Dumbly she shook her head in futile denial.

Kier smiled. Quite differently from before. This smile was knowing and confident and very, very male. It spelled trouble.

I must be crazy, Shahna thought. Why had she allowed him to do that?

"You'll want your clothes," she said, trying to appear unaffected by the kiss. "They're dry now."

"If there's anything else you need done…"

"You've done enough," she answered huskily. "And had your payment."

Immediately she wanted to bite her tongue. A stolen kiss that she hadn't made the least effort to avoid was hardly compensation for the amount of work he'd put in both yesterday and this morning.

Kier smiled again, tipping his head to one side as he

regarded her with lurking amusement. "And very nice too," he said.

Anger dispelled the warm afterglow of the kiss. Was it a game to him? Coming here, upsetting her hard-won equilibrium, intruding on the life she'd made for herself and Samuel, simply for some sort of whim.

"I'll get your things," she told him, and marched back to the house. As she climbed over the barrier keeping Samuel inside, Kier was right behind, entering after her.

Samuel was absorbed in poking wooden shapes into matching holes in a colored plastic bucket. He stopped to watch the two adults pass, then returned to his task.

Shahna picked up the neatly folded garments from the top of the washing machine and turned to present them to Kier. But as he held his hands out to take them she gasped, staring at his upturned palms.

He looked down too, at the reddened skin and broken blisters. "It's not as bad as it looks," he said, letting his hands drop.

"It's bad enough!" Shahna felt quite sick. "Have you put anything on them?"

"Disinfectant, last night when I broke the blisters I collected yesterday. And Alison gave me some salve."

But he'd been digging her garden this morning! Unaccountably angry, she said, "What the hell are you trying to prove?"

"Apart from the fact that I'm not accustomed to using my hands for physical labor," he said wryly, "nothing. But I'd hate to see this happen to you."

So he'd taken over the job when he realized she meant to dig the soil herself. "I wouldn't have gone on working if it had," she retorted.

He reached out again and took the clothes she held. "Thanks for this," he said, not moving away, and she found herself crowded against the washing machine. The laughter had left his eyes and they were searching, intent. "I'll be back," he said.

"What?" Her own eyes widened.

Kier frowned. "Why are you scared?"

"I'm not!" Shahna floundered, torn between a useless hope and the prospect of future heartbreak. "I just don't know why you'd bother."

"What is it with you?" He sounded exasperated. "I'd never thought you lacking in self-esteem."

"There's nothing wrong with my self-esteem, thank you! I told you, I've changed."

"Some things don't change." His gaze lingered on her mouth, then he lifted his eyes to hers in challenge and added softly, "Do they?"

What was the point of arguing? He was leaving anyway, and once back in his own milieu, absorbed in the world he knew and loved being a part of, he would forget her again.

After all, he hadn't chased her up until the sight of her name on her jewelry had reminded him of her existence. "It was nice seeing you," she said, striving for a pleasant indifference, "but I won't be holding my breath for another visit. Enjoy your life, Kier." She had to look away in case he saw sadness in her eyes, guessed at the tug of grief inside her.

"I intend to." A grittiness had entered his voice. "What about you?"

"My life is just fine. I have everything I need."

"Including a lover?"

She glared at him. "Like I said before, I don't need a man."

"You're a passionate woman, Shahna. How long do you think you can do without sex?"

"Just as long as I want to," she returned, meeting his eyes defiantly. "There are plenty of other pleasures in life."

He laughed. "None like that."

Samuel had all the shapes in the bucket now and was vigorously shaking it. It fell from his hands and rolled, coming to rest against Kier's foot.

Following in hot pursuit, Samuel found Kier's denim-clad leg a handy support, and hauled himself up by clutching onto the fabric.

Distracted, Kier looked down, and Shahna bent and scooped the child into her arms, holding him almost like a shield.

"Mum-mum," Samuel said fondly, grasping a handful of her hair.

Kier stepped back, allowing Shahna to slip past him into the living room. She removed Samuel's fist from her hair and held his hand.

He was the most important thing in her life now, she reminded herself. Sex was nothing compared to the on-going delight she took in her son. He was the center of her world.

Kier was looking at them both, a complicated expression on his face. "I'll be going then," he said.

Shahna nodded jerkily, not trusting herself to speak.

He stopped by them, and gently touched a knuckle to Samuel's cheek. "See ya, Scamp," he said.

Shahna stiffened as he scanned her face. Softly he added, "You too."

She didn't watch him go. When she was sure he was out of sight, she unclenched the teeth that she'd clamped together to stop herself from calling him back, and let out a long-held breath.

Samuel patted her cheek. "Mum-mum."

Shahna smiled at him with something like desperation, not realizing until he complained that she held him too tightly. "Sorry, darling," she said and loosened her hold, then put him down as he wriggled, intent on getting back to the floor. Remembering the plastic bucket, he crawled to it and banged at it. Shahna mentally shook herself, removed the lid and tipped out the shapes for him to begin the game over again.

Later she phoned the farmhouse to enquire about Morrie.

"He's in hospital," Alison informed her. "In Kaitaia. It's a nasty strep infection and he could lose his hand."

Shahna made a shocked exclamation. "Is there anything I can do for you?" she offered after expressing her sympathy.

"Thank you, dear, but you have a baby to look after. Your friend Kier is staying on for a few days to help out."

A leap of relief mingled with dismay. She'd braced herself never to see him again.

"He says he's a fast learner," Alison was saying, "and willing to try anything. Ace thinks he'll be quite useful."

He did? "Well..." Shahna said lamely, "...do let me know if I can help in any way."

After she had hung up she stood for a minute staring into space. So Kier hadn't left after all.

It didn't mean she would see him again.

But she did, the following day. While Samuel had an afternoon nap Shahna was hoeing the new garden when Kier arrived, carrying a cardboard box from which some green leaves protruded.

"Alison sent you these." He put down the box. "I told her you were starting a flower garden."

"That's good of her, only surely with Morrie in hospital she doesn't have time—"

"I think she's trying to keep her mind off it. She's been weeding and pruning all morning, but she's gone with Ace to visit him now."

Alison was a keen gardener who kept the farmhouse surrounded with flowers all year round. Admiration and envy had inspired Shahna to attempt growing her own, although it would take some ingenuity to keep Samuel's curiosity at bay while she established the flower beds.

The box held rooted cuttings and some divided tubers. As Shahna bent to look at them Kier asked, "Where's Samuel?"

"Asleep." She lifted out a plant with a good lump of earth clinging to its roots. "These are great."

"She said there's nothing with thorns in there, because of the baby." Kier frowned at her. "Don't you wear gloves when you're gardening?"

He could talk, she thought, considering the state of his hands yesterday. "Sometimes." She'd had some blisters herself when she was establishing the vegetable patch at the back of the cottage, but her hands were less tender now, and gloves would slip on the smooth handle of the hoe.

Kier said, "Didn't Alison tell you what Morrie's got?"

"Some nasty bug, she said."

"Streptococcus pyogenes. Apparently it's common in the soil, and can get into your bloodstream via the smallest thorn or splinter. If Alison hadn't got Morrie to the hospital in time he might have died."

From a *splinter?* "Alison must be worried sick," Shahna said. "She told me he might lose a hand. And that you're staying on for a while." She paused. "It's hardly your sort of holiday."

"It's a change," Kier admitted. "As a matter of fact I'm enjoying it in a masochistic kind of way."

She couldn't help smiling at that. "You're no masochist."

His eyes glinted as he surveyed her. "I wouldn't have said you were, either. You're not intending to spend the rest of your life buried here, are you?"

"I'm not buried! I feel more alive than I ever have."

"Ever?" The glint in his eyes intensified.

Heat raced through her, erotic memories chasing each other in her mind. Her hands clenched as she fought them. "I've learned," she said, "there's more to life than success and money and...sex."

"Hallelujah!" he mocked her. "You think the rest of us don't know that?"

"I'm not judging you...or anyone."

"Aren't you?"

"This has nothing to do with you, Kier! It's how I've decided to live *my* life."

"By walking out of mine!"

Shahna hesitated. "I had to." Did he think it had been easy?

"Without even discussing it?"

"What would be the use? I'd made up my mind."

"You were afraid I'd talk you out of it," he guessed.

That was almost too close. "I didn't want an argument. And I don't want one now."

"There's more going on here than a sudden desire for the simple life. Did that come before or after you met Samuel's father?"

Shahna steadied her voice. "That's my own business."

"Were you in love with him? Where is he now? Does he know he has a child?"

"I don't want to talk about it." Her heart was beating

suffocatingly. "And you have no right to ask these questions."

"We were together for three years!"

"We *slept* together," Shahna corrected him. And then added bluntly, "Not even that, quite often. We had sex, Kier."

His eyes darkened with temper. "We were lovers! It wasn't some casual one-night stand between people who barely knew each other's names."

"I don't recall you ever telling me you loved me," Shahna said.

Kier was taken aback, though he supposed that was true. He'd told her he loved her body, her laughter, her uninhibited sexual responses. But the words "I love you" hadn't been part of their bargain. "Did you want me to?" he asked.

Shahna gave him an oddly cynical smile. "Of course not."

Of course not, he echoed in his mind, with unreasonable anger. She'd never said she loved him, either. "You weren't in love with me," he reminded her. She couldn't have been, if she could leave him at the drop of a hat. And make love with another man so soon afterward. "Were you?"

"Would you have cared if I had been?"

"I cared a great deal about you!" he argued, dodging the question. "Why else do you think I followed you here?"

"Curiosity," she answered.

"More than that!"

"Oh? Don't tell me you suddenly discovered your undying love for me and tracked me down to tell me you can't live without me!"

"Is that what you'd have liked?" Tracking her down

had been his first, instinctive reaction—he'd wanted to find her and shake her senseless and demand an explanation. Or kiss her, make mad, violent love to her until she promised to come back to him.

"No!" Shahna vehemently shook her head. "Why do you think I moved so far away? I never imagined you'd find me here."

"Why was that important?" he pounced. "I've never hurt you, or even threatened you."

She looked away for a moment. "I just wanted a fresh start. A clean break from my old life. I know you don't understand. It isn't necessary for you to."

"Maybe it is, to me."

She made a despairing little gesture. "I can't help you."

Kier regarded her in baffled silence. One of the things that had first intrigued him about Shahna was the impression of hidden depths under the glossy, high-powered surface. Perfectly groomed, decisive and extremely good at her job, she'd preserved that surface right up to the night she first allowed him into her bed.

He had suspected—hoped for—passion behind the carefully maintained facade. And he found it, but even while making love to her he'd sensed a reserve, almost as though she were unsure of herself and her reactions, surprising in him a new sensation of tenderness.

In the habit of taking care of his partner's pleasure before his own, he had been especially solicitous of hers. And she'd seemed to grow in confidence, in trusting him. As their affair progressed he'd reveled in her increasing willingness to initiate and experiment.

But despite their physical closeness, allied to a mental attunement that he'd found with no other woman, he had never felt that Shahna was an open book. Somehow her innermost being remained elusive.

He'd realized after that first night that all the barriers weren't going to tumble at once, but he'd been confident they would in time.

Now he was discovering that he had known her even less than he'd thought. Never mind her casual clothes and relaxed lifestyle and apparent softening—the emotional barriers were more rigidly in place than ever. She wouldn't tell him why she'd left, had made it clear she wasn't pleased to see him, had shown nothing but relief when she thought he was leaving, and was tight-lipped about exactly what had sent her to live in the wilds of the Hokianga.

Watching her inspect the rest of the plants Alison had sent, he had a strong urge to grab her shoulders and make her look at him, force her to answer some pointed questions. Like, who was Samuel's father and why had she slept with him?

Instead he shoved his hands into his pockets and when she straightened asked her, "Would you like some help putting those plants in?"

"No, thanks. I want to fork in some compost first anyway."

"With gloves on, I hope," he said grimly. "Do you have a wheelbarrow?"

"Never needed one. I'll manage."

"I could put some in a bag and bring it 'round for you."

"I can do that myself. Say thanks to Alison for me, and tell her I'll phone her later."

She couldn't have made it plainer that he wasn't wanted. But he hadn't forgotten yesterday's kiss. He could still taste her mouth in his imagination, still feel the way her lips had opened to him, answered his, before she pushed him away.

He folded his arms. "If you won't let me help," he said, "I can watch."

Shahna blinked at him. "Watch? What for?"

His eyes challenged her. "Because I enjoy looking at you," he said. "And there was a time when you enjoyed me doing it too."

Mercilessly he watched the color fill her cheeks, making her eyes green and brilliant as emeralds. He knew she remembered, as he did, how often he'd lain on his bed or hers, waiting while she stripped to her undies. Often undies that he'd bought for her, because he'd liked knowing that under the conventional business suits she wore from nine-to-five she had on the most frivolous, sexy undergarments he could find, that would be revealed only to him in their private moments. And then she'd join him on the bed because he preferred to complete the task of undressing her himself.

Her voice was choked when she said, "I don't think that's a good idea."

"Then let me help."

"Your hands—"

"I brought gloves." He hauled a pair of worn leather work gloves from his back pocket. "Ace lent them to me."

"Aren't you needed on the farm?"

"Not until they get back this afternoon. I don't have anything to do until then."

Finally she shrugged. "If you're that bored..."

"There's a wheelbarrow at the farm. I don't suppose they'll mind if we borrow it. What about that sawdust Morrie promised you?"

"I'll spread that on top later, as a mulch."

He nodded. "I'll get the wheelbarrow. Won't be long."

When he returned with it and he'd silently noted that she'd found a pair of gloves too, they filled the barrow with compost and dug into the freshly hoed soil, working until Samuel woke. Then keeping the little boy happy and away from the garden became a major operation, and in the end Kier finished off the task while Shahna and Samuel watched.

"Thank you again," she said as he packed up the tools. "I appreciate your help."

He cast her a quizzical look. "No problem. I'll see you again."

And again, he promised himself as he pushed the wheelbarrow off through the trees. Somehow he was going to get to the heart of the mystery that Shahna presented.

Shahna put in the new plants after laying Samuel down for the night.

The lowering sun turned the clouds hanging in the sky over the hills to fiery red and gilded the harbor. By the time she'd finished, it was getting dark. She sat on the steps for a while, breathing in the calm, cool air of evening and watching the stars appear one by one.

There were no stars in cities. The artificial lights blotted them out, and no one had time to search for them.

She'd found a hard-won peace here, time to count the stars, but Kier's advent threatened to disrupt all that. He could turn her life upside down—again.

The following morning Samuel sported a new tooth.

After breakfast Shahna carried him to the rambling timber-clad farmhouse where Alison welcomed her into the big, cluttered kitchen and took Samuel for a cuddle.

Shahna was quite relieved to pass him over—he was getting heavier, but the walk across the farm paddocks was too rough for his stroller, so she kept it in the car.

Alison made tea that they drank while she told Shahna the latest news of Morrie, and Samuel crawled about the floor, discovering a cupboard full of plastic and stainless steel bowls that Alison indulgently allowed him to investigate.

They were still talking when Ace and Kier came in.

As Alison made another pot of tea for the men, Shahna hastily finished hers, but her move to leave was foiled when the older woman asked about the new garden and offered some advice on nurturing it. "And Ace will bring over some sawdust for you," she promised. "He just has to collect it from the mill."

"You and Ace have enough to think about," Shahna protested. "There's no hurry."

"I could fetch it," Kier offered, "while you two are visiting Morrie this afternoon—unless there's something else you want done, Ace?"

Ace shook his head. "Good idea. Take the pickup. I'll give you directions to the mill."

"Why don't you go with him, Shahna?" Alison suggested. "You can show him the way, and Samuel would enjoy the ride."

"We can't put his car seat in the pickup," Shahna pointed out. No way would she compromise Samuel's safety.

"Oh." Alison looked dashed. "I hadn't thought of that. But I feel guilty you're seeing so little of your friend. Kier came to visit you, after all."

"He wasn't intending to stay." Shahna avoided Kier's silently challenging look. "If Morrie hadn't got sick he'd have gone by now."

"Still…" Alison brightened. "Why don't you go this morning, and I'll look after Samuel. Ace can do without Kier for an hour or so, can't you?" She turned to her son.

"Sure." Ace grinned at Shahna. "You know Mum just loves to get her hands on the little fella. Besides, she needs to keep her mind off things right now. She's got nothing to do but worry."

Shahna was sure his mother had plenty to do, but when Alison said, "I'd love to have him, really…" Shahna gave in.

The men finished their morning tea and Ace handed Kier the keys to the pickup truck. "There you go, mate."

"If you're ready?" Kier queried Shahna, and she reluctantly left the table and followed him to the vehicle shed while Alison distracted Samuel from noticing that he was missing out on a ride.

Kier opened the passenger door for her but she evaded his proffered help and climbed into the seat.

Soon he had the truck moving down the long farm driveway, and she directed him to the village and then onto an uphill side road, unsealed and dusty but lined with trees and ferns and giving occasional glimpses of the harbor.

As they turned a tight corner, a large articulated truck and trailer rumbled toward them, and Kier maneuvered the pickup to the side, allowing the other vehicle, laden with cut boards, to pass. "Pretty hairy roads you have around here," he commented.

"You get used to them," Shahna replied. "You do have a license to drive this thing, don't you?" Ace wouldn't have bothered asking, she guessed. It was rumored that half the drivers in the Hokianga were unlicensed and half the vehicles unregistered, but she hoped it wasn't true.

"My license covers it," Kier assured her. "Can you drive it?" He accelerated as the road temporarily straightened.

"I've never tried. Do you want me to?"

"No. I thought maybe you don't trust me."

"I trust you."

He glanced at her briefly. "You used to, once."

Shahna looked away. The wheels bounced over a pothole in the road and Kier said, "Sorry."

"Not your fault," she said automatically.

"Is it my fault you don't trust me anymore?"

"I told you, I do!"

"Then tell me about Samuel."

"He's my son."

Kier's breath hissed between his teeth. "You know what I mean, Shahna. How did you come to have another man's child so soon after leaving me? Another man who isn't in the picture any longer as far as I can see. Does he even know he has a child?"

Shahna's hands twisted tightly together in her lap. She swallowed, and her voice lowered despite herself. "He doesn't believe Samuel is his."

She saw Kier's hands tighten on the steering wheel. Then he braked, and the truck slid to a stop. As he turned to her she saw glittering anger in his eyes. "What kind of a bastard did you sleep with?" he demanded. "What the hell were you thinking of?"

I was thinking of you. She'd almost said it aloud. "I can't blame him," she said. "I knew what I was doing."

Had she? Maybe at the time she hadn't been thinking rationally at all. Certainly no one would have said that she was acting wisely.

"There are tests," Kier said. "You can prove who the

father is, force him to take at least some financial responsibility.''

''No. I don't want anything more to do with him. I'd rather bring Samuel up by myself.''

Kier was scowling. ''It must have been a short-lived affair.'' His face suddenly changed, his cheeks going gaunt and sallow. ''You weren't *raped,* were you?''

''No!'' If only she could claim that. Not that she'd ever wish for such a thing.

''Then how could you have—'' He bit off the words in midsentence.

How could she have made love to someone else so soon after breaking off with Kier? He must know from his own careful campaign to get her into his bed that she wasn't in the habit of sleeping around, had no interest in casual sex.

''It was a one-night stand,'' she said, her voice brittle, her throat aching. ''A brief encounter, okay?'' She looked at him defiantly. ''So now you know.''

Chapter 5

"I don't believe that," Kier said flatly. It would be totally out of character for her.

Shahna unclenched her hands, shrugging her shoulders. "I can't help what you believe."

"It's not like you!"

She gave him a bleak smile that rocked him. "How would you know?"

"Dammit, Shahna, I know that much about you!" His imagination balked. "You're not the kind of woman who goes to bed with any stranger." If he was certain of anything about her, it was that.

"I didn't say he was a stranger, did I?"

"You said a one-night stand." Baffled, Kier ran a hand through his hair. Nothing in this computed in any logical way. "But you told me you *planned* to get pregnant."

"That's all it takes," she said. "I knew it was the right time."

She'd worked that out beforehand?

"And," Shahna added with deadly intent, "one night doesn't necessarily mean one...chance."

Sheer rage made him close one hand hard on the steering wheel, trying to control himself. He felt bruised, battered, and wanted to lash out, hit back. "So you picked out a stud to father your child?" he flung at her. "I hope his other attributes are an improvement on his morals."

She winced and turned white.

"Oh, hell!" he said. "I suppose I shouldn't have said that."

"You suppose?" She rallied quickly, casting him a sarcastic look.

"All right, I shouldn't have. I'm sorry." Kier knew he sounded grudging, irritated. He'd always hated being in the wrong. Increasingly frustrated by her refusal to explain, he was fighting a primeval urge to force the truth out of her, an instinct that shocked him by its violence. He had never physically bullied a woman. But then no woman had ever made him so angry.

He wasn't even sure why her secretiveness so infuriated him. As Shahna had pointed out, what she did and who she did it with were no longer any concern of his.

The reminder did nothing to improve his temper.

A car came toward them in a cloud of dust, and Shahna said, "Hadn't we better get on? We're almost blocking the road here."

Restarting the engine, Kier grated the gears and swore under his breath, letting off a bit of steam. The car swept by with inches to spare, leaving the dust to settle around them. It was a warm morning but Kier wound up the window as Shahna covered her nose and mouth.

For a while he drove in frowning silence, until they came to a junction and she said, "Turn right here. It's about a mile farther on."

She pointed out a wide gateway flanked by toetoe plants, silken cream flags rising from clumps of thin, sharp-edged leaves, and he swung into a yard half-filled with stacked logs and cut timber, parking near a hill of sawdust.

A balding man in overalls came out to see what they wanted, and fetched a front-end loader to fill the tray of the pickup. When they'd finished Kier took out his wallet, but the man waved it away. "We only charge if we have to deliver it. Glad to get rid of the stuff."

Shahna gave him a dazzling smile. "Thank you."

It occurred to Kier that she hadn't once smiled at him like that since he'd arrived. And that it was plain stupid to be jealous of the middle-aged, paunchy sawmiller.

He helped Shahna into the truck again with a firm hold on her arm and slammed the door, giving the man a curt but pleasant nod before going around to the driver's side.

"You've been here before?" he queried as he drove out.

"I collected a few bags of sawdust in my car when I started the vegetable garden."

"I'd never have picked you for a gardener."

Shahna laughed. "I'm no expert, but it gives me a buzz, cooking and eating my own vegetables. And they've got to be better for Samuel, fresh and not sprayed with all kinds of chemicals."

"Have you turned into a greenie?"

"I'd rather not use poisons. Alison says the bugs haven't found my garden yet and in a couple of years I'll probably have more pests. By then maybe I'll know enough about organic gardening to keep them away naturally."

A couple of years? Did she really expect to stick it out

here for that long? He glanced at her. She was staring out the windshield.

"Look out!" she said.

He braked as a family of Californian quails crossed in front of them, the lean adult sleek and gray, a feather bobbing on its head, followed by a dozen or so chicks like tiny pom-poms on matchstick legs.

Shahna laughed. "Aren't they incredibly cute?"

For a moment the wariness and strain she'd been showing vanished. He couldn't help smiling back at her.

"Incredibly," he agreed, sliding the pickup to a halt.

One of the chicks tumbled on the rough road and struggled to its feet again. The other birds had already disappeared into the dust-caked grass and ferns that edged the road. The stray headed off in another direction, and Shahna said anxiously, "He's going the wrong way, he'll get lost."

She had grasped the door handle, but Kier was faster, his long legs allowing his feet to hit the road while she was still scrambling out of the truck. He tried to shoo the chick in the right direction, but it darted away with remarkable speed. Shahna headed it off, sending it back to toward him, and he stooped, his hands cupped, allowing the chick to run into them.

As he stood up with the minute ball of fluff enclosed in his hands, tiny feet scrabbling at his palms and the down on its body tickling, Shahna said, "Be careful!"

"I will." He strode to the side of the road, waded into the grass and fern and stooped to free the chick from its prison. Shahna joined him as it hurried after its family.

An approaching rumble warned of more traffic, and Kier urged Shahna back to the pickup. A long stainless steel milk tanker roared by, the driver giving them a nonchalant wave.

More dust clouded about them as they reentered the truck cab, and Shahna grimaced, trying to brush some of it from her clothes.

Not wanting to put her on her guard again, Kier turned the conversation to neutral topics, asking questions about the district and making her laugh with his account of his incompetence at herding cows. "That's probably why Ace was so keen to get rid of me this morning," he finished. "He's realized I'm the world's most useless farmhand and he'd do better on his own."

"Alison said for a townie you pick things up pretty fast, and you're not afraid of hard work."

"I've never been afraid of that."

"Are you ever afraid of anything?" She gave him a sideways look of curiosity.

"Not much, these days." He wasn't going to admit to the panic he'd felt when he had come back to his apartment and found her note telling him she'd gone out of his life. Nor to the increasing dread he'd felt when, after contacting her friends and her employer, he'd realized that she'd deliberately, systematically, taken herself beyond his reach.

Brushing aside the sweat-inducing memories, he said, "When I was a kid I hated heights." He'd never admitted this, either, but it was a safer subject. "Taking up skydiving cured me of that."

Her eyes widened. "I remember the photo of you with the members of your club. You never told me it scared you!"

"After a while it didn't. And once I wasn't scared anymore I gave it up." The sport had served its purpose, and although he missed the adrenaline rush he'd had more constructive things to do with his time than jump out of airplanes every weekend.

"It's a pretty drastic cure," Shahna murmured.

He dropped her at the farm to collect Samuel while Ace hopped in the pickup and the two men drove to her place to unload the sawdust. By the time she got back they had almost finished piling it on the new lawn, and she thanked them both before they went off again.

Shahna felt oddly lonely as the truck disappeared among the trees. Most of the time she reveled in the peace and silence, but the outing had made her restless.

Samuel objected when she put him down for his afternoon nap, fussing until she picked him up again. He was tetchy for the rest of the day, and she fed him and put him to bed earlier than usual in the evening.

Remembering guiltily that she hadn't got around to phoning Alison after visiting hours, she called the farmhouse.

Ace answered. "The antibiotics are working," he told her. "They think they can save the hand, sort of, but they have to operate and it might end up crippled and useless."

They talked for a while, Ace telling her his sister was coming up from Wellington at the end of the week, and she gave him messages of support for both his parents before hanging up. Shaking off an empathetic depression, she went outside to attack her pile of sawdust.

A quick rustling in the trees made her turn toward the track from the farm. A fat native pigeon lifted into the air and flapped laboriously away, its blue under-feathers a flash of color against the paling sky.

A pang of disappointment made Shahna realize she was expecting Kier. She dug her spade into the sawdust, trying to banish the dismaying emotion, and worked on spreading the stuff over the garden until dark.

* * *

Overnight Samuel developed a sniffle and a slight fever. Although it was playgroup day, if he was incubating something infectious Shahna didn't want to pass it on to other children, so they stayed home and Shahna watched him anxiously for spots or other symptoms.

It was difficult to work when Samuel was grumpy, and after spending an hour or so in her studio, she gave up and devoted herself to keeping him occupied with toys and cuddles.

To her great relief, after lunch he went to sleep. Shahna was in her studio, setting a piece of polished mother-of-pearl into a silver surround that she'd shaped into irregular pleats, when a shadow fell across the open doorway. She turned, a punch and hammer in her hand, and Kier said, "Don't let me stop you. Do you mind if I watch?"

She shrugged, returning to painstakingly closing the edges of the narrow silver bezel around the piece of shell to keep it in place.

When she laid down her tools Kier said, "That looks great."

Shahna lit her gas-powered blowtorch and played a gentle flame on the jewelers' wax holding the pendant in place, then lifted it from its prison with a pair of tweezers.

She swung around on her stool. "Did you want something?"

"I thought you might need help with spreading the sawdust, but I see you've done that."

"Yes. Thanks."

"And you're busy." He looked again at the pendant she had laid on the work surface. "Sam's asleep?"

"For now."

Kier looked at her closely. "Something wrong?"

"Not really. He's got a cold or something."

"You're worried."

Surprised at his perceptiveness, Shahna admitted, "Well, a bit. He's had all his shots but...you can't guard against everything. Meningitis is a killer, and it's very fast."

"Why don't you take him to a doctor?"

"I can't run to the doctor every time Samuel has a runny nose." She might have asked Alison's advice but the older woman had enough problems of her own right now.

"For Samuel's sake," he suggested, "shouldn't you be living somewhere less isolated? I'd have thought readily available medical care would be a priority when you have a child to care for."

Shahna stood up, letting the stool slide away. "You think you know what's best for my son? Alison's a trained nurse, and Samuel's a very healthy child now," she said. "If he's really ill of course I'll get him to a hospital."

"I didn't mean to imply you wouldn't—just that it could be difficult."

She supposed that was a sort-of apology. "I appreciate your concern," she said, only half-sarcastically. "And I take my responsibility for Samuel very seriously. He's more important to me than anything else in the world."

"I know that." He moved, rather edgily, and she thought he was going to leave. She ought to let him, but she heard herself say, "Would you like a coffee?" An olive branch.

He glanced at the pendant. "I don't want to interrupt."

"I promised myself a break before I clean the wax off this and do a bit more finishing."

"Then thanks. I'd like that."

She made coffee for two and they sat at the kitchen table.

"Ace's sister is coming up for the long weekend," he said.

"Yes, he told me. Alison will be glad."

"I look forward to meeting Ginnie," Kier remarked. "Her family's very proud of her."

Ginnie held a top job in a go-ahead computer company in the capital. "She's extremely good at what she does, I gather. Very clever." On the couple of occasions they had met, Shahna had resisted the urge to boast about her own past achievements in the business world.

"Did she make you wish you hadn't thrown in your job after all?"

"No. She made me glad I wasn't a part of all that anymore."

He looked at her skeptically and she looked back, unblinking. "I'm happier now than I've ever been."

It was almost true, as long as she ignored the fierce inner ache that sometimes attacked her in the middle of the night, or when something—a business magazine lying in the dentist's waiting room, a news item in the paper she bought infrequently, a snatch of overheard conversation—brought into her mind a disconcerting picture of Kier's face. Or of his body.

His lips tightened. "You weren't happy when you were with me?"

She couldn't help laughing at the blatant egotism, though the laugh caught in her throat. Kier had never suffered from a lack of confidence. "That was a kind of happiness, I guess."

He was positively smoldering now, his brows a line, his eyes hostile.

"It was different," she said quickly. "What we had...it couldn't last. Neither of us expected it to, did we?"

He didn't answer immediately. "I suppose not," he conceded. "But things can change."

Shahna blinked. Her heart turned over, painfully. "You...never suggested that you wanted them to."

"I might have," he said, sounding almost resentful, "if you'd given me a chance."

"You had three years," she reminded him.

For a moment he seemed discomfited. "I was thinking of asking you to move in with me," he told her.

Something inside her hurt. "Oh...and then what?"

Kier shifted irritably, his eyes leaving hers before returning at full glare. "Then...who knows? I thought we'd take one step at a time."

"To where?" she challenged him. "You were going to ask me to give up my home and move into yours—for what? So you wouldn't have the inconvenience of living in one place and sleeping half the time in another? Sex on tap?"

"Why are you so determined to cheapen our relationship?" he demanded, furious. "You know we had more going for us than just sex!"

"Did we? It seemed pretty important to you."

"Sex *is* important between a man and woman. You had no complaints at the time."

She certainly hadn't voiced any. Sex with Kier had always been a satisfying, exhilarating experience. And on the rare occasions she hadn't been in the mood, he'd seemed content to hold her in his arms while they watched TV or listened to music after she'd showered and dressed in a cosy robe. Sometimes she'd fallen asleep against his shoulder and had been dimly aware of him carrying her to bed and placing the covers over her. And then he'd leave.

In the lonely reaches of the night when she relived their

time together, it was often that rare, asexual tenderness she missed more sharply than their sizzling lovemaking.

In the end she'd been the one to leave, for good. And if he found that unconscionable, it was his problem. "I never had any complaints about your lovemaking," she said. "You were superb in bed."

His brows lifted, and to her surprise his cheeks colored. "*We* were superb together," he said. "We still could be." His eyelids flickered and his eyes glittered as his gaze slipped over her. "If it wasn't enough for you, why didn't you say so?"

"Was it enough for you?"

Their eyes met and clashed. Shahna regarded him warily, and realized that her hand was tightly clenched on her cup. Deliberately she relaxed it, surreptitiously flexing her fingers.

It was sexual fascination that had first drawn them to each other, that had been the strongest tie. True, they enjoyed other things together, but not deep emotional intimacy. *That* he hadn't asked for and hadn't offered. She sometimes wondered if his charming company was the price Kier felt he must pay for access to her body.

"It was never the only thing," he said. "As you said, any woman could have satisfied my physical needs. But I wanted *you,* not any woman. I still want you, Shahna."

Sitting there at the small table, the sun spilling through the window in a shaft of dancing dust motes, she felt as if she'd been suddenly transported to another plane, where the air was rarefied and anything was possible. A longing that she hadn't felt so keenly since she'd first left him took hold of her, capturing her breath.

Then common sense reasserted itself. In essence, he was offering no more than he had before. And anyway, her life had become more complicated now. "We can't go back again, Kier."

He shoved back his chair, and it rocked as he got to his feet. She wondered if he was going to haul her up as well, perhaps make uncurbed, passionate love to her until she capitulated and admitted she wanted him. But after a moment he shoved his hands into his pockets and swung away from her, going to stand in the sunlight pouring through the window.

"You should have talked to me before you left," he said. "You could have told me what was wrong."

Could she? Not without entangling him in a situation he'd never wanted. "You're so sure something was wrong," she said. "Can't you accept that I simply felt it was time to move on?"

He turned then to face her. "Is that all you're going to say about it?"

"Maybe it's all there is to say."

His look pierced her. "It's there again. I thought you'd left it behind in Sydney."

Shahna was bewildered. "I don't know what you're talking about."

"The first time I saw you, you had this tantalizing glass armor wrapped around you. I thought I'd get through it when I took you to bed, but it was always there, keeping me from reaching the real woman inside."

"That's nonsense," Shahna said uncomfortably.

But didn't she feel more "real" now than she ever had? Wasn't that what she'd been saying to him since he arrived?

Kier shook his head. "You're different here." Confirming her thoughts. "I knew it when I first stepped off the boat." With unexpected urgency, he said, "Don't shut me out again, Shahna!"

"I'm not." But she knew he was right, she'd always had a strong sense of self-preservation. Just as well, because in the end it became necessary to her survival.

"No?" He looked at her with patent disbelief.

"Anyway," she said, "it's all in the past."

"This—" he looked around them "—isn't the past." His eyes swept back to her. "We're here *now*. Both of us."

"But you're only visiting. When you're gone..."

When he was gone life would return to normal. She'd be safe again in her painfully constructed cocoon, looking after her baby. Even the memory of Kier and her old life would fade in time.

It must.

"I'm not going anywhere...yet," he promised, almost threateningly. "I suppose you wouldn't care to take up where we left off?"

"You're joking!" she exclaimed, despising her stupid heart for its involuntary little skip.

Kier tipped his head, regarding her consideringly. "Not entirely. I didn't expect you'd jump at it. But I'd love to know what's holding you back."

Shahna fought a shameful yearning to give in. Even if only for one night. He looked wildly sexy standing there with the sunlight gleaming on his hair, black and glossy as a tui's wing, his eyes holding an invitational gleam, and a slight curve to his beautiful male mouth.

"Been there, done that," she said flippantly. "And I threw away the T-shirt."

He laughed, easing the tension a little. "That's the old Shahna," he said. "The one I thought I knew."

"You bring it out in me." A protective device, something to deflect him from what was going on inside her mind, her heart.

"What else do I bring out, Shah-na?" He drawled her name, low-voiced, in a way he'd done only in private, making her shiver right down to her toes.

He knew very well—she didn't need to tell him and had no intention of doing so. His ego was heavy enough as it was. Shahna stood up, muttering something about getting back to work.

She picked up the cups and took them to the sink, assuming he would move aside. But he stood rock-still and she had to go around him to deposit the cups on the counter. As she straightened he raised a hand and grasped her arm. His breath stirred her hair against her temple.

Shahna pulled back and he let her go. Her heart was pounding and her breath came fast. She saw the gleam in his eyes intensify, a look of satisfaction cross his face. "Why fight it?" he asked.

"Why push it?" she retorted.

"For old times' sake?" He was turning on the charm, smiling down at her, teasing her with those come-to-bed eyes.

"No, thanks. The old times are long gone. You made a mistake coming here, Kier, if you thought I'd fall into your arms for a few nights and then send you on your merry way."

His brows drew together. "I didn't think that."

"But it's what you'd like." Maybe he needed to prove to himself that he hadn't lost his touch, that she couldn't resist his masculine attraction. She must have made a crack in his pride by leaving him flat.

"I'd like to make love to you," he said bluntly. "It's the other part I don't fancy. Leaving you here while I go back to the real world."

"This is my real world," she insisted. "So you see,

there's no point in us being lovers again. I've grown beyond temporary affairs, relationships without promises.''

He frowned again at that, a sudden alertness in his eyes. ''You want promises?'' he asked. ''Commitment?''

''Don't worry,'' she said, her voice very dry, ''I won't expect it from you. But you can't expect any…sexual accommodation from me. I'm not available.''

''Sexual accommodation,'' he repeated. ''It sounds like a sleazy boardinghouse—or a brothel. And I've never frequented either.''

She didn't suppose he had. The thought of a boardinghouse would probably have horrified him as much as, if not more than, the other.

He straightened and moved out of the sun, so when she looked at him again his face was dark and enigmatic. ''If it's commitment you want,'' he said, ''I'll give it to you.'' As if throwing down a challenge, he said, ''How's this for commitment? Marry me, Shahna.''

Chapter 6

Kier couldn't believe he'd said that.

It was uncannily like the time when he'd first stood in the open doorway of a moving aircraft and felt the wind whip at his nylon jumpsuit. When he'd looked down and seen the earth dizzyingly far below, and thought, *What the hell am I doing?*

Shahna looked as stunned as he felt. Her eyes were dark and huge, and her lips had parted softly as if she had trouble breathing. He had a strong urge to close them with his own, to kiss her and go on kissing her until...

Until she said yes. He wanted her to say yes. Yes to his kiss, yes to making wild, wonderful love the way they used to. Yes to shared laughter, to eating a whole plate of crisp, winged wontons for breakfast, to squabbling over the Sunday paper as they had invariably done when he'd stayed on Saturday night, to being his partner when he had to attend a boring business function, exchanging wicked murmurs that lightened the proceedings considerably—to being the part of his life that he missed more than he'd ever admitted even to himself. Yes to coming back to him.

Yes to marrying him.

When he'd taken that step from the plane and thrown himself out into empty blue space he'd been terrified, but then he'd discovered he was flying without wings, and although his heart thumped and the fear was still there, he'd found the freefall unexpectedly exhilarating. His parachute had opened without incident and he'd had time to begin enjoying himself before it deposited him safely on the ground, giving him a triumphant sense of achievement.

"You're joking." Shahna's voice was flat, expressionless. Disbelieving.

He could have said yes, of course he was, he didn't really mean it.

But he took the step into unknown space instead. "No joke," he told her, free-falling. No going back, the plane was off into the wild blue and he had only instinct now to rely on. "I want to marry you, Shahna."

He was dizzy, euphoric. Why hadn't he done this before? What had he been afraid of? It felt so right! So...exciting.

"No." She took a step backward, as though removing herself from him. "It's not possible."

Kier abruptly came to earth, a rough landing without a 'chute. "Why not?"

"Well, because..." She was looking at him almost fearfully. "I can't just...there's Samuel. And everything I've built here. You're not suggesting you want to come and live with us, are you?"

"*Here?*" He might be crazy, but he wasn't that far gone.

She smiled, but it looked like an effort, and her eyes were sad. "You see?" she said gently. "It *is* impossible."

An uncomfortable echo of the panic he'd felt after her departure from his life stirred in Kier's stomach. "Nothing's impossible."

"Your credo," she said. "But you can't run people's lives the way you do your business, Kier. Not even your own."

He'd always done pretty well at running his life, thank you. Until Shahna up and left him.

"It would never work," she said despairingly. "Surely you can see that?"

"I don't see that at all. We could make it work, if you really wanted it to."

"And what about you?" she countered. "What would you give to make it work? Your business, your lifestyle? Everything you've worked so hard to achieve?"

"Are you asking me to?"

"I'm trying to point out what you're asking of *me*."

Exasperated, he looked around them. "Like giving up a tumbledown hovel that isn't even yours, in the back of beyond? And working in a converted washhouse? Of course, you couldn't possibly trade that for a decent studio in a civilized part of the world where your work would get the attention it deserves and you could live in comfort! What are you punishing yourself for, Shahna? What heinous sin did you commit that you've condemned yourself to a hermit's existence?"

"The cottage isn't tumbling down, and I've committed no sin—at least, none that my lifestyle is a penance for. I've put a part of myself into this place. I take inspiration from it for my designs. It has a *soul* that I could never find in Sydney."

"It's a *place!*" Kier said. "That's all. Are you claiming

some mystical connection with it? The spirit of the harbor cast a spell on you or something?''

There were people who claimed that, or something very close to it—not only those descended from the vikings of the Pacific who had sailed centuries ago from the legendary islands of Hawaiiki and discovered the Hokianga, who had named the hills and rivers that modern Maori claimed as their spiritual ancestors. Others from Europe and America had come to visit and stayed, because something told them they had found home, the place where they wanted to spend their lives. The harbor and its rugged hills had always held some special magic.

''If you don't feel it,'' she said, ''there's no use trying to explain.''

His mind in overdrive, Kier took a deep breath, prepared to persuade, reason, cajole.

''Don't!'' She stopped him before he'd begun.

''Don't what?''

''Think you can talk me round,'' she told him, rocking him back on his heels. He'd forgotten how well she knew him. ''I said *no*, Kier. And I meant it.''

His instinct was to secure her capitulation by any means he could, even grab her and make love to her and show her what she'd been missing...

After all, she'd told him he was a magnificent lover.

But he was a strategist, accustomed to working his way around problems using his mind and not his emotions.

Something warned him a head-on attack wasn't the way to go. He dipped his head, hiding his eyes. ''If that's how you feel,'' he said. When he looked up again she was regarding him suspiciously. ''But if you change your mind you only have to say so.''

''I won't change my mind.''

Kier put a clamp on his tongue. He nodded curtly, letting her see his disappointment.

She looked miserable and a little uncertain, Kier was rather pleased to see. He needn't give up yet. He *wouldn't* give up.

After he had gone, Shahna stood at the window, gazing in a bewildered haze at nothing in particular, until she was startled by a half dozen parakeets flashing by in a blur of red, blue, green and yellow and disappearing into the trees.

Kier had asked her to marry him. It was so unexpected that she found it difficult to believe.

When had he ever shown any interest in marriage? On the contrary, when he'd made his first move he'd been very clear that he wasn't looking at any long-term commitment.

Even today he'd begun by offering much less. Only when she'd laid out the issues had he played the marriage card.

A last-ditch ploy?

Did he really want her back so much he'd go that far?

Putting away the cups, she tried to ignore a flutter of excitement. Of yearning. If only he had suggested marriage before everything changed…before it all fell apart.

She stood staring at the cup he'd used, remembering his big hand curled around it, and how his hands used to feel on her skin, molding the shape of her breasts.

Steadying her breath, she briskly rinsed the cups and dried them, then opened a cupboard to shove them out of sight.

He hadn't said anything about love. So what motive did he have? Surely not just a determination to net the one that had got away? Kier hated to be beaten on any front, but that was taking things too far.

Decisively she closed the cupboard door. Everything she had told him still applied. Whatever his motives, she'd said no, sensibly, and that was the end of it.

Depression washed over her. Suddenly life looked bleak and empty. Did she really want to spend the rest of it alone?

Then Samuel let out a wail, reminding her she wasn't alone. There would be plenty of love and laughter in her life as long as she had him.

She certainly couldn't marry without taking her son's needs into account.

Kier didn't want to be a father. Had he realized he couldn't have her without her son? She suspected that when he'd made his rash proposal, Samuel's very existence had slipped his mind. He'd been intent on carrying her along with his will.

No. As she'd told him, marriage wasn't an option. There were too many reasons why it wouldn't—couldn't possibly—work.

But the painful sense of what-might-have-been stayed with her all day.

It was still there in the morning. And so was Samuel's fever, despite the baby paracetamol she'd dosed him with. He was flushed and unhappy, and she phoned Alison who said, "Bring him over and I'll have a look at him."

She hurried across to the farm, entering the house as usual by the kitchen door.

The room smelled of freshly fried bacon, and at the table Kier and Ace were tucking into crisp-edged rashers accompanied by eggs and sausages, while Ginnie nibbled a finger of toast. A cool, elegant blonde, she was already perfectly made up with not a strand of her sleekly styled hair out of place, although she wore an exotic-looking blue satin robe.

Alison turned from putting more bread into the toaster when Shahna stopped in the doorway, Samuel's hot face resting against her neck.

"I'm interrupting your breakfast."

"Not at all, dear." Alison moved toward her and plucked Samuel from her arms. "Let's have a look at this wee fellow. Have you had any breakfast yourself?"

"I'm all right."

"Starving yourself won't help you look after Samuel, you know."

"I'm not starving myself—"

But Alison was already directing Ace to pour some coffee for her, and Kier pulled out another chair.

"Just toast, then," she said, taking the chair as Alison put a hand on Samuel's forehead.

Ginnie pushed a plate of toast toward her and Shahna helped herself to a slice. "Thank you, Ginnie. It's nice to see you again."

"Virginia," the young woman said. "Please." But she smiled back quite kindly.

Ace put a cup of coffee in front of her and then a plate, knife and fork.

Kier passed her a dish of butter. "You should have more than that." He took a rasher of bacon from the side of his plate and placed it on hers.

Alison said, "There are eggs in the pan." She sat down with Samuel on her knee and lifted his T-shirt to examine his chest.

"He doesn't have a rash." Shahna waved away the egg Ace offered her. "This is plenty, honestly."

Alison replaced Samuel's shirt. "Has he been rubbing at his ears at all?"

Shahna shook her head. "I don't think so."

Ace returned to his breakfast and Ginnie—Virginia— sipped a cup of coffee, but Kier was watching Alison and the baby.

Samuel began to cry and Shahna pushed back her chair.

Alison said, "I'll look after him while you eat. It might be wise to have him checked over at the hospital in Rawene, but a few more minutes won't make any difference. The ferry won't be going for half an hour."

She took Samuel into the next room. A tinkling tune indicated she'd picked up the musical snowball that never failed to distract him, and the crying stopped.

"Eat that," Kier said at Shahna's side.

She ate quickly and downed a cup of coffee, then went into the big living room. Samuel's head rested on Alison's breast and he was almost asleep.

"It's a pity to disturb him," Alison said, "but you could make the next ferry if you go soon. Will you be all right on your own?"

As Shahna bent to take the baby Kier's voice behind her said, "I'll drive you, so you can hold him."

"He has to be strapped into his car seat anyway."

Samuel objected to the transfer, and she soothed him with her hand on his back, but he went on miserably wailing.

Alison said, "Let Kier take you. I'm sure *you* will be happier and less distracted."

"Come on then," Kier said. "Do you have the keys?"

Arguing would only waste more time. "Yes," she said, and followed him outside.

Being put into the car seat upset Samuel, but Shahna

sat in the back and stroked his hair until he fell into a tear-stained sleep.

When the car was safely on board with several other vehicles and a few foot passengers, people left their cars to enjoy the view. Kier looked over his shoulder at the sleeping child and wound down his window. "Might as well get out."

"If you like." She meant him, but he climbed out and opened the rear door for her. She glanced at Samuel, hesitated, and then joined Kier a few steps away at the railing.

Shahna tried to concentrate on watching the water slide past the hull, admiring the long sleek clouds that hung low over the hills. Among a few houses nestling in a hollow, the narrow spire of a white wooden missionary church stood against the sky.

She had always loved this short journey, and usually Samuel would be in her arms, crowing with delight at the movement of the vessel and smiling at the other passengers.

"I can see why you like it here," Kier admitted. "I guess if one wanted peace and tranquillity, it would be the ideal spot."

Peace and tranquillity wasn't his style. He was into challenge, stimulation, the intellectual cut and thrust and financial risk of big business.

Well, it made the world go 'round, but she'd opted out and was happy to be away from it all. "The harbor's dangerous in a storm," she said.

"Hard to believe."

"Appearances can be deceptive."

"Tell me about it." He looked at her sideways, until she turned her head and said defensively, "What?"

Kier grinned. The breeze had ruffled his hair and left a few strands rakishly straying across his forehead. His eyes were bright and teasing. He looked incredibly handsome and sexy, and a familiar, melting sensation stole over her, a sexual longing that was impossible to hide.

He knew. She saw the leap of answering desire in his eyes, and he bent his head and kissed her.

It was very short, lasting scarcely a second, but electrifying. No one but Kier could pack so much punch into a brief meeting of mouths. Her lips had scarcely parted under his when he withdrew, and she felt cheated. Longing for more.

It was probably what he'd wanted, she warned herself as he looked down at her, calculating the effect of his kiss. Kier was a player, skilled and experienced. She'd been on the receiving end of his subtle sexual tactics before. But she was older and warier now. And there was more at stake.

She glanced toward the car, checking that Samuel was still sleeping.

Kier's left hand came over her right one where it clutched the rail. "He'll be all right. Try to relax."

Relax. Between worrying over Samuel and fighting the urge to turn and bury herself in Kier's arms, there was small chance of relaxing.

Kier said, "We'll hear him if he cries."

She moved her hand under his, but as she pulled it away from the railing he curled his fingers about hers. "It must be hell being a mother at times like this," he said.

Startled at his understanding, she agreed ruefully. "In a way. But I've never been sorry."

"Never?"

"Not for a minute."

He nodded, but she thought he wasn't wholly convinced.

''Fear is the other side of love,'' she said. ''You can't have one without the other.''

He looked as though she'd struck some unexpected chord then. His eyes glazed slightly for a moment. ''I guess that's right,'' he said thoughtfully.

Kier was thinking about the dreams that had plagued him after Shahna left him. Dreams of dire disaster overtaking her while he struggled to reach her—fighting against giant waves sweeping her out to sea, farther and farther from him, or trying to leap across chasms in the earth that opened threateningly between them; running up gaping stairs in crumbling buildings to reach her on some precarious parapet before she fell.

Had his subconscious been trying to tell him something?

Love. He tried the word out in his mind. He'd never admitted to loving Shahna. Not even to himself. If she had ever used the word to him perhaps he might have reciprocated. But he'd learned long ago that if you wanted something from someone you didn't give any advantage, show any weakness.

And Shahna had certainly shown none. She'd kept him guessing to the end—glorious in bed, smart and sharp out of it, lovely to look at, and maddeningly mysterious under the lustrous surface that was all she'd allowed him to touch.

She was different here—still determined to keep him at an emotional distance, but Samuel had done what Kier had never managed, penetrated the veneer and reached the hidden recesses of her heart, made her vulnerable. There were cracks in the glassy outer shell and Kier meant to exploit them to the full. Until the shell shattered and fell to dust.

* * *

The ferry arrived at the foot of the main street, where the road ran straight uphill between old wooden shops hooded under corrugated iron overhangs.

Samuel didn't wake until Shahna removed him from his car seat to carry him into the emergency room when they reached the hospital at the brow of the hill. He whimpered a little, and his eyes looked glazed, half-closed.

Kier waited in the public area while Shahna took Samuel in to be examined. When they emerged he shot to his feet. "What did they say?"

"A mild throat infection. I have to get a prescription filled and if it doesn't clear up in a couple of days they want to see him again."

Even Samuel seemed slightly happier, and when Shahna had persuaded him to take some medicine even before they left the pharmacy, Kier said, "Let me buy you lunch?"

"I don't know." Shahna looked doubtfully at the little boy in her arms. "He should have a drink, maybe. I have to make sure he doesn't get dehydrated."

In a little café at the water's edge, Samuel downed diluted orange juice and was tempted into eating a bite of Shahna's sandwich and a few potato crisps.

"He's looking better, isn't he?" Kier observed.

"I think so." Relief had softened the tight expression she'd had earlier and brought a hint of color to her cheeks.

"Anything else you want?" he inquired as they left the café and began walking toward the car parked near the water.

"Maybe some fresh fish. Samuel might be hungry by dinnertime."

She hitched Samuel higher on her hip and Kier said, "Let me take him."

He took the child from her, and Sam seemed to debate

whether or not to protest, but then his eye was caught by a bobbing balloon held by a child of five or six skipping along the path with her parents.

His pudgy hand reached out. "Uh?"

"Balloon," Kier said. He'd noticed that Shahna named things for him when he showed an interest in something new.

"Boo." Samuel was still reaching after it as the family walked in the other direction. He started to cry.

"Sorry, mate. It belongs to someone else," Kier said. How did one explain things like that to a baby? The kid sounded heartbroken. "I'll buy you one," he promised, looking around to see if there was a shop that might sell the things. Maybe they could run after the family, find out where the little girl had got hers.

Shahna said, "He has to learn he can't have everything he wants."

"He's too young to understand." How could she be so hard-hearted?

"He doesn't understand why he's feeling sore and sick, either." She dug in the bag she'd slung over her shoulder and brought out a small plastic toy, offering it to Samuel, who promptly batted it away, knocking it from her hand. But he stopped crying, apparently waiting to see what happened next.

Shahna laughed. "And cross," she said, bending to pick up the toy. "That was naughty," she told Samuel, and kissed the top of his head. "Never mind, darling, you'll soon feel better."

Perversely, he reached for the toy, and she handed it to him. "But next time you throw it away," she warned sternly, "you don't get it back."

Kier didn't suppose Samuel understood that, either, but

he immediately began chewing on it, which seemed to be his highest accolade.

There was nothing Kier could do about him being sick and sore, but at least he could buy him a balloon.

There was a sort of general store-cum-souvenir shop open and he insisted they visit it, finally finding a packet of balloons sitting in a corner with decks of playing cards and some whistles and streamers.

"You shouldn't," Shahna protested as he paid for the balloons. "He's forgotten all about it already."

"I want to." He perched Samuel on the counter where the shop assistant cooed at him while Kier broke open the packet and blew up a red balloon, then a blue one. The assistant found a piece of ribbon and helped tie them, and Samuel looked on, his eyes rounded and his mouth forming a small, rosy O.

"He loves them," Kier pointed out, fastening the ribbon around Samuel's wrist. Samuel obligingly confirmed his opinion, waving his arm and watching the balloons bounce in response. He tried to catch one, but it floated down out of his reach.

Kier placed it between his baby hands, and for a moment Samuel regarded it with absorption. Then he opened his mouth and leaned forward.

"Hey!" Kier hastily moved the balloon away again. "You can't eat it." Glancing in consternation at Shahna, he confessed, "I didn't think of that. Will his teeth get through it?" If it burst in his face might it harm him? Maybe traumatize him?

"I don't think he'll be able to get enough purchase to bite it," Shahna said. "I hope."

Kier had never realized there were so many pitfalls to raising children.

On the wharf they found a man selling freshly caught fish, and Shahna bought a couple.

Kier asked, "Do you think Alison would like some?"

"Maybe. Ace goes fishing but he won't have had much time this last week."

He bought two large snapper and a smaller one, and carried the plastic bags to the car in time for the next ferry crossing.

This time Shahna held Samuel while they chugged over the water, pointing out a swooping seagull and sitting him on the railing, safely enclosed in her arms, so he could see the blue-green water turning milky as it foamed at the ferry's side, leaving a broad wake behind them.

When they returned, the family car was gone from the farm, and Kier said, "I guess they're all at the hospital. I'll just drop off the fish and carry Samuel home for you."

"I can manage from here," Shahna said, sliding into the driver's seat as he retrieved the plastic bag. "Thanks for your help...and lunch. I'm very grateful."

"How grateful?" He couldn't let the opportunity pass.

She looked at him warily.

He grinned down at her, reading the suspicion in her face, and said blandly, "If I bring my own fish would you invite me to dinner? With Virginia home the family may prefer to be on their own after being at the hospital."

He could see her thinking it over, and pressed his advantage. "I'll help you cook," he offered.

"Oh, all right," she said. "Come to dinner."

Not the most gracious invitation, but he'd settle for it.

When he arrived, bearing a wrapped fish, a bottle of wine, and a single, just unfurling pink rose from Alison's garden, Shahna greeted him at the door, wearing a dress instead of the jeans she'd had on that morning, and low, strappy sandals. She'd changed for him, probably showered first.

For a second he allowed himself to picture her in the shower, water cascading over her naked limbs. Then she smiled at him, a conservative movement of her lips, and stepped back to allow him inside.

Her lips were glossy and pink, and her eyelids had a smudge of soft gray-green shadow on them. Her hair curled lightly about her ears—he knew it would be soft and satiny to his fingers—and a subtle waft of some scent like spring blossom teased his nostrils when he passed her. "Nice perfume," he said appreciatively.

"Shampoo," she said. "I'm not wearing perfume."

She'd put on makeup, though. A good sign, surely?

He handed her the rose and she took it tentatively, as though it might conceal a mini-bomb amongst its petals. But she couldn't resist lifting it to her nose. "Lovely," she said. "Thank you." Eyeing the bottle in his hand, she asked, "Where did you get that?"

"From Morrie's wine rack. Don't worry, I'll replace it."

"I haven't had wine for…ages," she said—rather wistfully, he thought. "I don't even have proper goblets."

She really had retired from the world. Shahna had always drunk sparingly, quite often sticking with soft drinks or juice, but she had enjoyed a decent vintage now and then. "Why not?" he asked. "I mean, why haven't you drunk it?"

She turned away from him to place the rose on the counter and open a cupboard. "I gave it up when I was expecting Samuel. Wine is supposed to be dangerous for an unborn child."

He vaguely recalled hearing that somewhere, but as it hadn't affected him he'd not taken much notice.

"And then," she continued, "I suppose I just lost the habit."

She took down a bloodred glass vase and placed the rose in it, taking it to the table for a centerpiece, then turned to unwrapping the fish. "You can scrub some potatoes if you want to help. What's the latest on Morrie? I heard the car come back."

She kept him busy and talking about his hosts until the meal was done and they sat down to eat it.

The fish looked white and moist, drizzled with lemon butter and fresh chopped parsley, and the potatoes gave off a faint aroma of mint. Baby carrots and barely cooked spinach sprinkled with ground black pepper added color.

Kier decided he'd tasted nothing better in the finest restaurants. "Have you always been this good a cook?" He didn't remember that she'd been any more than average, on the rare occasions when she'd prepared a proper meal.

Shahna laughed. "There's nothing like food straight from the garden—or the sea—to the pot."

For dessert she served firm, fresh plums, not peeled but chopped into slivers on top of a warm sponge base, and handed him a jug of cream to pour over it.

Between them they had almost finished the wine, and she was pensively turning her glass on the checked cloth, her eyes hidden from him under lowered lashes.

Kier picked up the wine bottle and poured what remained into her glass.

She looked up. "I think I've had enough, really."

He gave her his most charming smile. "You're not driving anywhere. Nothing to worry about."

"Isn't there? I have a feeling I should keep my wits about me."

"You don't trust me?"

She gave him a candid, considering stare. "Can I?"

The direct question challenged his clever stratagem, making his plan to seduce her into acquiescence look sordid and somehow despicable. Carrying the attack into her camp, he said, "Did you ever?"

A strange, almost guilty expression came over her face. She looked away. "You know I did. I trusted you not to cheat on our...arrangement."

The word left a nasty taste. *Arrangement* sounded so cold and businesslike.

Brushing away an uncomfortable part of his conscience that reminded him he'd been approaching this whole dilemma in the same way as he would any tricky business transaction, he said, "You mean our relationship."

Her eyes came back to him, the considering look returning. "Whatever you want to call it," she said politely.

He wanted to call it a love affair. Certainly something a lot more meaningful than an "arrangement."

Chapter 7

Shahna pushed away her glass. "I can't finish this."

For an instant she saw chagrin in Kier's eyes. Then he shrugged. "Your choice. It's good wine, though."

"Very good," she agreed. "Thank you for bringing it."

It had made her feel mellow and less guarded, tempted to let her natural response to him escape the rein she held it under.

Once before she'd allowed herself to follow blind instinct and blamed it on too much wine. A single such massive mistake was enough for one lifetime.

She stood up and busied herself with coffee as he finished the last of his wine.

"Shall we have it here or..." She indicated the living area where the chairs were more comfortable, and he said, "There."

He sat on the two-seater sofa, but she chose a chair

opposite. Kier said nothing, although the glint in his eyes challenged her choice.

The uncurtained window reflected them, two people apparently cosily at ease, only a few feet separating them.

The reality, Shahna reminded herself as she sipped at her coffee, was that they were poles apart. Wanting different things, different lifestyles. The only thing they had in common was that they also wanted each other.

And what Kier wanted, he was accustomed to getting.

Not this time. Powerful though the temptation was, this time she had to deny herself, deny him. Inviting him into her bed would encourage him to nurture false expectations. And she would be handing him a potent weapon that he would have no hesitation in using.

The further she allowed Kier to insinuate himself into her painstakingly built new life, the harder it would be to say goodbye…again.

Lowering her coffee cup, Shahna turned her eyes to the window. Behind the reflection in the glass she could vaguely see the distant stars. Sometimes she stood outside before going to bed, watching the opulent display that hung over the hills and stretched across the black arch of the sky, reflected in the still night waters.

"What are you thinking of?" Kier broke into her thoughts.

"How lovely the harbor is at night," she replied. Better than admitting to temptation.

He glanced at the window. "Show me?" He was up before she could answer, placing his empty cup on the floor by the sofa. "When you've finished," he added.

She had, almost. After draining the rest she put down her cup, rising reluctantly. It seemed a dangerous thing to do, walk into the star-filled night with Kier.

He opened the door for her. "Will you need something warm?"

Shahna shook her head. "No, it's warm enough in this weather. Shut the door, or the place will be full of moths and mosquitoes and huhu beetles in five minutes."

And five minutes, she vowed, was all the time this would take.

She led the way to the new gate. "This is far enough."

"You think so?" His voice held quiet amusement.

"I don't want to go too far away because of Samuel."

"I do understand that." His tone was dry. He leaned his arms on the gate, while she stood to one side. "You're right. It's pretty spectacular."

The night was almost cloudless and every inch of the sky seemed crowded with tiny dazzles of light. A full moon spread a soft cloak of white-gold over the harbor, broken by a leaping fish that appeared, bright and twisting, for an instant and left tiny ripples dancing on the surface.

Something pale whirred by them, caught for an instant in the light reaching out into the darkness from the cottage. Kier straightened and, looking at the bright square of the window, he said, "Shouldn't you have blinds or something? Anyone looking in could see you're a woman alone."

"Out here?" Shahna queried. "There aren't too many prowlers who'd take the trouble."

"I suppose not."

"There are curtains in the bedrooms."

"I hope you use them."

She did, more from force of habit than anything, when she was undressing, but often pulled them back before getting into bed. It was the next best thing to sleeping directly under the night sky.

"I'd have thought," Kier said, "that a city girl would be nervous, all alone in a place like this."

"I'm not a nervous type. And I haven't always been a city girl." That was an assumption on his part that she'd never bothered to dispel.

"I thought you came from Auckland." He sounded surprised.

Shahna shook her head. "I lived not too far from here until I was ten, in a little country town where my father had a small printing business."

"You never told me that."

"It was hard going and he gave it up to move to the city and take a job with a daily newspaper. We weren't on the harbor, but we used to visit. The ferry was my favorite outing."

She fell silent for a moment, staring at the moonglimmer on the black water. "Do you know what 'Hokianga' means?"

"No idea."

"The place of returning," she said softly. "Deep down, I think I always wanted to come back."

The only time she'd returned before she came to live here was during the last holiday she'd had with her parents. For once they hadn't been quarreling, and Shahna remembered it as a time of blue skies and gently ruffled water. A time of tentative happiness that turned to tears and recriminations after they left this magical place.

Maybe her parents had made one last-ditch effort for her sake. But by then it was too late.

"Don't you feel vulnerable at night?" Kier broke into her reverie.

"I'm not afraid of the dark."

"What *are* you afraid of?" he asked.

She said cautiously, "Why should I be afraid of anything?"

Kier said, "Come on, I told you about my fear of heights. There must be something that frightens you."

You do. He could make her lose control of her emotions, as well as her peace of mind, self-respect and common sense. None of which she wanted to part company with. "Lots of things," she said lightly. "Telling people my fears, for one."

"Ah," he said. "Let me guess." Then, slowly, as if feeling his way, "You're afraid of giving away too much of yourself, aren't you? Of letting anyone get really close to you. You're afraid of…this."

He reached for her and drew her into his arms, but this time she held her body stiff and unyielding, turning her head away from his kiss, her hands flattened against his shirt, pushing at him in unmistakable rejection.

His breath was warm on her averted cheek, teasing the sensitive skin just below her ear. She said, "Don't do this to me, Kier. Please."

If she'd fought him, shown a righteous feminist fury, he might have overridden her denial, reverted to thoroughly retrograde male chauvinism and kissed her until she gave in—as he was certain she would have in the end. He could feel the faint trembling of her body despite its determined rigidity. And it wasn't caused by fear—not fear of him taking her against her will. It was desire, and he recognized it, sensed her longing to let it take her over and carry her where it would.

Her own needs would have betrayed her and given him victory.

But instead of resisting she stood in the circle of his arms and said, *Please.*

Begging. Desperate. A note he'd never heard before in her voice, even when she was naked in his arms and he'd taken her to a new pitch of sensual experience and, with a supreme effort of will, made her wait for the exquisite moment of fulfillment. She had never sounded like this.

Shamed and shaken, he loosened his hold, allowing her to step out of his embrace, but caught at her hands, holding them tightly. "I'm sorry, Shahna," he heard himself say, not sure what exactly he was apologizing for. "I didn't mean to…"

"Frighten me?" He saw her square her shoulders in the dim light. Composing herself. "You didn't."

Liar, he thought. She was scared witless of her own sexuality and where it might lead her. Since when? He frowned. That was surely an aspect of her personality he hadn't come up against before.

Unless…unease stirred. Unless he'd been too preoccupied with his own pleasure, with making sure she shared in it, to notice. "Was I a selfish bastard?" he asked her. "When we were together."

"No!" Shahna shook her head. "You always considered my needs. I told you, as a lover you were all any woman could want."

High praise, and a year ago he'd have accepted it at face value and been satisfied with it. Even smug, congratulating himself.

Somehow it didn't sound so wonderful now. *As a lover,* she'd said. A limited, qualified role. He'd read somewhere a psychologist's analysis of the great lovers of history— Casanova, Don Juan, he forgot the others—arguing that they'd suffered from some personality disorder, that despite their formidable reputations for bedroom athletics they were unable to connect emotionally with a woman and had gone from one to the next and the next, ever more desperately seeking something that eluded them all their lives.

He'd taken the theory with a grain of salt, and anyway, that wasn't him. There had been few women before Shahna and none after. But now he felt uneasy.

Shahna's fingers moved in his, tugging, and he released her hands. His felt empty and cold now.

"And as a man?" he asked, unable to stop himself.

For a moment she didn't answer, and he braced himself for a crushing reply, something cutting and clever.

But she said, "You surely don't need me to tell you what kind of man you are, Kier. Don't you know?"

Did he? He was no longer sure.

He left her soon afterward, knowing she was relieved that he'd said good-night without reentering the cottage.

Not having thought to bring a light with him, he stumbled a couple of times as he made his way through the trees. Crossing the paddocks was easier, the bright stars and a sliver of moon guiding him across the sheep-shorn grass.

When he let himself into the house a light was still on in the living room and as he made to pass it Ginnie's voice called, "Hi. You're early."

He stopped in the doorway and glanced at his watch. It was just after nine, but in this household they tended to keep what in his normal life—and hers, he supposed— were ridiculously early hours. Up before five, into bed by nine.

She was in one of the armchairs, her slender legs elegantly disposed to one side. A magazine lay in her lap, her thumb resting on a page, the nail long and oval, varnished with shiny pink. Shahna kept hers barely past the tips of her fingers now, he recalled, natural and unglossed.

Ginnie's eyes, a clear pale blue, regarded him with undisguised feminine curiosity. "I thought maybe you'd be staying the night." Her carefully shaped brows rose delicately, making the remark a question.

He couldn't help a smile. "Shahna and I don't have that kind of relationship," he said, and took a step into the room.

"Oh?" She smiled back at him, pleased.

This was the kind of woman who was prepared to let her desires be known, who would even take the initiative if he indicated he was interested. Refreshingly uncomplicated.

Then she cocked her head, allowing her curiosity to show. "But you did once?"

Her family was right about her—she was no fool. Kier shrugged an acknowledgment.

"And you came looking for her."

"Yes."

"She didn't welcome you with open arms?"

"Hardly."

A frown appeared on the flawless skin between her brows. "Is that baby yours?"

"No." The angry regret that shook him then came as a shock. And sharp on its heels followed a wholly irrational feeling that his bald negative was a kind of betrayal.

"Sorry," Ginnie said lightly. "It's none of my business. Only he does sort of look like you—the same coloring."

She'd thought his anger was directed at her. He shook his head. "Don't apologize. It's…complicated, that's all."

"Obviously."

"You don't want to get involved."

She looked faintly amused. "I'm going back to Wellington on Monday."

The put-down was subtle but calculated. He had to laugh. With Ginnie a man would always know where he was. Despite her aura of sophistication, at heart she retained the straightforward, no-nonsense characteristics of her family.

She closed the magazine and stood up, letting it plop onto her vacated chair. "Oh, well…I suppose I might as well go to bed." Stretching discreetly, her arms held out from her sides, head back so that her neat, full breasts were enticingly thrust into prominence, she regarded Kier through half-closed lids.

Distantly he registered that she was a very attractive woman, with all the superficial attributes any red-blooded male could wish for. But his body failed to respond, his heart didn't skip even one beat. He gave her a rueful look of mute apology.

It was her turn to laugh, sounding only slightly put out as she relaxed and began to saunter past him.

"Ginnie?" He stopped her. "I mean, Virginia."

"Yes?" Hope and speculation lurked momentarily in her eyes, replaced by a resigned amusement.

With unusual clumsiness he said, "You're a woman."

She laughed again. "I believe so."

"Have you ever thought of coming back here—I mean to live?"

"God, no!" She shuddered. "I couldn't wait to shake the cow dung from my feet. If you're asking me why Shahna would choose to live here, I have no idea. Frankly, I think she's mad—on several counts."

She batted her eyelashes at him, and he grinned. They understood each other perfectly. He wished he could say the same of himself and Shahna. "Do you think she'd talk to you?'' he asked urgently. The idea had only just entered his head, but he was clutching at straws.

"Me?'' Ginnie shook her head. "I hardly know her.''

"But you must have things in common. You're about the same age, and...'' He frowned, trying to explain. "She was like you when I met her. A career woman. Successful, dynamic. Going places.''

"You've been listening to my family.''

"They're all extremely proud of you.''

To his surprise, she flushed at that.

He followed up swiftly, giving her his most persuasive smile. "I know it's a lot to ask, and of course you don't owe me a thing—'' his conscience twinged "—but I'd be grateful.''

Alison and Ace had told Ginnie when they introduced him that he was generously working for nothing, embarrassing him with their gratitude. She'd given him a long, considering look, but when she cornered him later he'd explained that he didn't need wages, and helping out on the farm gave him the opportunity to see something of an old friend.

Now he was taking unashamed advantage and he didn't care. "You might be able to get her to tell you...''

"Tell me what?'' she queried. "We're not likely to exchange girlish confidences.''

"No, but...'' He was seldom so hesitant about expressing his thoughts. "She might give you some clue as to why she's changed, and why she refuses to leave.''

"Has it occurred to you,'' Ginnie asked, "that she doesn't want *you?* I mean—'' her appreciative gaze discreetly assessed him, the tip of her tongue appearing between her teeth "—there's no accounting for taste.''

"Of course it has,'' he said, rather curt. "But it isn't

that, I know it. Could you make some excuse to visit her before you go? Please?''

"And pump her?'' Ginnie shrugged. "All right. But you'll have to come too.''

"That would defeat the object.''

"Look, if I turn up there on my own she'll smell a rat for sure. Besides, seeing you together I'll have a better idea how she feels.''

"You saw us together this morning.''

"She was totally wrapped up in the kid this morning,'' Ginnie said. "Not really seeing anyone else. It's a mother thing, I guess.'' Her tone implied she didn't understand it. "Don't worry, I'll figure out a way to get her alone at some stage. Or you can.'' She regarded him with a slightly jaundiced eye. "And you are going to owe me after this, buddy.''

Kier grinned at her again. "Anytime.''

Samuel had slept all night and was miraculously almost himself when Shahna lifted him from the cot. His skin had cooled, and he cooed and smiled at her as she cleaned him up, sprinkled his plump bottom with baby powder and got him changed and dressed.

"Just as well you're so cute,'' she told him. "Because you have some disgusting habits.''

He laughed at her and she laughed back, tickling his tummy and making him squirm delightedly.

She was hanging washing while he played on the grass when Kier and Ginnie—Virginia, she reminded herself again—appeared from the trees.

Kier wore jeans and a white T-shirt; Virginia, blue linen trousers and a paler blue shirt. Country casual, Shahna thought, straight out of *Vogue*.

They walked side by side, close together although not

touching, and there was something intimate about the way Ginnie looked up at him, listening as he bent his head toward her.

Firmly Shahna quelled a surge of jealousy. Kier was a free agent and as far as she knew so was *Virginia.*

But he'd asked Shahna to marry him.

You turned him down, she censured herself sternly. She had no rights over him.

He looked up and her heart thudded as she saw his eyes light. She comforted herself with the thought that he had only just met his hosts' daughter.

"Hi there," he said when they drew closer. "How's Samuel?"

"Much better," she said briefly, the wet towel in her hand making her baggy T-shirt and comfortable old shorts damp. "See?"

Samuel sat back on the grass, clutching a squishy stuffed ball to his chest and regarding the newcomers. "Kee," he said, finally deciding to recognize Kier.

"Hi, little fella." Kier went down on his haunches. "What have you got there?"

Samuel instantly offered the ball to him, and Shahna returned to pegging the towel.

Ginnie stepped forward, picked out a cot-sheet from the basket, and began helping.

"Thanks." Shahna was surprised.

"No problem."

Kier had rolled the ball away and Samuel giggled and took off on all fours, chasing it. Kier strolled after him.

Ginnie was fast and efficient and they were soon finished.

"Um...can I offer you two a coffee?" Shahna asked, picking up the empty basket.

Kier didn't seem to hear, still playing chase-the-ball with Samuel. Ginnie said, "Sure."

The two women went into the cottage and Ginnie accepted Shahna's invitation to sit at the table while she put the coffee on. Filling it with water, Shahna glanced out to where Kier was rolling the ball toward a bright-eyed, expectant Samuel. As if he felt her gaze Kier looked up and waved. She lifted the kettle, indicating an invitation, and he nodded, then turned back to the game.

He seemed to be enjoying himself. An insidious optimism wormed into her heart and she sternly banished it.

Ginnie said, "You've made this place quite…interesting."

"I try." Shahna flicked a switch and followed her guest's critical gaze around the room.

"My brother and I used to play here when it was empty," Ginnie said. "I'm surprised it's done up so well."

Shahna wondered if Ginnie felt she was an interloper. "Do you mind?" she asked. "Me being here now?"

Ginnie blinked. "Of course not." She looked around again. "It's good to see the old place being used." Then, as if remembering something, she said, "What *are* you doing here? Kier says you had a pretty high profile in Sydney. Public relations, wasn't it?"

Getting cups out of the cupboard, Shahna repeated what she'd told Kier. "I wanted a change."

"Don't you miss the bright lights?"

"Hardly at all."

"You must have missed Kier."

In the act of opening a packet of chocolate wafers, Shahna dropped it. Fortunately the wafers spilled onto the counter. Picking them up one by one, she started arranging them carefully on a plate. "What did he tell you?" she asked, her voice low.

"Not much. I gather you were…close."

Shahna couldn't help shooting a quick look at the other woman. Why did Ginnie want to know? Did she have designs on Kier?

"That was…some time ago." Shahna almost choked on the words. The cliché *Just good friends* came to mind, but she couldn't bring herself to utter it. Nor *The coast is clear; if you want Kier, I have no claim on him.*

Her hand closed around a wafer and it broke in two. "Damn," she muttered. She would give it to Samuel later. But recently he'd been rejecting broken cookies. One of the child development books she'd brought home from the library had expounded a Freudian explanation for it.

Freud might have had something to say about Shahna's inner conflicts too.

Ginnie would make an ideal partner for Kier. They moved in similar circles, probably shared similar views, and neither of them had any time for the country lifestyle Shahna had embraced so wholeheartedly.

Ginnie didn't seem to have inherited her mother's maternal instinct—she had hardly glanced at Samuel this morning, and Shahna didn't recall her touching him or speaking to him on her other visits. *She* wouldn't be bringing any inconvenient baggage to a new relationship. Or hanker after having a child.

Unless her biological clock kicked unexpectedly into gear. Shahna couldn't suppress a slightly malicious little smile.

Mentally she shook herself. The two of them had only met yesterday, and Ginnie was leaving tomorrow.

Then she remembered with unsettling clarity Kier telling her he'd decided at their first meeting that they were going to be lovers.

She shivered.

"Something wrong?" Ginnie's eyes were blandly blue, uncomfortably interested.

"It's not as warm in here as it is out in the sun."

Didn't Kier deserve someone who was on his wavelength, a woman who would complement him in both his business and his private life? It wasn't as though Shahna hadn't been given the chance herself. She ought to be wishing the other woman well, saying good luck to her.

She wanted to scratch *Virginia's* eyes out.

I'm being a bitch, she scolded herself. *A bitch in the manger.* Putting the plate on the table, she gave the woman her best smile. "Help yourself."

"Thanks." Ginnie picked out a wafer and took a tiny bite. "Did Kier do something? He wasn't violent, was he?"

"No!"

"He doesn't strike me as the type," Ginnie said, "but you never know. And you obviously removed yourself as far as you could from him." Her eyes queried the denial.

If Ginnie was interested in him, Shahna reasoned, she'd want to be reassured about that. It explained why she had decided to accompany him on this visit. "Kier would never raise his hand to a woman. He isn't like that."

"What *is* he like?" The question sounded idle, but the curiosity in the woman's eyes belied her tone.

Tempted to say, *You'll have to find that out for yourself,* Shahna swallowed a mixture of pain and unwarranted rage and made her voice even, uncaring. "He's…a decent man. Honest. Generous in his way."

"In his way?" Ginnie murmured.

"I mean…" Shahna floundered. "He's generous with

material things—gifts. And with women...I mean, to them. Considerate.'' She remembered he'd been sensitive to her moods, her needs—except for her deepest need that she'd deliberately kept secret from him—without revealing his own needs much at all.

"Good in bed, you mean," Ginnie said bluntly.

Shahna flushed. "Not only that..."

She wasn't in the habit of discussing her private life, but Ginnie had already guessed that Shahna and Kier had been lovers. Or he'd told her.

Stupid to feel betrayed by that. It was no secret. She said, "He cares for...for a woman."

Maybe he had been warning Ginnie off. After all, he'd asked Shahna to reconsider her refusal to marry him. Her mood lightened. "He wouldn't just move on without a backward glance," she said almost to herself. Perhaps the attraction was all on Virginia's side.

"The faithful type?" Ginnie suggested.

What did the woman want? A testimonial? "When he's with someone," Shahna said, "she's the only woman in his life." A shaft of regret at what she'd turned her back on stabbed at her—a physical pain that momentarily stopped her breath. She turned away on the pretext of checking the coffeemaker.

"A prince." Ginnie nibbled at the chocolate wafer, regarding her thoughtfully. "But you dumped him?"

Shahna was clattering cups at the counter. "We wanted different things."

"Like?"

Shahna shrugged. "Kier is a city animal. I needed to get out of the rat race. Coffee's ready. I'll go and call him in."

Kier gave her a penetrating look when she went out to tell him there was coffee poured and to pick up Samuel.

She put the baby in his high chair, helped him not to spill the orange juice she gave him while the adults sipped their coffee, and wiped chocolate off his hands when he'd finished eating his wafer. He refused the broken one and she ate it herself. But despite fussing over him she was aware of the provocative glances passing between Kier and Ginnie across the table.

She forced herself to smile and be nice, to pretend interest when Ginnie talked about her work and her social life in the capital. There was no mention of any man.

Ginnie was making no secret of the fact that she found Kier attractive, catching his eyes with a bold, laughing gaze, teasing him with flirtatious body language. And Kier, though at first he seemed somewhat morose, wasn't immune. He gave her an appreciative grin, and an answering gleam in his eyes made Shahna swallow hard and bite on her soft inner lip until it hurt.

If they were heading for an affair, she wished they'd conduct their opening skirmish somewhere other than at her table.

When she noticed Samuel grunting, red-faced, with an air of concentration, she was relieved at the excuse to whip him up and leave them for a few minutes.

When she returned to the kitchen Kier and Ginnie were leaning across the table, heads only inches apart, conducting a murmured conversation.

Kier looked up at Shahna. "Is Samuel okay?"

"Yes." She wanted to scream at them both to get out. Her throat was hurting almost as if she had. "He's fine." As if to confirm it he came crawling after her and went to the settle, demanding his toy basket.

She got it out for him, then realized Kier was standing up, downing the last of his coffee as he did so, and pushing his chair under the table. "I told Ace I'd be back

before eleven," he said. "I'll leave you two girls to talk."
His gaze skittered over Shahna, his eyes not quite meeting
hers. "I don't suppose you get much chance to chat with
women of your own age and…business background."

He was gone before she had a chance to say anything.

Shahna guessed Ginnie was as disconcerted as she was
by his abrupt departure. Stiffly she said, "Would you like
some more coffee, Gi—Virginia?"

"Oh, give it up and call me Ginnie." The other woman
sighed. "I can see it's a losing battle when I come home.
I'd like another cup, but I'll get it."

Shahna's smile apologized. "It's just that Alison and
Morrie and Ace always call you Ginnie."

"I know." She poured coffee for herself. "More for
you?"

Shahna nodded. "Thank you."

They sat down and Ginnie stirred sugar into her cup,
absently watching Samuel solemnly remove everything
from the toy basket. "Is he the reason you stopped working?"

"I haven't stopped working."

Ginnie shot her a glance. "Sorry. I mean, the reason
you left your job in Sydney."

"No, that was before…"

"Before you had him or before you got pregnant?"

Shahna hesitated. "Before I got pregnant with him."

Ginnie leaned back in her chair, thoughtfully sipping at
her cup. "Kier said the…Samuel…isn't his."

"That's right," Shahna said steadily. "He isn't."

Ginnie's gaze slid back to the baby. "Did his daddy
stick around for the birth?" Her eyes left Samuel.

"No."

"Bastard," the other woman said laconically.

"It was my own idea to have a baby, so it wasn't fair to involve him."

"It takes two," Ginnie pointed out. "*I* would have involved him," she added feelingly, "up to his neck."

"Yes, well…he didn't want any part of it, and I'm happy to have Samuel to myself."

Shahna supposed that sounded selfish. Maybe she *had* been selfish, depriving Samuel of a father who loved and wanted him. Or rather, not taking care to provide him with one.

She recalled Kier playing ball with Samuel so patiently on the lawn. Kier, who had once stated with conviction, "There's no room for kids in my life." Who had laughed and said, "I'd make a rotten father."

But who had also said, Marry me.

She looked at the woman across the table and told herself, *Being kind to a child for a few minutes is quite different from living with one, responsible for it night and day, wiping its dirty bottom and cleaning up bedclothes, walls and floor when it's been sick, and pacing the floor with a howling infant at two o'clock on a winter morning.*

He hadn't taken all that into account when he proposed, she was sure. In fact, she was nearly certain it had been a spur-of-the-moment thing, a misguided impulse. He probably hadn't given a thought to Samuel. But being Kier he wouldn't back down once he'd asked her to marry him.

He was probably relieved that she'd said no.

Chapter 8

"I don't know," Ginnie said, when Kier cornered her in her mother's rose garden after lunch, where she was picking flowers for her father. "She didn't say much at all. But I'll tell you this much—she's in love with you."

He felt as though she'd punched him full on. Then as though his head was floating in the clouds. "She said so?"

"Of course not." Ginnie snipped off a bloom with a lethal-looking pair of secateurs. Her hands were gloved, he noted. After Morrie's mishap this family was taking no chances. "But she'd have liked to bite my head off." She laid the rose onto newspaper spread on the ground.

That was hard to believe. When Virginia had flirted with him he'd known she was testing Shahna's reaction, but even when he cottoned on and reciprocated, he'd seen no sign of jealousy. Shahna had been very friendly to the other woman. "I thought you two were getting on quite well."

"Funnily enough, I think she likes me better now."

"Shahna didn't like you?"

"I don't think she cared one way or the other, but she was sort of...prickly. Maybe it was my fault."

"How?" Kier demanded. Shahna was prickly with him too, and if Virginia had any insights as to why, he wanted her to share them.

"I guess I thought she was...I don't know. Some pathetic creature who'd messed up her life and couldn't get it together. I mean, Mum and Dad just said they'd leased the old cottage to a solo mother who'd asked if she could live there."

"A charity case?" Kier shook his head. Shahna would have made it clear she wasn't begging.

Ginnie snipped another rose. "Why would anyone *want* to live so far from...everything? Unless they're farming."

Perversely he defended Shahna. "It's peaceful," he said. "Healthy. A good place to raise a child."

"I wouldn't know about that."

"You grew up here," he reminded her.

She picked up the roses, wrapping the newspaper loosely about them. "And got out as soon as I could."

Kier resisted the urge to return to the cottage in the afternoon, instead taking out his laptop computer and dialing up his office in Sydney. Each day he spent several hours working on the computer and transferring data, sometimes late into the evening. And he talked to his deputy, who obviously didn't understand his sudden urge to "see something of the country" while he was in New Zealand but was valiantly holding the fort. Because Sydney was a few hours behind New Zealand, Kier was able to work around the time difference.

It all seemed very distant. Something about this place

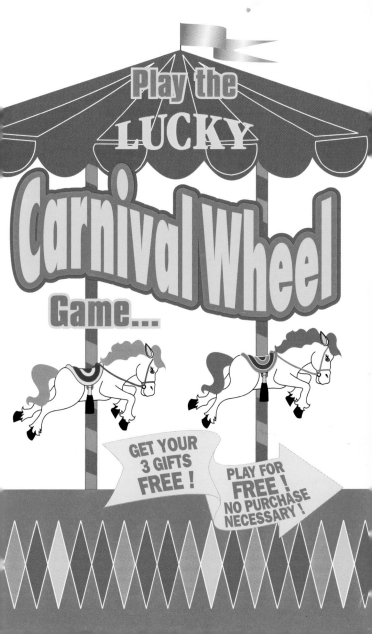

HOW TO PLAY:

1. With a coin, carefully scratch off the 3 gold areas on your Lucky Carnival Wheel. By doing so you have qualified to receive everything revealed—2 FREE books and a surprise gift—ABSOLUTELY FREE!

2. Send back this card and you'll receive 2 brand-new Silhouette Intimate Moments® novels. These books have a cover price of $4.75 each in the U.S. and $5.75 each in Canada, but they are yours ABSOLUTELY FREE.

3. There's no catch! You're under no obligation to buy anything. We charge nothing—ZERO—for your first shipment. And you don't have to make any minimum number of purchases— not even one!

4. The fact is thousands of readers enjoy receiving books by mail from the Silhouette Reader Service™. They enjoy the convenience of home delivery...they like getting the best new novels at discount prices, BEFORE they're available in stores... and they love their *Heart to Heart* subscriber newsletter featuring author news, horoscopes, recipes, book reviews and much more!

5. We hope that after receiving your free books you'll want to remain a subscriber. But the choice is yours—to continue or cancel, any time at all! So why not take us up on our invitation, with no risk of any kind. You'll be glad you did!

A surprise gift

FREE

We can't tell you what it is...but we're sure you'll like it! A

FREE GIFT!

just for playing LUCKY CARNIVAL WHEEL!

Visit us online at

www.eHarlequin.com

almost gave the impression of time slowing down, the ever-present harbor pervading the atmosphere. He couldn't even see the water from here, yet he sensed it, fancied he heard the whisper of the waves as they rippled over each other on the way to the shore.

Shahna had said it was dangerous in a storm.

It occurred to him that she was like the harbor, its unknown depths hidden under a glassy calm. Even the breezes that sometimes ruffled the surface had no effect on what lay beneath.

What sort of storm would it take to shake Shahna's determined composure, stir the emotions he was sure lay deep within, and lay bare her secret, inner self?

He must stop thinking about her. Concentrate. He had a business to run.

Why didn't it seem so important anymore?

The next afternoon Ginnie was scheduled to leave after visiting the hospital. When the family had gone, Kier made some business phone calls, carried out a couple of small jobs that Ace had left for him, and then made for the cottage.

Shahna was in her studio, working on a pair of earrings in wrought silver with opals. She greeted him briefly and invited him to make himself a coffee.

"One for you too?" he asked, and she nodded, absorbed.

He placed hers before her, watched her work for a minute, then sat in the open doorway of the studio, staring at the trees as they moved restlessly in an invisible breath of wind, and listening to their faint rustlings, the constant licking of the water along the shore, and the occasional chirp and whistle of a bird.

A whirring of wings and a swift shadow on the lawn

made him look up, to see a flash of blue as a kingfisher flapped by, heading for the water.

He heard a faint chink when Shahna laid down a tool and picked up another. He thought he could hear her breathing.

After finishing the coffee he remained where he was.

How long was it since he'd sat in the sun with nothing to do? How long since he'd been this close to happiness?

Not since childhood, and perhaps not even then.

He remembered his mother as a quiet, contained woman with a wistful smile, who smelled of roses when she hugged him, which had been less often as he grew from a baby into a boy and then a teenager. She died when he was fourteen.

The night she finally gave up her long fight against cancer he and his father had cried together in each other's arms.

That seemed to him to have been the last time they'd been close. Not knowing what to do with a bereft teenager, two months after the funeral Alan Remington had sent him off to an exclusive boarding school, and Kier had spent most of his holidays with various relatives and the families of school friends who took pity on him. He'd learned to fend for himself, and had buried a nagging inner sense of betrayal under an uncaring facade.

He'd made some good friends but allowed none of them to get really close, confiding in no one his continuing grief and secret feeling of abandonment. Adolescent boys weren't comfortable exposing their emotions, or dealing with the feelings of others.

A daisy grew on the lawn at his feet, and he leaned down and plucked it.

His father had compensated for the loss of his wife by throwing himself into work, and his solid accounting practice thrived. He attended Kier's school prize-givings and praised him for his academic and sporting achievements. And excused himself for being busy at other times. "You're all right, aren't you? You understand I have a business to run? Your mother would have wanted you well looked after."

Kier understood. Being well looked after meant a good school, an occasional outing or a few days of the holidays spent together when they made stilted conversation and he was questioned about his marks and his interests. The same questions every time, to which he mostly gave the same answers. Later it meant his fees and accommodation paid while he gained his degree, working toward a guaranteed place in his father's firm after university.

Twirling the daisy in his fingers, Kier studied the faint pink flush on the edges of the white petals. He hadn't realized daisies had so many petals, arranged in interlocking rows.

His one act of teenage defiance had been joining a group of friends on a backpacking holiday during the long university break when he was nineteen. Not that his father had forbidden him to go, but he'd made his disapproval plain, even resorting to, "Your mother wouldn't have liked it."

"She isn't here to know," Kier had pointed out, and been sorry when he saw the quiver of grief on Alan's face. But he'd gone all the same. It hadn't occurred to him that his father was anxious for his safety.

Running a thumb over the butter-yellow cushion of slightly furry stamens in the center of the daisy, he felt a pang of compunction.

He had inherited the practice when Alan Remington died of a heart attack without warning, only weeks after

Kier had qualified. Almost as if he'd been waiting to hand over the firm and now he could let go.

By that time Kier didn't feel he knew his father anymore. Subconsciously he'd been promising himself that when they were working together he and Alan would regain the relationship that had been lost with his mother's death. He'd been cheated of that, and after the funeral his chief emotion was resentment. He carried on with the practice because he owed it to Alan for all those years of hard work, of making sure his son was looked after.

Ironically it was because he hadn't really cared that he'd been successful beyond his father's wildest dreams. Beyond his own. He'd taken reserves that his father had cautiously invested in sound, long-term, low-interest stocks, and played the money markets.

The sun beat on his head. Behind him a buzzing noise indicated that Shahna was using some kind of machine. He touched the narrow petals on the tiny flower in his hand, trying to count them.

Sheer dumb luck had accounted for most of his early success, but he'd learned quickly that luck couldn't be relied on. Boldness, acumen and knowing when to call a halt to speculation were more important. He'd turned to investment broking, begun buying and selling companies himself, and before he was twenty-five he'd gained a reputation, respect, accolades in the cut-throat sphere he'd entered. And money. Enough money to do what he liked, buy what he wanted, barring such extravagances as gold-plated Rolls-Royces or private jumbo jets.

Or the woman he wanted.

He'd had her, once. Not bought—even back then he'd known Shahna wasn't the kind of woman to be impressed by his money. He'd learned before then, having been burned a couple of times, that a pretty face could hide a mercenary heart, that real women had more to give than sex and wanted more from him than access to his credit card. More than he was able or willing to give. They became demanding, or reproachful. In the end it was kinder to them and less stressful for him to let them go.

He'd not offered Shahna flashy baubles or extravagant dates, had never flown her to Paris for dinner or suggested a weekend in New York. He had wined and dined her and wooed her with discretion and panache and persistence. Treated her as an equal, not a conquest. Respected her independence and her integrity. Persuaded her into his bed.

But he'd never captured her heart.

He'd tried not to hanker after that, reminded himself that he'd never wanted it of any other woman, tried to pretend she was no different. But deep down he'd known all along that she was like no other woman he had known. She had entered into some place within his own heart that he'd denied to those others who had briefly shared his bed.

He turned his head, watching her. Bent over her work, she was oblivious of his presence, her expression intent, focused. Her profile had a delicate strength that he'd always loved. Her hands were the same—slim, but capable. She closed one over some small implement, lifted, twisted, and made a soft sound of satisfaction. The kind of sound she used to make when he touched her in certain ways, while she lay with him in the night in a wide bed.

Then her head lifted, and she stilled. She had put down her tools and was pushing back her stool before Kier heard what had roused her. Samuel was awake.

She turned and blinked at Kier, as if she too had just woken. He realized she'd forgotten he was there.

And Virginia had said Shahna was in love with him.

So much for feminine intuition. He moved aside to let Shahna pass him in the doorway, breathed in her clean, warm scent for a moment, and followed with his eyes as she hurried into the house.

The sun slipped behind a high, silver-edged cloud, and he stood up, finding his limbs had stiffened. How long had he been sitting there in a reverie?

What the hell was he doing here anyway? Shahna had refused his proposal; she hardly remembered he existed. Alison and Ace would manage without him. He knew that neighbors had offered help, and the family could probably afford to employ a proper farmhand anyway—someone who knew what he was doing and didn't need to be instructed at every turn. His second-in-command in Sydney kept asking when he was coming back, and he'd put the man off with vague excuses, saying he was taking a break, he hadn't had a holiday in years and New Zealand was a great place to relax.

"I thought you were only there for a few days checking on the feasibility of expanding the business across the Tasman," Quentin complained. "You didn't tell me you were going on holiday."

"It wasn't planned," Kier had explained patiently. Quentin, he guessed, had never done anything unplanned in his life. That was why, although a good deputy, he'd never make it to the top. An occasional leap of faith in one's own judgment was what separated the doers from the planners.

Quentin probably thought his employer had flipped his lid.

And maybe he had. Certainly the other man would be convinced of his opinion if he could see Kier mooning about admiring the sunlight glimmering on blue-green water and counting the petals on a daisy.

He realized he was still holding it, and dropped it on the grass. This was crazy. *He* was crazy. Hoping for the impossible.

Then Shahna came out of the house, holding Samuel in her arms, smiling at the baby as he stared adoringly into his mother's face. And Kier's heart turned over.

Crazy—yes.

Impossible—she'd said so.

They'd said it was impossible to make his father's practice pay more than it did. He'd been told he was taking impossible risks when he ventured capital on long shots, and doubled their value almost overnight.

He was accustomed to making the impossible possible. All it took was some imagination, an informed assessment of the potential, quick thinking, and a willingness to take risks.

He wasn't beaten yet.

Shahna noticed him studying her with a peculiarly intent expression, his eyes narrowed and his jaw stubborn. "What's the matter?" Involuntarily she hugged Samuel closer.

"Nothing." He moved, and the impression of a forcefully channeled will disappeared. Shahna relaxed.

"Would you like me to watch Samuel while you work?" Kier offered.

Chiding herself for wondering if there was a catch in the idea, Shahna shook her head. "No, I can spend time with him now. We might go for a walk."

"Mind if I tag along?" It sounded casual. He'd thrust his hands into his pockets and was standing easily, sneaker-clad feet apart on the grass. A daisy near his right foot was in imminent danger if he moved, and she was surprised to see it had been plucked from its plant. "I suppose," she said. "Samuel likes you."

"Sam has good taste." Kier reached out a hand to ruffle the baby's hair.

She couldn't help a small laugh. Samuel chuckled in imitation.

Settling him securely on her hip, she led the way to the gate. "He likes the water," she said. "Sometimes we see fish, and birds diving for them. Or boats."

Kier closed the gate behind them.

"Bo'?" Samuel pointed to the water.

"I don't see any today," Shahna told him, scanning the harbor.

Samuel babbled something incomprehensible that sounded as if he were scolding.

"What did he say?" Kier asked.

"I've no idea."

They walked along the grass near the water's edge. A few sheep scrambled away, fleeing up the slope as if all the devils of hell were at their heels, and Samuel laughed delightedly.

"Silly things, sheep," Shahna said. "They run when there's no need."

He flicked a glance at her. "They don't have that on their own." A tree bowed arthritically over the water, and Kier stepped forward and pushed back an overhanging branch so Shahna could duck under it with Samuel.

Shahna didn't answer. They'd had this argument when he first arrived, and reprising it would get them nowhere.

A motorboat cruised into view and Samuel pointed excitedly, declaiming in something that certainly wasn't English but lacked nothing in expressiveness.

Shahna matched his enthusiasm. "Yes, a boat! I think it's Timoti's boat."

As it came closer a figure in the cockpit waved to them, and she waved back. Samuel followed her example.

The boat veered toward them and came nearer the shore, the motor cut. A couple of fishing rods stood at the stern, but Timoti appeared to be alone.

"Hi, Shahna," he called across the intervening water. "How's things?"

"Fine," she called back.

Timoti turned his attention to Kier. "You still here, then?"

"For a while."

"Kier's helping Ace on the farm while Morrie's in hospital," Shahna explained.

"Good on ya, mate," Timoti approved. "Bummer eh, about Morrie?"

"They think he'll be all right now," Shahna told him. "He could be out of hospital next week."

"Yeah? Great. Can you do with a couple of fish?"

"Love some," Shahna answered.

"I'll leave them on the jetty for you." He revved the motor, backed the launch up and puttered along the shoreline out of sight.

Shahna shifted Samuel to her other hip and began walking on over the uneven ground.

Kier said, "Let me take him."

She gave him up with relief. He was getting too heavy to carry for long. But they both enjoyed their walks over the farm and around the shore, and the terrain was too rough for his stroller. "I'll be glad when he's walking," she admitted.

Kier arranged the boy on his shoulders, plump legs on each side of his neck, tiny hands held securely in his. Shahna watched the maneuver a little anxiously, and Kier said, "I won't let him fall."

Samuel crowed down at her from his unaccustomed perch. She smiled back at him.

"More fish?" Kier commented.

"It's always welcome. Timoti's generous with his catch." She laughed softly. "I think he's sorry for me."

"Why?"

"Because Samuel and I are alone. I think, it's almost incomprehensible to him, being Maori, that I have no family. He and Meri sort of adopted us when we first came. They were a huge help when we moved in, bringing furniture and stuff over in the boat."

"How did you find the cottage?"

"I saw it from Timoti's boat. I'd heard that accommodation in Rawene was cheap, and I booked into Timoti and Meri's while I looked for a place. Timoti had some tourists wanting a cruise along the harbor and he offered me a free ride. When we passed the cottage I knew it was what I was looking for. Until then I hadn't known what that was." She stopped gazing at the view of the ever-changing harbor. "Timoti said it had been empty for years and he didn't think it would be much good. But when we got back he phoned Morrie for me. It needed quite a lot of work but the rent was cheap and Morrie and Ace helped me fix it up."

I knew it was what I was looking for. Until then I hadn't known what that was.

The words stayed in Kier's mind as Shahna led the way back to the jetty. That was how he'd felt the instant he saw her standing outside the cottage, waiting for him. Waiting to fill the gap in his life that she'd left when she walked out of it. The aching, empty space that had been inside him ever since.

Two gleaming silver fish lay on the weathered wood of the jetty, tied together with a piece of greenish twine.

Striding ahead of Shahna, Kier crouched, releasing one of Samuel's hands to pick up the fish.

Immediately Samuel grasped a fistful of hair.

"Ow!" Abandoning the fish, Kier raised his hand to disentangle the tiny clutching fingers.

Shahna laughed. "I'll take the fish."

"Take Sam!" he said urgently, realizing his balance was precarious.

She plucked the child away, asking no questions, and Kier stood up. "I was afraid I'd drop him." He looked at the water gurgling beneath the narrow boards of the jetty. "Aren't you nervous about being so close to the water, once he's walking?"

"That's what the fence is for."

"How soon will he learn to climb?"

Shahna shot him a look. He wondered if she'd thought of that, despite her apparent intention to live here forever. "Not for another year or two," she said.

Kier intended to have them both well away from here long before that. He held out his hands to Samuel.

"I can manage him now," Shahna said. "You bring the fish."

She let Samuel down and held his hands while she walked him along the jetty in front of her. When she let go one of them he teetered and Kier bent, offering a finger.

Samuel grabbed at it and for a few steps he walked between them, then with a grunt sat down. Shahna picked him up again and carried him the rest of the way.

Kier put the fish on the kitchen counter while Shahna lowered Samuel to the floor and gave him some toys.

"Do you want these in the freezer?" Kier asked.

"I'll gut and fillet them first, and have some tonight."

"Gut them?" He looked down, realizing there were no telltale slits in their bellies. "You can do that?"

"Meri showed me."

She sounded so casual about it. Somehow it made the distance between them seem greater. What else had she learned since leaving the city behind? "Do you shoot rabbits?" he asked, watching her take a lethal-looking knife from a drawer.

Shahna was spreading a sheet of newspaper on the counter. For an instant she looked bewildered, then she laughed. "No. But Ace does, and I've eaten them." She cut through the twine and began operating on the fish.

"A real country boy, Ace."

Shahna gave him a sideways glance. "There's nothing wrong with that."

"Of course not." Ace was no fool. He enjoyed physical, outdoor work, but he also kept the farm accounts, studied stock control and breeding programs, and could conduct a pretty good argument about international economics.

There was a picture of him in the farmhouse lounge, holding an enormous cup as captain of his high school debating team, and a certificate proclaiming him a district finalist in the Young Farmer of the Year contest. A tough contest, Alison had told Kier proudly, involving knowledge of current affairs and the latest developments in farming and business as well as practical skills.

An ideal mate for an intelligent woman who enjoyed life in the country.

Shahna was right here on Ace's doorstep. A stunningly attractive woman, and not attached...

Kier looked away as she opened up the first fish. Samuel was walking around the furniture again, and reached the gap between the armchair and the dining chairs. As Kier watched, he debated, then relinquished his hold on the armchair and daringly took a step, then another. Three steps to safety. He flung himself at the dining chair and rested on his laurels, then slumped to the ground and crawled back to the abandoned toys.

''He walked!'' Kier said.

''What?'' Shahna looked around.

''Samuel just walked. Three steps without holding on to anything.''

''I don't believe it.'' Now he was absorbed with his xylophone, banging away with a plastic mallet.

''He did,'' Kier insisted. He crouched, holding out his hands. ''Come on Sam, show your mum what she missed.''

Sam stared uncomprehendingly, then began crawling across the floor.

''No, not like that,'' Kier admonished him. As Samuel reached him, he swung the child up, laughing, holding him between his hands above his head and giving him a gentle shake. ''Don't you make a liar out of me!'' he said sternly.

Samuel giggled at him.

Shahna was smiling. She shook her head and returned to her task.

Kier let Samuel down into his arms. The little boy pointed to what Shahna was doing, demanding to be taken closer. Kier obliged, not allowing him to touch the mess on the newspaper, though it seemed to fascinate him. ''You're raising a ghoul,'' he said to Shahna.

She laughed. He loved her laughter. Her hands were slimed with blood and other revolting stuff he didn't even want to think about, her hair was windblown and her nose was shiny. She wore a shapeless shirt and cheap cotton

trousers, faded and stained at the knees. Her feet were
bare since she'd kicked off her shoes at the door. And the
smell of fish killed any other scent.

Kier didn't care about any of it. The sound of her laughter, the light in her eyes when she turned to share it with
him, made his heart do a flip and then take up its beat
faster than before.

He leaned forward, still with her son in his arms, and
kissed her, took her laughter into his own mouth, inside
himself, something to keep.

She made an odd little sound in her throat and stood
very still, but her mouth answered him, sweetly open, giving, yearning.

Then Samuel wriggled and the moment was over.
Shahna said, "O-oh," on a strangely broken note. And
then, "You shouldn't have done that." She went back to
filleting the fish, her head down so he couldn't see her
eyes.

Samuel pursed his lips and blew bubbles of saliva
through them, looking from her to Kier with what seemed
a knowing air. "Samuel seems to approve," he said.

She didn't answer, merely throwing him a withering
look.

He said soberly, "I couldn't help it, Shah-na. It just
happened."

Shahna shrugged. "It was only a kiss. Let's not make
a production of it." She turned the fish under her hand,
slapping it back onto the counter, and sawed the knife
vigorously along the bones. He supposed he was lucky he
wasn't a fish.

Shahna kept her eyes firmly fixed on her task, trying to
still a mad longing to fling her arms about Kier and cry
"Take me, take me!" If Samuel hadn't been there, she

wasn't sure she wouldn't have done it, or something like it. It just wasn't fair what Kier could do to her.

Kier had carried Samuel back to the living area and was trying to persuade him to repeat his feat. It didn't seem the kiss had affected him nearly so powerfully as it had her.

By the time Shahna finished and washed her hands, Kier had Samuel happily walking, clutching his fingers. But as soon as Kier let go, the baby plumped down on his bottom.

Shahna laughed again, and Kier looked up at her, a smile on his lips. "Hey," he said to Samuel. "Look, there's your mum." Crouching, he hoisted the child to his feet and nodded encouragingly toward Shahna. "Show her what you can do."

Samuel looked earnestly at him, then at Shahna. Holding on tight to Kier's finger, he took a step, and as Kier refused to move with him, he let go and toddled the half-dozen steps to his mother, giving her a pleased, toothy grin.

As he reached her she stooped and swept him into her arms for a congratulatory kiss. "Clever boy!"

Kier straightened, grinning almost as widely as Samuel. "I told you he could."

Shahna gave Samuel another kiss that he returned with a generous, slobbery one of his own. She looked at Kier. The grin was still there, along with something else, an almost wistful look that was at odds with it. "So you did," she said softly. "You're very good with him."

"He's a great little guy."

Kier had only known him for a matter of days, an inner voice warned. No real test. "I thought you didn't like children."

"Who told you that?"

"You said you had no room for them in your life."

Kier frowned. "I don't remember. Anyway, it's not the same thing."

Shahna brushed that aside. "At the christening of Quentin's baby. You were talking to Quentin and Jill and some other people."

Kier shook his head. "I might have. I really don't remember," he repeated.

"You hadn't shown much interest in the guest of honor."

"Quentin's baby?" He looked baffled. "I'm sure I made all the right noises. But it wasn't a *person,* not like Sam."

Sam, hearing his name, turned to give Kier a sunny smile, and wriggled to get down. Shahna bent and set him on his feet. He stood for a moment, then headed off toward Kier, lurching the last few steps into his arms.

It was a new game, and he toddled proudly from one to the other of them until he abruptly sat down and stuck a thumb in his mouth. "He's tired," Shahna said.

"I'm not surprised after all that exercise."

When Kier was leaving he stopped in the doorway and with a hand resting on the frame he looked down at the step, then at Shahna. "Why are you depriving yourself?" he said. "And me."

Following up his advantage, she thought. He knew how she'd reacted to that kiss. But nothing had changed. Mutely she shook her head, and he looked upward as if beseeching the fates, then leveled a brooding gaze at her before nodding a curt farewell.

Chapter 9

Frustrated and more determined than ever, Kier made his way along the rough track.

What would make Shahna consider moving back to Australia?

He could build her a studio, one with every amenity she needed. They could have a house outside the city if she wanted to be in the wilds. There were settlements among the gum trees in the Blue Mountains he could commute from. Buy a helicopter and whisk off to the office daily if necessary. Or some of the time he could use the computer and telephone to keep in touch, as he'd been doing here. At least over there he'd be able to use his cell phone.

Compromise. He was willing to compromise, but Shahna seemed fixated on the Hokianga.

Alison and Ace were back and the news was good. Morrie should be released from hospital by the end of the week, and although he wouldn't be able to use his hand for a while, the doctors were hopeful that with intensive physiotherapy it might return to almost full functionality.

Alison wanted an early night, but after dinner Ace said he was going to the pub to celebrate, and would Kier like to come?

"And who's going to drive you home?" Ace's mother asked sternly.

"I'll drive," Kier volunteered. Maybe a convivial atmosphere would dispel the mood of depression that had descended on him. "I won't have more than a couple of glasses of beer." It was no hardship, he had never been a heavy drinker.

Ace looked relieved, and Alison grateful.

The hotel bar was noisy, smoky and crowded. After Ace had introduced him all round, Kier made his two beers last, then switched to ginger ale. He talked with farmers, commercial fishermen and the local garage proprietor, then found himself in a group that included the retired editor of a local newspaper, a poet who drove a school bus, and a political journalist who wrote for magazines all over the world.

"And you live here?" Kier asked, incredulous.

The man laughed. "About six or eight months of the year. The rest of the time I'm swanning around the world, but I do a lot of the in-depth stuff at my place in the bush. A two-room shack but it's got a phone and power and I can get on the Internet—usually."

"Are you married?"

The man gave him a peculiar look. "Not anymore."

It figured.

Next day Shahna and Samuel spent the morning in a small church hall with other young mothers supervising a noisy bunch of adventurous preschoolers, and Samuel showed off his new and still shaky walking skills. Afterward they were invited to lunch with a woman whose child was a little older than Samuel. It was late afternoon by the time Shahna stopped at the garage-cum-store for groceries, and then drove home.

While Samuel pottered around she made sketches for a necklace using a cabuchon aquamarine from a broken brooch that she'd picked up cheaply on her last visit to Kaitaia. The color reminded her of the waters of the Hokianga, and she wanted to set it into a free-form design reminiscent of the harbor and its hills.

It was difficult to concentrate. When she wasn't watching Samuel her mind kept wandering—to Kier kissing her as she laughed, ignoring the fishy smell and the nasty slime on her hands, and the fact that he held Samuel in his arms. Kier grinning with pleasure when Samuel took those triumphant, tottering steps toward her.

And Kier at the christening in Sydney, his deep voice carrying and emphatic. "There's no room for kids in my life." Then his laughter, and, "Anyway, I'd make a rotten father."

He claimed he'd forgotten the incident, but she remembered it clearly, remembered the death of hope, her heart thudding until it drummed in her ears, until it was the only thing she could hear, so that she had no idea what the person talking to her was saying, only kept on nodding inanely and smiling until her facial muscles ached. Because she had to pretend she was having a good time, that her world, her future, her life, had not just crumbled into dust.

She recalled someone saying, "Are you all right? You're awfully pale." And giving them some vague reply. Someone else thrust a glass into her hand. Water. Only water, but it had nearly choked her.

And then Kier was at her side, his strong hand under her arm. "What is it? You look like death."

"I'm all right," she told the small ring of concerned faces. She couldn't look at him. "The heat...I'm probably a bit dehydrated." Although she'd been steadily sipping apple juice.

It was high summer in Sydney and they'd accepted the excuse. "You must remember to drink water," someone said. "Lots of it, in this weather."

She'd said she would, and Kier had taken her home, putting her into his car as if she were fragile, and casting worried glances at her all the way back to her apartment, where she lay on her bed while he brought iced water. "You're still pale," he said. "Is it that bug you had before, do you think? Should I take you to a doctor?"

"I don't need a doctor. I feel better already."

"I'll stay tonight."

"No!"

"Shahna, you're sick. I can't leave you."

"I'm not sick. It's just all that standing around in the heat. And the time of the month," she lied.

His worried expression cleared a little. "Still..."

"I'd rather be left alone."

They compromised. Kier made her a sandwich while she showered and undressed. He fed her and waited until she was in bed, and made her promise to stay there, before he left.

And then she cried.

That was the last time she had indulged in self-pity. After a sleepless night she'd forced herself to pragmatism. *Think the problem through, make decisions, plan a strategy and carry it out.*

Just like designing this necklace, she told herself, looking critically at the drawing in front of her. Dissatisfied, she screwed up the paper and started over, but her mind was still in the past.

The first, most difficult but most necessary decision had been to get out of Sydney, take herself as far as she could from Kier. It meant leaving her job, her home, her friends, and abandoning a large part of her life.

She'd done it, and had few regrets. Realistically, the friends she'd had in Sydney would have little in common with her now. Contact would probably have withered away in time, even if she'd made the effort to keep in touch. It had been simpler not to.

Her pencil drew a circle, her mind seeing silver—a thin, delicate wire.

After flying to New Zealand she'd taken a temporary job in Auckland, the country's largest city, though nowhere near the size of Sydney. The firm that hired her was small and the position less challenging and lower-paid than the one she'd left, but her new colleagues had been pleasant and welcoming. She had begun making friends.

At the base of the circle under her fingers she sketched in a line, making a long, horizontal crescent.

Friends were easy to find. She'd found some here when she moved to the Hokianga. Timoti and Meri, the McKenzies, the other playgroup mothers.

She had never found anyone to take Kier's place. She'd told herself that Samuel would fill the empty places in her heart, and she'd soon forget.

Now she knew she'd been lying to herself all along.

The pencil in her hand had stilled. She applied it to the paper again, blurring the top of the crescent and making its outline uneven, reminiscent of the bush that softened the brows of the distant hills.

Shahna picked up a colored blue-gray pencil to shade the upper part of the crescent. *Enamel?* she queried in a notation beside it. No, too shiny and hard. Better to use silver and give it a matte finish with steel wool. She crossed out "enamel."

She couldn't marry Kier…could she?

Samuel. She didn't want to bring Samuel up in the city.

Lots of people found suburbs pleasant places for children, where it was perfectly possible to bring up a family.

A family? Brothers and sisters for Samuel? How would Kier feel about that?

She divided the lower half of the crescent with a curved vertical line and, choosing another pencil, colored one side dark green. The other section should be…*driftwood*. A sliver of whitened wood set into the silver.

She derived her inspiration from the changing patterns of nature on the Hokianga. Another reason not to move back to Sydney.

Of course, if she didn't love Kier, all other arguments were irrelevant.

Love. The word emerged reluctantly from her subconscious even as she tried to shy away from it.

Shahna sat with a pencil poised in her hand, not seeing the design before her anymore, staring into her own heart.

Of course she loved Kier. Deep down she had known that all along, from the night she'd invited him into her bed, but for a long time she'd tried to hide it even from herself, a defense mechanism, because he had never used the word to her and because loving a man who didn't love her was tantamount to emotional suicide. In the last days, knowing that admitting to love would make it harder to leave, she had refused to think about it at all.

By deserting him and fleeing Sydney, coming back here, she'd put him out of reach—until he came looking for her and turned her carefully constructed alternative life-plan on its head.

Her gaze focused again on the sketch in front of her. She drew in a slender curve of silver to hang below the crescent, made it a loop…no, an off-center heart shape.

Had she meant to do that?

She sat staring at it. The translucent gray-blue aquamarine would hang nicely within the finely wrought frame.

Kier had never said anything about loving her, only wanting her. Perhaps he didn't know the difference. Or he was holding it as a trump card, waiting for her to show her feelings first. He'd made all the moves so far, and he wasn't in the habit of revealing his hand.

Hope and doubt battled for supremacy. Could he learn to love her son? A crucial question.

For all his claims that he'd make a rotten father, he was surprisingly at ease with Samuel.

But when Samuel lost the universal charm of babyhood, would Kier's feelings alter? He'd never shown any interest in children before.

Samuel was her first concern. Everything came back to that. She'd knowingly, perhaps selfishly, brought him into the world and it was up to her to make it a good place for him throughout his childhood. Her own needs, and whatever Kier wanted, must come second.

She drew in the shape of the aquamarine and colored it, her imagination seeing it swinging freely within the silver heart, glittering in the light.

Like a teardrop.

Kier was arguing with his second-in-command.

"You can deal with it, Quentin," he reiterated. "I trust your judgment."

Quentin said, "Yes, well...I appreciate your confidence. But I'd be happier if you were here to deal with it yourself. I'll...er...let you know the outcome."

"Do that."

Kier put down the McKenzies' phone and sat frowning, drumming his fingers on the inadequate table in his room, experiencing an unusual mood of indecision.

Damn, why couldn't he just cut his losses and shrug Shahna and her inexplicable stubbornness off? Plenty of women would jump at the chance to marry him. Women who would happily give him his own child.

A stab of jealousy brought him up short, and he stood staring unseeingly through the darkened window. A distant glimmer of light through the trees told him Shahna was awake, probably working in her studio after putting Samuel in his cot. He gradually focused on the light, seeing her in his mind's eye absorbed, concentrating as she shaped a piece of metal into a marvel of delicate workmanship while Samuel slept.

Samuel, the baby she had made with someone else, some anonymous male, in what she claimed was a one-night stand.

Kier clenched his hands into fists, gripped by a combination of anger and unexpected heartache, taken unaware by the depth of his emotion.

Children had hardly figured in his life at all. With no siblings, and nurturing no ambition to found a dynasty, he had never thought seriously about having children of his own. But Samuel had somehow charmed his way into Kier's heart.

With a shock he discovered that he wished quite fiercely the little boy was his. Maybe because he was

Shahna's. But also because he was Samuel, in his own right. A small person with his own personality already. Kier liked him enormously.

He wanted Shahna. And he wanted her son.

Kier took the truck to Rawene to collect some farm supplies for Ace. Afterward he had time to kill before the next ferry, and as he strolled along the waterfront Timoti hailed him from his boat, where he was cleaning some fish.

"Show me how to do that?" Kier asked him.

Timoti grinned. "Come on down."

It was a messy job and Kier was clumsy, but Timoti said encouragingly, "You'll be right, with a bit more practice. Ever done any fishing?"

"I tried once when I was kid, but I didn't catch anything."

"I could take you out sometime. Tomorrow if you like. After lunch."

"Thanks. If Ace doesn't need me, I'll take you up on that."

"Go for it," Ace said. "Have a good time."

Timoti picked him up from the new jetty near the big farmhouse and motored up the harbor to anchor at a spot where the bush grew down to the water.

He handed Kier a rod and showed him how to bait a hook and cast the line into the water. Then they sat back in comfortable chairs on the deck, and waited.

The boat rocked gently, the water slapping at its sides, and white wisps of cloud floated in a blue sky. Timoti had his feet up on the railing, and his eyes were half-closed. A couple of gulls flapped lazily by, then turned and circled the boat before skimming down onto the water and tucking their wings neatly to their sides.

Kier shifted, growing restless, and without moving Timoti said, "Fishing takes patience."

He could be patient, Kier told himself, settling his behind into the chair and trying to emulate Timoti's relaxed air. But he was used to making things happen, not just waiting for them.

"Fish are like women," Timoti said. "You show them the bait, let them think you're not interested, and sooner or later curiosity gets the better of them. Let them have a nibble or two, then they want more, and pretty soon you've got 'em hooked."

"Is that how it was with Meri?"

Timoti's laugh was rich and full. "Ah, Meri. She was different. A proud woman. Like your Shahna."

"Shahna?"

Timoti gave him an oblique look. "She's got her pride, hasn't she?"

"What did she tell you?"

"Not much. Didn't want any favors, though, when she arrived here with a new baby and no place to live." Timoti's dark gaze turned speculative. "No man, no family to help her."

"She told me she didn't need a man."

Timoti nodded. "Same thing Meri told me." He laughed. "She wanted me, though. Even if she would never admit it." He paused, watching a black shag land with a discreet splash on the water and pleat its wings, arranging its long neck into a graceful S-curve. "But then, I didn't give her a baby until we were married."

"Samuel isn't mine," Kier said.

Timoti cast him a skeptical glance. "I guess that makes a difference."

"No!" Kier said involuntarily. "I mean, not to me."

It was true, despite his jealousy of Samuel's father. He supposed he should resent Samuel, but he couldn't.

Timoti lapsed into silence again. The shag had disappeared, but then broke the surface yards away, and rested before diving again, coming up seconds later with a small fish that it tossed down its throat.

"He's got one," Timoti commented. "Fish are around, all right."

He seemed content to sit there all afternoon.

The motion of the boat and the silence, except for a few twittering birds and the rippling water, gradually had their effect, an unusual calm stealing into Kier's soul.

When his line twitched it took him a moment to realize what was happening. Then it twitched again, and Timoti said, "Got a bite?"

"I think so." He sat up, his hand tightening on the rod.

Spurred on by Timoti's advice and encouragement, he landed a respectable kahawai, and was tempted to throw the wriggling, gasping thing back. But Timoti dispatched it quickly and efficiently, and Kier banished a pang of regret for the shimmering silver beauty that immediately became dull and lifeless.

He caught three more to Timoti's half dozen before Timoti headed the boat back along the harbor, and Kier asked to be dropped off at Shahna's place. Ridiculously, he wanted to show off his catch to her, like primitive man bringing home some trophy of the hunt to his mate.

She opened the door with Samuel in her arms. The sight of them together gave him a strange warm feeling. She smiled, then a slightly wary look shut the smile down. "Kier," she said. And then, almost reluctantly, "Come in."

He held up the fish, strung together on twine. "Are you tired of eating fish?"

"Not if it's fresh." She led the way to the kitchen, while Samuel gazed interestedly at the fish. "I heard Timoti's boat. Did he give those to you?"

"Nope. Caught them myself."

"*You* caught them?"

"And gutted them," he told her. "All cleaned and ready to cook." He deposited them on the counter.

"I'm impressed." She looked it too. Impressed and surprised. "But I can't use all of that." Samuel reached toward the fish and she hitched him higher on her hip, moving away.

"Take what you want, I'll give the rest to Alison."

"Thank you. I'll have one." She put Samuel down, and he sat back against her ankles, gazing up at Kier.

"Make it two, and I'll cook," he offered rashly. He didn't do it often, but he could produce a decent meal when necessary. "Seeing I caught these, I'd like to do the rest."

Samuel suddenly clapped his chubby hands together.

Kier looked down at him, grinning, and Shahna laughed.

"See, he approves," Kier triumphed.

"He's not *that* bright," Shahna said. "He's just showing off for you."

"Kee." Samuel lifted his arms.

Kier bent and picked him up. "He likes the idea," he said firmly. "Don't you, Sam? You tell her."

Samuel regarded him solemnly. "Mum-mum," he said.

Shahna laughed again. "Oh, all right," she agreed. "I'll do the vegetables and you can cook the fish. You'd better let Alison know you won't be there for dinner."

Reminding himself not to push his luck, Kier made sure

to keep the conversation light and neutral while they shared the preparations and Shahna fed Samuel.

They ate after Samuel was put to bed, while it was still light outside under a lazily lowering sun. Shahna pushed away her empty plate and said, "That was delicious. Thank you, Kier. Coffee?"

"I'll make it. You stay there."

She settled back in her chair as he got up, and he heard her sigh.

"You must get tired," he said. "Samuel's never still when he's awake, is he?"

"I don't mind." She yawned, though, stretching briefly.

"It's worth it?" He spooned dark, aromatic grains into the coffeemaker.

"Samuel? Oh, yes."

He poured water into the jug and brought it to the table.

"You have no regrets?" he asked, sitting down again.

Her eyes darkened. "I don't regret having Samuel."

"Or leaving me?" He kept his voice low, even, as though the answer didn't matter too much.

"Oh, that—" she looked away "—that was…inevitable."

She sounded sad. While he groped for some less direct question than the simple and obvious, *Why?* she added, "Please don't ask me anymore."

It was a huge effort, but he nodded, accepting that he'd get no more from her tonight, and pushed down the plunger in the coffeemaker, not too fast. *Patience,* he heard Timoti's voice in his mind.

The light was fading outside, making the room shadowy, somehow more intimate.

"You never told me much about your parents."

He'd assumed they died in a traffic accident, and when

he asked she'd nodded and shrugged off further questions.
The subject hadn't come up again.

And—he faced the fact—he hadn't wanted to know
more. Neither of them had been keen to pour out their
life story to the other. They'd lived for the present. Their
past lives seemed irrelevant.

But nothing about Shahna seemed irrelevant now.

"My parents?" Shahna blinked at him.

"You must remember them," he said. "You were
twelve, you said, when they died. What were they like?"

Shahna shrugged. "At that age, parents are just parents.
I hadn't really begun to see them as individuals with their
own lives."

"Did you love them?"

"Of course I loved them. But…" She paused, then said
quickly, "I didn't say they'd died."

She'd certainly implied it. Carefully he said, "You told
me you lost them both when you were twelve…what happened?"

She flickered a glance at him, and he saw her reluctance, as if she regretted saying so much. "My father
left," she said. "Walked out for good. He'd done it before, but this time he had another woman. Well, maybe
she wasn't the first, I don't know. He went to live with
her, and my mother was so bitter she wouldn't let me
visit. I used to meet him secretly in town, but he never
bothered to try for legal access, and then he and his lady
moved away and…we lost touch."

"Doesn't sound like he was much of a father."

"He was the only one I had."

Kier's lips were compressed. "What happened to your
mother?"

She shrugged, and seemed to struggle within herself,
and he waited. Patiently.

"After Daddy left, she began seriously drinking. She'd bring home a bottle of vodka from work—she was a hotel receptionist—and sit at the kitchen table with it for hours before going to bed. First it was Friday nights, then nearly every night. She managed to hold down her job but at home she barely functioned."

"With a teenager to look after?"

"By the time I was fourteen I was looking after myself pretty well. I would have liked to have left when I turned sixteen, but I stayed because she needed me. Then one night after I'd gone to bed she went out...I don't know why. Maybe to buy more drink, she'd finished a bottle. Walked in front of a car, and died a few hours later. That's when I sold the house and came to Australia. I was eighteen."

"And you never heard from your father again?"

"It doesn't matter anymore." A wistful expression crossed her features. "I would have liked Samuel to have grandparents, though. Real ones, who cared."

"They're missing out on something there, all right."

She gave him a rather wondering, considering look.

"His father too," Kier added. "Idiot."

Shahna continued to stare at him. She said uncertainly, "You've only known him a couple of weeks."

He felt as if he'd always known Samuel. "He's a terrific kid."

She seemed to be groping, her voice going husky. "Would you...would you have liked a baby?"

Kier lifted a shoulder. "I never thought about it." He looked back at her, accusing despite himself. "You didn't give me the chance."

Abruptly she pushed away her chair and got up, turning from him, almost running into the kitchen area, fetching up against the far counter as if she'd blundered into it unseeing. He saw her hands clutch its edge, her shoulders hunch as he left his own chair, crossing swiftly to take her arms and bring her to face him.

She ducked her head, gasping like someone short of air, and he felt her shudder before she braced herself and tried to pull away.

He wouldn't let her. "Shahna?" he queried. "What is it? What's the matter?"

"We never talked enough," she said. "I'm sorry, Kier. I've messed up, and there's no going back."

"It's not too late."

"But it is!" She looked up and he was shocked at the stark anguish in her face. "It is, much too late."

Chapter 10

"You don't understand," Shahna said. Despair filled her, choked her.

Kier gave her a small shake. "Talk to me now!" he urged. "Tell me what you feel."

She wouldn't have known where to start. There was so much he didn't know, and what good would it do to tell him? What would *he* feel if she told him the whole truth? Anger, grief? Disgust?

"I can't," she said. "I don't know what I feel."

His hands moved to her face, cupping it between his big palms, tipping it up so he could search her eyes. "Maybe this will help," he said, and kissed her.

It held a desperate, angry hunger, and she tried not to return the passion that finally overwhelmed the other emotions, telling herself this was an unfair weapon and he had no right to use it.

At first she clenched her fists between them, keeping him at bay. Then her fingers uncurled of their own accord and she kissed him back helplessly, needily, returning the passion in kind, letting her emotions spill into this bittersweet moment, giving him all he asked for, demanded from her.

But when he lifted his mouth again from hers, his thumbs caressing her cheeks, he found tears there, and a low, explosive exclamation escaped his lips.

It brought her to her senses, and she pushed against him, freeing herself at last.

"Shahna—" He reached for again. "What is it?"

She shook her head, evading his touch. "Nothing you can help. Please just go away, Kier. I was all right until you came."

It was unfair to blame him. She was equally, if not more, responsible for the mess she'd made of things. But she needed to think, sort herself out, and she was less and less able to do that while he was here, enticing her with kisses and making her realize how much she'd missed him.

He raised a hand, brushing away a tear, but when she flinched from him he dropped it again. "It was only a kiss, Shahna."

Angrily she dashed the back of her hand across her eyes. Only a kiss? "Fine, let's leave it at that."

He scowled at her. "I've never seen you cry before."

Of course he hadn't. She'd hidden any tears from him, not wanting him to know how vulnerable she was. "Well, this is a first, then," she said flippantly. "Don't worry, I'll get over it." Already the tears had stopped flowing, and she silently thanked God.

"I wish you'd tell me why you're so upset."

"I'm tired," she said. "All I need is a good night's sleep."

"You haven't been sleeping?" He searched her face.

"I had some broken nights with Samuel," she reminded him. "And haven't had time to catch up yet."

"All right, I can take a hint," he said, "if it's heavy enough."

"I don't mean to be rude."

"I can't complain," he admitted, "after inviting myself."

He was on his way to the door when the telephone burred.

While she hurried to answer, Kier hesitated with his hand on the doorknob.

"It's Alison," she said, holding out the receiver to him. "For you."

He took it from her, frowning. The frown didn't lift, and when he hung up he said, "Quentin's wife has been trying to get hold of me."

"What's happened?" She was sure Jill wouldn't have phoned him without a very good reason.

"Quentin is in hospital. They suspect a heart attack. Damn!"

"Oh, poor Quentin. And poor Jill! He's young for that, isn't he?" Surely he was still in his thirties.

Kier ran a hand through his hair. "I'll have to go home, as soon as I can get a flight."

Her heart lurched. "Yes, of course. Jill must be frantic."

He looked at her as though he didn't see her, and she knew his brain was working fast, making plans, sifting priorities. Then his eyes cleared, focused on her. "When I've sorted this," he said, "we'll talk."

Shahna didn't answer. Once he returned to Sydney and what he'd called real life, maybe he'd change his mind, look on this interlude as an aberration, a short holiday from reality.

She wouldn't count on his returning, she promised herself, repressing a stupid instinct to cling, beg him not to leave her.

Hadn't she known this moment would come? But not quite so abruptly. She said, "You can use my phone if you want to arrange travel plans."

Kier shook his head. "I'll go back to the farm and try from there. I hope Ace and Alison won't feel I'm leaving them in the lurch."

"They'll understand. Morrie will be home in a day or two. And they have friends who will help out."

His mouth twisted as if the thought didn't please him. "I guess I'm not really needed here." He looked around the room as though memorizing it, before his eyes returned to her face. A hand lifted to her cheek again and this time she didn't jerk away.

His fingers barely touched her skin. "I'll see you," he said softly, and hesitated a brief second before walking back to the door.

Shahna watched it close behind him and wondered if she would ever see him again.

Sydney was noisier than he remembered, crowded and hot, and the driver of the taxi he hired at the airport was bad-tempered. So was Kier by the time he'd paid the man and carried his luggage up to his apartment. He changed and shaved and drove himself to the hospital, finding Jill pale and tense and faintly hostile.

Quentin, despite his pallor and the machines and tubes surrounding him, insisted on giving Kier a rundown of all that he'd done before collapsing on his desk.

"He's been working himself into the ground," Jill said, following Kier into the corridor as her husband sank against the pillows, having passed over the burden of administration. "He's stressed out."

And it was all Kier's fault. "I'm sorry, Jill," he told her. "I should have known I was expecting too much of him."

"He has a family to think of. It's all right for you, Kier. You don't have children." Then she flushed. "I shouldn't have said anything. Quentin would be mortified."

"Say whatever you want. Maybe Quentin should have said it before."

"Would you have listened?"

The resentment in her voice bothered him. "I always listen to my staff," he said evenly. "Why wouldn't I?"

"Because you're so wrapped up in the business, and he tried to be the same. He thought he had to be, to meet your standards."

"To the detriment of his family?" Kier guessed. "I certainly didn't mean to give him that impression." But he'd hardly thought about Quentin's other commitments, had he?

Quentin had never pleaded family commitments when Kier asked him to work out of office hours or go on a business trip at a moment's notice. He had requested some time off to be with Jill during her labor with both their children, and for some days after she came home. Kier had not complained at the inconvenience. After all, he knew where Quentin was and could phone him if he needed to discuss something.

He thought he'd been an understanding employer. But perhaps not understanding enough. "Quentin will need time to get over this," he said.

Jill looked anxious. "He won't lose his job, will he? He's worried you'll find someone else."

More and more Kier was feeling like some Scrooge

who had no feeling for his employees. "I can't do without him," he told her firmly and almost truthfully. "Where would I find another deputy as good as he is?"

"Can I tell him that?"

"Sure. And I'll tell him myself the next time I see him. How are you holding up, yourself? Do you need some help at home?"

"The children are with a neighbor but I can't impose on her too often or for too long. I should go home and check on them." She looked distracted. "I hate to leave Quentin."

"He seems pretty stable at the moment. I'll stay if you like. Take my mobile phone, and I promise I'll contact you right away if things change."

"I have Quentin's, you know the number. But...don't you want to go to the office?"

He did, there were things that needed his attention, but he tried to reassure her. "That can wait." His secretary would stave off any urgent queries. "Go and make whatever arrangements you have to. The sooner you start, the sooner you'll be back here with your husband."

The next few days were hectic. Normally Kier wouldn't have minded, but the usual adrenaline rush was missing, perhaps because of a nagging guilt over Quentin. And the continuing sense of having left something unfinished when he departed the Hokianga so abruptly.

He kept seeing Shahna's face as she'd watched him go. Composed, serene, but with something behind it that he couldn't read.

And he missed Samuel. Missed the little boy's round-eyed wonder at the world, his habit of gazing solemnly upward while he sized up an adult, his gurgling laughter and the warm shape of his tiny body when Kier lifted it into his arms.

He had intended to phone Shahna with the excuse of relaying news of Quentin's condition, but Jill told him she'd had a call from Shahna herself, expressing her concern.

''It was nice of her,'' she said. ''I always liked Shahna. I didn't know you two were still in touch. She told me you were visiting her when I phoned the number you gave Quentin. I'm sorry if…well, if I dragged you away from something important.''

''Quentin's health is more important at the moment. I told Shahna I'd be back.''

Jill looked relieved. ''I'm glad.''

He telephoned the farmhouse and learned that Morrie was home and on the mend. Alison sounded pleased to hear from him, but she interrupted the conversation with a quick ''Excuse me a minute,'' leaving him dangling for a while.

''I have little Samuel here,'' she told him, after apologizing on her return. ''I'm looking after him for Shahna.''

''Shahna isn't sick, is she?'' Kier queried sharply.

''No, no. She had a dentist's appointment in Rawene. I told her to take her time and treat herself to lunch over there. She's been looking a bit peaky lately. It's not easy bringing up a little one on your own, and now he's mobile Samuel's a handful, into everything. He's a bonnie little chap, for such a wee thing as he was when they first arrived here. Well, it was nice to hear from you, Kier. I'll tell Morrie you were asking after him.''

Kier put down the phone with a feeling of dissatisfaction. Shahna was looking peaky? Did she miss him, or was Samuel running her ragged now he was walking?

A clear picture floated into his mind of those first steps, Samuel toddling precariously between his mother and Kier, laughing with delight at his own achievement. And the glow of pride on Shahna's face.

He ached for her. For them both.

It was two weeks before Quentin was home, and Jill invited Kier to dinner to celebrate. An olive branch, he figured. "It will be heart-healthy food," she warned. "And Quentin can't stay up too late."

He promised to leave early.

The food was delicious, he assured her when they'd eaten. Quentin seemed to have enjoyed it.

"You should eat healthy too," Jill told Kier. "You could be heading for a heart attack yourself if you're not careful."

"I'm very fit," he protested.

"Still, if you don't slow down a bit…"

A wail from the children's bedroom interrupted, and she sighed and got up, to reappear a few minutes later holding the three-year-old in her arms. "He missed his daddy when Quentin was in hospital," she explained to Kier as Quentin took the child on his knee.

Kier wondered if Samuel had missed him. He was younger and maybe he'd forget more quickly.

"I'll bring coffee," Jill said. "Milk and sugar for you, Kier?"

"Just sugar." He was watching Quentin's son snuggle into his father's arms. Within minutes the child was asleep, and Quentin made to get up. "I'll put him back to bed."

"Let me." Kier stood up, sure Quentin shouldn't be

carrying three-year-olds about. He took the child carefully and Quentin led the way to the bedroom.

Kier watched the tender way the man tucked his son in, smoothed fair hair back from the fine-skinned forehead and bent to kiss it. Something tugged at his heart, a sharp, almost painful longing.

When they returned Jill was placing coffee cups on the table. "You didn't carry him back to bed?" she asked Quentin anxiously. "You shouldn't—"

"Kier did it for me."

"He did? Thank you, Kier, that was nice of you."

"I can be nice." He smiled at her.

She gave him a doubtful look, and then a slightly shamefaced smile in return. "It's been a stressful time," she said. "I'm grateful for your help."

He had done very little, in fact. Provided paid home help and what moral support he could, and tried to keep Quentin from fretting over business affairs, constantly assuring him everything was under control. And making sure that it was.

But for the first time in years his mind was never wholly on his job. In the middle of a meeting he would find it wandering to a quiet cottage on the Hokianga, and after working late one night, while he sat at a traffic light, drumming on the steering wheel and breathing in fumes from a truck belching evil brown smoke in front of him, he had a sudden clear vision of the broad gray-green waters, disturbed only by the spreading wake of Timoti's boat.

When he got home he went straight to the phone and called Shahna's number. It rang several times before she picked up.

"Hello?" She sounded surprised, sleepy.

"I'm sorry," he said, and silently cursed himself. "I'd

forgotten the time difference." It must be midnight over there. "Did I wake you?"

"Kier!" Her voice was husky with sleep. "It doesn't matter. Is everything all right?"

"Yes." *No, everything is all wrong, as long as we're apart.* "I just wanted to—" *hear your voice* "—make sure you're okay. Alison said you look tired."

"She told me you phoned. I'm fine, really. How's Quentin?"

"Recovering fast. Jill won't let him come back to work yet, though. It'll be a while before I can go to New Zealand again."

There was a short silence. "I didn't really expect you to."

"I said I would."

"I know, but…"

The telephone was a frustrating means of communication. He couldn't see her face, guess at what she was thinking, feeling.

"I disturbed you," he said, "and you need your sleep."

"That's all right, I don't mind," she answered quickly. "It's nice to hear from you, Kier."

Even nicer, perhaps, if he hadn't called in the middle of the night. It occurred to him that she might not have a bedroom phone. "Where are you, in the kitchen?"

"Yes."

"Go back to bed," he ordered. "I'll call again at a more civilized hour."

She laughed, the sound warming him right down to his toes. "I'll look forward to it. Good night, Kier."

After he'd hung up he sat for a while with a foolish smile on his face. She'd said she looked forward to hearing from him again.

He'd told himself he was giving her time to miss him, to wonder if he'd forgotten her. Strategy.

Now, his heart pounding with relief, he realized to his chagrin that he'd been putting off phoning her because he was afraid she'd give him the brush-off, say she didn't want him to contact her anymore.

But she hadn't. The lines were still open.

There was light on the horizon after all.

Shahna too was smiling as she climbed back into her bed. Ever since Kier left she'd been feeling depressed and listless. His silence had confirmed her guess that back in Sydney he'd come to his senses and put her out of his mind. A belief that was reinforced by Alison's casual mention of his phone call to her.

She ought to have told him not to call again, because surely keeping in touch was merely prolonging the inevitable agony of parting again, but at the sound of his voice her heart had lifted, and despite it being the middle of the night she could have sworn she heard birds singing.

Suddenly, denying the darkness that surrounded the cottage, the world seemed a brighter place.

Kier called several times in the next few weeks. He asked about Samuel and seemed genuinely interested in the baby's progress, his increasing mobility, the new forms of mischief he was able to indulge in, and even the latest tooth to make its appearance.

She described the jewelry she was making and some new markets she'd found, and he told her about his meeting with a particularly pompous member of a government regulation board, and his problems tying up the loose ends Quentin had left when he became ill.

They didn't touch on personal subjects, and Shahna decided she would treat these intermittent contacts like bubbles, beautiful while they lasted, but fragile and bound to disappear into nothingness without warning.

Kier called at Quentin's house one afternoon to find Jill looking exhausted, and as she picked up the toddler who had followed her to the door he realized she was pregnant again.

"I'm sorry if it's a bad time," he said. "I just need to see Quentin for a few minutes."

"He's resting," she said shortly. "Can it wait?"

Not for long, but he could see she wasn't going to allow her husband to be disturbed. In the background the younger child was crying, and she looked behind her, one hand on the door, and made to put down the boy in her arms, who whimpered and clung.

"Shh." She swung him up again. "Be a good boy. If I don't pick up your sister she'll wake Daddy."

Kier stepped into the hall and held out his arms. "Let me take him while you attend to the other one."

"You?"

He smiled. "I'm quite good with babies. I looked after Shahna's once or twice."

"I not a baby," the boy in her arms said darkly.

"No, you're a big guy," Kier agreed. "Want to show me how big?"

The child wriggled down to the floor. "This big," he said, standing against Kier's trouser leg and holding a hand above his head.

"That's pretty impressive." Kier nodded to Jill as he closed the door behind him, then looked down. "How big will you be when you grow up?"

The boy stretched his arm as high as it would go. "Big as my daddy!"

Kier laughed, then sobered as Jill quietly left them. Would Samuel ever be able to say that? He didn't know his father, and according to Shahna he probably never would. The man had no idea what he was missing.

When Jill came back carrying the little girl, Kier was sitting on the floor of the lounge, while the boy explained a complicated game involving blocks and toy cars.

Jill watched for a few moments, then sat on one of the armchairs with the girl on her lap. "So Shahna did have the baby," she said.

Kier looked up. "I didn't know she'd kept in touch with you."

"She didn't," Jill denied. "But I suspected, before she disappeared so suddenly, that she was pregnant."

Kier experienced an odd sensation, as if the ground underneath him had shifted. "She wasn't pregnant when she left."

Jill's brows rose. "Are you sure? I could have sworn...she had that look."

"What look?" Even if Shahna had been pregnant, she could hardly have known it herself. It would surely have been far too early.

"It's hard to describe," Jill said. "Just a look that some women have...hormonal, I suppose, but it's kind of an inner glow that comes and goes."

"The baby's eleven or twelve months old." Would Samuel have had a birthday by now? Kier wondered, with a pang.

Jill's expression was puzzled. "I guess time goes faster than you think," she said. "But I remember at this one's christening—" she looked down at the child she held "—you took Shahna home early because she wasn't well."

"Some kind of tummy upset. It wasn't the first time

she'd had it." She'd been sick weeks before, for several days.

"Tummy upset, or morning sickness?"

"It wasn't morning," he pointed out.

Jill laughed. "I don't know why they call it that. It can hit you any time of the day—and anytime during pregnancy," she added bitterly. "I've been having it since day one, I swear. It was my first inkling that I was expecting again, and I suspect it's not going to stop for the full forty weeks."

Kier's heart began to pound uncomfortably. "Forty weeks? Nine months, I thought…"

"Babies don't read calendars. Forty weeks, give or take a few days—or even a few weeks."

"Weeks?"

"You really don't know much about it, do you?" Jill queried pityingly. "That one—" she indicated the child at his feet "—was three weeks late, and had to be induced in the end."

Kier vaguely recalled Quentin being twitchy at the time, muttering about the baby being overdue, snatching up the receiver of his office phone every time it rang.

Eyes glazed, he stared at Jill. "She can't have been pregnant then," he said.

Jill's mouth opened as if she would dispute the diagnosis, then she firmly closed it. "Well, it's none of my business anyway," she muttered, looking unconvinced. "Sorry."

Quentin came into the room, running a hand through his rumpled hair. "You didn't tell me Kier was here," he reproached his wife. "Come into my study."

"We didn't want to disturb you," Kier said, following the other man. "I've been making friends with young Morgan, and I see congratulations are in order again."

Quentin smiled as he closed the study door behind them. "It was kind of unexpected," he said ruefully, "but the best-laid plans, you know." He waved Kier to a chair but didn't sit down himself, standing by his desk looking rather awkward. "The doctors said I could go back to work next week, as long as I ease into it."

Hugely relieved, Kier forced himself to caution and consideration. "You must take it slowly. Jill will never forgive me if I allow you to do too much too soon."

"We appreciate you holding my job, and all you've done for the family." Quentin hesitated. "But...well, I want to spend more time with them. If that doesn't suit you, I'll tender my resignation."

"And then what?" Kier asked, his mind working furiously. If he had to find and train a new deputy it would be ages before he got back to the Hokianga, to Shahna and Sam.

"Jill's happy to take a cut in income in return for more of my time and to safeguard my health. Having a heart attack gives you a different perspective on life."

"You must do whatever seems right for you," Kier said, his voice clipped. "And for your family."

"Once you have kids," Quentin said apologetically, "you have to think about them. The job has been the first priority in my life, I always thought a good income for the family was essential, but as Jill says, it's more important that the kids have a father. And with another baby on the way..."

"Surely it's not a good time to throw in your job and your salary. I don't want to lose you, Quentin. I hope we can work out some arrangement that will suit us both."

Quentin looked happier. "So do I. Jill hasn't been as well with this pregnancy. The doctor wanted to put her into hospital for bed rest, but she wouldn't hear of it.

Anyway, you didn't come here to discuss babies. What did you want?''

Kier contained his frustration while he went over the queries he'd come with.

All the way home, he was doing the same calculation over and over in his head. As soon as he got there he pulled out a calendar.

His head began to pound, and the figures in front of his eyes swam.

It was possible…just. Jill might have been right.

The more he looked at the dates the more sure he became. The only question was whether Shahna had known she was pregnant when she left so abruptly.

Jill had.

His first thought was to confront Shahna, demand reasons, explanations. Why had she never told him? Why lie to him when he offered to take responsibility for Samuel, why deny that the child was his?

Because she hadn't wanted him to have anything to do with Samuel's upbringing.

A black anger took hold of him. He'd more or less accused her once of finding a convenient stud or a sperm bank. Now he realized that she had, in fact. And he was it.

The thought brought a sour taste to his mouth. She'd thought him good enough to impregnate her, but not good enough to help raise his own child?

Had she planned it from the start of their affair? When had she stopped taking her pills? Had she ever taken them, or was that a lie too?

But surely it wouldn't take three years to conceive? Something had made her want a child, but she'd decided not to involve him.

Or…she'd lied about the pregnancy being planned. Had

she forgotten her pill, and decided that was her fault, her responsibility, so she would deal with it on her own?

That would be like Shahna, all right. Too proud to admit a mistake, too self-sufficient to ask him to share in the consequences. His fists clenched and his mouth tautened. If she were standing in front of him right now he didn't know if he'd kiss her or kill her.

He'd always thought that story about getting purposely pregnant in one night with a man she must have barely known was close to incredible. But she'd been very convincing. Putting him off the scent because he'd pressed her, coming too close to the truth. A truth that stunned and terrified and thrilled him, all at once.

Samuel was his child.

He was a father.

He thought about his own father, how they'd grown apart in the latter years of Alan Remington's too-short life, and he made a silent vow that he would never again be a stranger to his son.

Somehow he had to persuade Shahna to marry him.

He would damn well make it happen.

Chapter 11

The phone calls had stopped. A week went by, then two, and Shahna no longer expected to hear Kier's voice whenever she picked up the receiver.

It was only what she'd anticipated, she told herself, trying not to feel the crushing disappointment that threatened to overwhelm her. Kier had finally become absorbed back into his normal life, and in time he would forget her. As she must forget him.

It proved to be far from easy, and there were nights when she stared into the darkness, listened to the muted, sad cry of the morepork in the trees near the cottage, and was filled with a loneliness so deep it was almost unbearable.

She could have been with Kier now if she had accepted his proposal. Was she all kinds of fool for not doing so?

Sometimes she was tempted to pick up the telephone, no matter what time it was, and dial his number, which she still knew by heart.

And say what? *I changed my mind. I'll marry you and live wherever you please?*

If he had phoned once she might have blurted it out. But his chilling silence indicated he was no longer interested. Kier was a man who knew when to cut his losses. She'd had her chance and turned it down. He'd given her time and she had still said no. Shahna couldn't blame him for finally giving up.

Then one evening when the setting sun was painting the water with gold, she opened the door of the cottage at the sound of Timoti's boat, saw it approaching the jetty, and experienced a sense of déjà vu.

She couldn't at first make out the two figures in the cockpit, and while her heart leaped in foolish anticipation, her mind said, *No, it can't be.*

But it was.

She stood as if nailed to the doorstep when Kier leaped onto the jetty and waved Timoti off.

Then he turned and lifted his head, and time seemed to stand still for an instant as they looked at each other across the intervening space.

He climbed slowly up the slope, his bag slung on his shoulder, and pushed open the gate to come toward her.

She said, "What are you doing here?" Then remembered saying exactly the same words the last time he'd arrived like this.

Kier gave her a glittering smile and swung his bag to the ground. Without bothering to answer, he reached out and hauled her into his arms, making her lose her footing on the step, but it didn't matter because he was holding her securely, kissing her with an edge of violence that made her shudder against him and sent her heart into overdrive.

She felt him check, forcing himself to gentleness, tenderness, but his arms still imprisoned her as the kiss turned to a persuasive, sweet torment.

She breathed in his potent male scent and felt the beat of his heart against her breast, and her mouth opened for him like a rose to the kiss of the sun.

When he finally drew away a little, still holding her, his eyes smoldering with a dark flame, he said, "I needed that."

And so had she, Shahna admitted silently. "You'd better come in," she said, the mundane words breaking into the moment. "Will you stay tonight?"

His eyes blazed a question, and she met them squarely, almost defiantly. The words had almost spoken themselves, out of her loneliness and longing and the sweet shock of his presence, but she didn't want to take them back.

There was no point in being coy. She wanted him, fiercely, unequivocally, and the time was past for pretending otherwise. Even if it was only for tonight.

"Thanks," he said, his eyes cooling abruptly, disconcertingly, as if he'd switched on another part of his brain. He bent and retrieved his pack.

Perhaps he was unsure that she'd meant it. "There's just one thing," she said, stepping back to let him in. "I'm not on the Pill anymore."

He cast her another piercing glance. "I'll take care of it," he said. "Where shall I put this?" He hoisted the pack.

"My bedroom." She led the way down the narrow passageway.

Her room overlooked the harbor and was minimally furnished with a double bed, a freestanding wardrobe and a dressing table. He put down his pack on the floor and looked about, his attention caught by a wall-hanging over the bed, a construction of driftwood, beaten copper, shells and feathers, woven into natural twine.

"Did you do that?"

"Yes. Do you like it?" She was still in the doorway, feeling diffident now, nervous.

"Very much. What happened to the silk scarf?"

"It fell to pieces when I took it down," she said. At the time it had seemed symbolic of their fragile, insubstantial relationship, which wouldn't stand the rigors of daily life. "I burned it."

Kier walked toward her, rested his hand on the doorjamb beside her. He scanned her face with probing eyes. "Where's Samuel?"

As if he'd heard his name, Samuel came toddling out of his room clutching a large toy rabbit. He stopped abruptly on seeing the visitor.

He looked bigger than Kier remembered, and his hair had been cut. But the clear blue eyes were the same, surveying the newcomer suspiciously.

Kier stepped toward him and went down on his haunches before the boy. "Hi, Sam. Remember me? Kier?"

Samuel looked at his mother inquiringly, then, reassured, he returned his round-eyed gaze to Kier.

Kier picked up one of the rabbit's floppy ears. "Who's this? Bugs Bunny?"

Samuel said clearly, "Bunny."

"He's talking?" Kier turned his head, lifting his brows at Shahna.

"A few words," she confirmed.

"He's grown."

"They do that."

"He's forgotten me."

"He'll soon get to know you again. I mean, if…"

Kier straightened and turned to face her. He was feeling his way. Her invitation to stay had taken him by surprise. He'd expected defensiveness, wariness, a raising of the barriers. She had preempted his plans for a determined, carefully calculated seduction. He searched her face, looking for clues. "One-night stands don't interest me," he said. "I thought you knew that."

"I wasn't sure how long you could spare."

"As long as it takes," he returned grimly, and when her look turned inquiring he didn't elaborate.

Kier had hired a new deputy manager from a raft of highly qualified candidates and retained Quentin on salary with the title of executive advisor, given them phone numbers and packed his computer.

He'd told them he couldn't give them a date for his return, but the new deputy had hardly had time to warm his chair, and Jill would have Kier's hide if he left Quentin in charge again for any length of time. He was fully determined that he'd get what he wanted with the minimum of delay.

Samuel dropped the rabbit and trotted to his mother's side. She picked him up, and from this new perspective he inspected Kier's face. "Man," he finally pronounced.

"Kier," Shahna reminded him. And Kier said, "We had this conversation before." Only last time Samuel hadn't been able to pronounce the word properly. The changes in only a couple of months were astonishing.

Shahna had changed too. She was a shade thinner, and there was a brittle air about her. He hoped that was because she'd missed him. There had been a hint of recklessness in her invitation that he found both exciting and disturbing. When he looked at her she met his eyes boldly and color tinged her cheeks, so that his body stirred hotly in response.

Only Samuel's presence prevented him from grabbing her, tumbling her onto the nearest bed, taking her without finesse and satisfying the craving that had gnawed at him ever since he'd left her.

Instead he made himself coffee and a sandwich at Shahna's invitation while she bathed Samuel and dressed him in cotton pyjamas patterned with teddy bears.

"Say good-night to Kier," she instructed him, holding him in her arms.

"'nigh', Kee," Samuel said obediently over her shoulder. He waved a pudgy hand.

Kier went over to him, taking the tiny fingers in his. Obeying an irresistible impulse, he bent his head and kissed the soft baby curls. "Good night, Sam."

After they left the room he heard Samuel give a protesting whimper, and then Shahna's soothing voice. It was several minutes before she returned to the kitchen.

"Coffee?" Kier asked her, getting up to pour it.

"Thanks." She waited until he'd passed it to her before sitting down.

"Have you eaten?" he asked her.

"Yes, a while ago." She looked at the empty plate before him. "Did you have enough?"

"I'm not really hungry." He gave her a deliberately predatory smile. "Not for food."

Her answering smile mocked him. "Very original."

"Cat."

Shahna laughed, shook her head, and bent it over her coffee cup. Her hair had grown a little longer, and it fell across her cheek so that he couldn't see her expression.

Something about her manner bothered him. The new softness that had intrigued him was gone. She was more like the Shahna he had known in Sydney, with that shield of sophistication that deflected his attempts to penetrate it.

He wondered what she'd say if he told her he knew about her deception. But he needed to be sure of her before introducing that complication. She had made it very clear that she would never put the father of her child under an obligation, and he certainly didn't want her suspecting his motives.

Hiding his eyes under hooded lids, he watched her finish her coffee.

Aware of his scrutiny, and increasingly of the fragile thread of tension between them, Shahna took her time.

The light was dimming outside, dusk enfolding the cottage in a quiet embrace. Kier seemed disinclined to break the silence.

"How is Quentin?" she asked.

"He'll be fine. He has to take it easy, though. That's one reason it's taken so long to get back here. Jill would have killed me if I'd left him in charge too soon."

He didn't volunteer any reason why he'd stopped calling her, and she didn't ask.

Finally she put down her cup. "It's hot in here. I'd like to go outside for a while."

Kier pushed back his chair and stood up. "Good idea."

There was still some light. They left the door cracked ajar and walked to the gate. Kier unlatched it and she glanced back at the house but didn't protest. They wouldn't go far.

His arm came about her shoulders as they strolled down the slope to the jetty.

The water slapped and gurgled against the piles, and silver ripples betrayed a school of tiny, slender fish just breaking the surface.

Shahna stopped walking, and Kier stood behind her, his arms linked around her waist, strong but gentle.

She sighed, and leaned against him, letting go of doubts, fears, her suspicion that he was playing some deep game with her, that he'd deliberately withheld communication these last weeks precisely to catch her off guard and bring about her capitulation.

At this moment none of that mattered. He was here, he wanted her, and it was enough, for now.

His arms tightened around her, and she felt his breath on her temple, then his lips trailed down her cheek, until she turned her head to him and he found her mouth. One hand moved from her waist and closed about her breast, accelerating her heartbeat. The other hand slipped under the edge of her loose shirt and his warm fingers splayed on her skin. She felt his arousal at her back, and heat raced through her. Then he turned her, both hands on her back, one holding her firmly to him, the other roaming, unimpeded.

He lifted his mouth from hers, and she saw the brief gleam of his smile. "No bra?"

"Too hot," she mumbled. "Are you complaining?"

She felt his silent laughter. "Hell, no."

She hooked her arms around his neck, and his hands moved to her breasts, the thumbs teasing the already aroused centers as he watched her face for her reaction.

She couldn't hide it. Her lips parted, her breath quickening, and her head dropped back, eyelids lowered. He bent to kiss her throat, his mouth trailing hotly over the taut curve.

Her hands went to his shirt, pulling open the buttons, pushing the fabric aside. She touched his skin, aware that her fingers trembled, ran them over the rise of his rib cage, felt the beating of his heart.

Kier hissed in a breath and almost roughly put her a little farther from him, yanking her shirt over her head and throwing it down on the worn boards of the jetty.

Then he was hauling her close again, skin to skin, her throbbing breasts crushed against the hard, warm wall of his naked chest. And he was kissing her with a fierce, wild hunger that something equally fierce within her leaped to meet.

It was a long, deep, devouring kiss, an acknowledgment of passion too long denied. A promise of consummation. When at last they drew apart, both of them knew they had passed the point of no return.

"Back to the house?" Kier enquired, his voice uneven.

"Yes. Samuel…"

He understood. She wouldn't lose herself to everything here, even though the cottage was within sight, less than twenty yards away.

They stumbled up the slope in the fading light, and Kier latched the gate behind them, then swung her into his arms and carried her the rest of the way, kicking the door shut behind them, not putting her down until they reached her bed.

Her window was open, the curtains stirring in a whisper of a breeze.

Kier opened his backpack and tossed a small packet onto the table by the bed. He shucked his shirt and the rest of his clothes before lying down beside Shahna, who had lain still and silent, one knee slightly drawn up, a hand behind her head while the other rested on her midriff. He knew she had been watching his silhouette against the window, and the knowledge intensified his arousal.

Forcing himself to keep the pace slow, he opened the snap fastener of her jeans and parted the waistband, dropping a kiss on her navel before sliding down the zip and caressing her intimately.

She sighed sharply when he touched her, and he removed the jeans with her ready cooperation, taking the scrap of silky fabric underneath with them. Her eyes were half-closed but brilliant in a shaft of moonlight, her mouth invitingly full, parted and waiting.

He intended to make her wait, although his body clamored for release.

He kissed her mouth and she turned to him, her hand on his flank, her thigh lifted over his, and he lost his mind, totally, flipped her onto her back and drove into her without preliminary, without finesse. He heard her cry out and hesitated, momentarily stabbed by fear that he'd hurt her. Then she wrapped her legs around him, drawing him even deeper, and relief gave way to triumph and then sheer physical sensation, beyond thought, beyond emotion.

Dimly he heard her sobbing cries as her body convulsed around him. Her breath was on his cheek, then in his mouth as he covered it again with his. She clung to him as if he were the only stable thing in her universe. And at last she was still, one graceful arm flung against the pillow, her hot face nestled on his shoulder.

He didn't want to let her go. Instead he turned, letting her rest on his body, the whole exquisite, light weight of her. His hands explored the enticing curves and contours, and she gave a tiny shudder, caught a breath, and tensed, then he felt the rhythmic contractions of her second climax.

He met it with a renewed surge of desire, and minutes later they both lay quiet and pleasantly lethargic, arms still locked around each other, his hand stroking her hair, her mouth dropping small kisses across his shoulder, at the base of his throat, on his chest.

"If you keep doing that," he said, "I'll never let you sleep."

"Who wants sleep?" she murmured, a smile in her voice.

He kissed the top of her head. In a minute he'd have to get up and...

The thought hit him like a sledgehammer to the head. The packet he'd so carefully left ready on the bedside table was still there, unopened. He hissed an expletive through his teeth, and Shahna lifted her head. "What?"

"Hell!" he said. How could he have forgotten? He had *never* done so before. "I didn't use the damned condom. I'm sorry, Shahna. I broke my promise."

She was silent for several seconds. Then she said, "It probably doesn't matter. Although...I do seem to conceive easily."

"Next time I'll make sure."

He would, he told himself. It wasn't fair to risk an unwanted pregnancy. Not to her nor any child.

But he couldn't help reflecting that it would give him a powerful lever to induce her to marry him. Maybe his subconscious had been at work when he forgot his promise.

Samuel's indignant cry woke Shahna to sunlight streaming in the window.

Immediately she was aware of not being alone in her bed. Kier lay on his back, his cheeks shadowed, an incipient smile on his lips. His bare chest rose and fell above the sheet that barely covered his hips.

But she didn't have time to admire him, stumbling out of bed and, remembering that she'd left her shirt lying on the jetty, hastily pulling on Kier's over her nakedness.

She was in the kitchen giving Samuel his breakfast

when Kier appeared in the doorway, freshly showered and naked from the waist up. His eyes kindled as his gaze lingered on her legs, then traveled upward to her face. "So that's what happened to my shirt," he said. "I must admit it looks better on you. What do you say, Sam?" He sauntered over and hooked an arm around her waist, looking down at the little boy.

Samuel looked from his mother to Kier and waved the spoon in his hand. "Mum-mum."

"Mine's still down there by the water," Shahna pointed out. "And whose fault is that?"

"At a guess," Kier drawled, "you're blaming me." He bent and kissed her, his lips lingering. "I'll go and fetch it." He caught Samuel's wondering eyes and grinned down at him. "It's a grown-up thing," he explained. "One day I'll tell you about birds and bees, and all that stuff."

Shahna couldn't help laughing, but her gaze followed him thoughtfully as he went out the door. One day? Wasn't he taking a lot for granted? A shiver of apprehension cooled her flesh.

She put three toast fingers in front of Samuel and went to the bathroom for a shower. The room was warm and steamy and smelled of soap and some faint, indefinable male scent.

She was heading for the bedroom, wrapped in a towel, when Kier appeared with her T-shirt in his hand. "You look delicious," he told her, and followed her. "How long will Samuel be occupied with his breakfast?" He dropped a kiss on her shoulder, the other hand stroking her arm.

"Not long." She evaded the caress. "Go away, I have to get dressed."

"Can't I watch?" He slanted her a provocative glance.

"No. Go and talk to Samuel." She held the towel to her as if expecting him to try tearing it from her.

"Too bad." He dropped the T-shirt on the bed and made for the door, turning as he reached it to say, "But hey—do me a favor and don't put on a bra."

Shahna jerked open a drawer and withdrew a pair of panties, then a matching, soft-cup, silky bra.

Buttoning a sleeveless shirt, and pulling on a simple short skirt, she told herself that the fact she'd let him into her bed didn't mean he could call all the shots. Her mind, and her body, were still her own.

When she went back to the kitchen Samuel had started to complain, and Kier was trying to find the mechanism to free him from the high chair.

"It's here." Shahna showed him and lifted the baby out, setting him down. He toddled to the still open door, and Kier made to go after him, but Shahna said, "He's all right."

Kier watched as Samuel halted, inspected the steps, then went down on all fours, turned himself around and negotiated the steps safely. "Smart kid."

"He learns fast. Do you want some breakfast?" She was already boiling the water for coffee. "If you'd let me know you were coming, I'd have bought some bacon. I can do a couple of fresh eggs for you."

Kier stood in the doorway watching Samuel while she fried the eggs and made toast. The child had found a large ball that he threw with great enthusiasm, hurrying after it and occasionally falling over his feet, but each time he picked himself up and went on with the game. Then he noticed a sheep on the other side of the fence and toddled over to talk to it, leaning against the wire mesh. The animal turned its head, nonchalantly chewing at a mouthful of grass, and apparently decided that so small a human was no threat.

A sweet scent lifted to him by the breeze made Kier look for its source. The plants in Shahna's new garden were thriving, green leaves almost covering the sawdust mulch, and flowers lifting their faces to the sun. A low picket edging divided the garden from the lawn. "Who fenced the garden?" he asked. "Does it keep Samuel away from the plants?"

"Ace helped me with it," she said. "And Samuel knows he isn't allowed to touch them. The fence helps to remind him." She slid two eggs onto a plate, and one onto another for herself. "It's ready."

When they had eaten, Shahna picked up the plates and carried them to the sink. Last night she'd tried not to think at all, but this morning questions crowded her mind. Questions she didn't dare to ask.

Kier said, "Do you have any plans for today?"

"Nothing special. I do have some work I want to finish, though."

"Care to go for a drive later? There's something I want to show you."

"What are you up to, Kier? Why are you here?"

"I thought that was obvious. I'm here because I can't keep away from you."

Samuel was laboriously climbing up the steps, a more difficult task than going down, entailing much huffing and puffing. She kept a watchful eye on him in case he tumbled.

Kier said softly, "You weren't exactly unwelcoming when I arrived."

"You took me by surprise." She looked back at him as Samuel reached the top step and triumphantly stood up, making for the settle that held his toys. Automatically Shahna left her chair to go and get some out for him. "I never expected you'd come back."

"You should know I don't give up that easily."

She had her back to him, placing several toys on the floor. Straightening, she faced Kier across the room. "Yes," she said, a slight, warning prickle traveling from the back of her neck down her spine. "You're used to getting your own way. But I have to think of Samuel."

Kier stood up. "Then think about giving him a father!" he said, startling her with his vehemence. "Doesn't he deserve that much?"

She stared at him in dumb astonishment. He looked angry, and she didn't know why he should be. "You?" she asked.

"Of course me!" His brows drew together. "Who the hell else?" Then he seemed to pull himself together, and in a milder tone, continued. "I asked you to marry me, remember?"

Her eyes went to Samuel, who was sitting on the floor, regarding them with wide eyes, interested but apparently unafraid.

A remembered bitterness rose in her throat, nearly choking her. Almost two years ago Kier had broken her heart with his carelessly voice opposition to the idea of children in his life. And now he was prepared to be a father to Samuel?

There was a sad irony in that. She couldn't suppress a surge of resentment.

Supposing he changed his mind again when having a child constantly underfoot became a day-to-day reality? For some reason he'd taken a liking to Samuel, but the novelty might wear off.

"Don't say anything now," Kier said finally, as the silence stretched. "I can wait."

He would lay siege, if she knew him at all. He would use every means at his command to persuade her. She said, "How long are you staying?"

"I told you, as long as it takes. Or until you ask me to go."

His eyes challenged her, daring her to do it, and to her own shame she couldn't quite bring herself to. "What about your business?" she said. "How long can they manage without you?"

"They can get hold of me if they need to. At the moment this is more important."

More important? The memory of last night was fresh in her mind, and her body still tingled with the aftermath. Maybe she was weak, and maybe she would regret it later, but she nodded a tight acquiescence and said, "What time do want to go out?"

"Whenever it suits you."

"Before lunch, then," she said. "Samuel still has an afternoon nap."

Chapter 12

Samuel gurgled with delighted anticipation as Shahna strapped him into his safety seat. He loved riding in the car.

Kier was holding the driver's door for her. It was silly to be touched by such a small thing, she supposed, but it was nice.

When they crossed the cattle stop from the farm driveway to the road, Kier said, "Turn left."

She could have guessed that much. The road to the right passed another farm and then petered out at a piece of swampy ground that was a drawcard for hunters in the duck shooting season but deserted for the rest of the year.

Kier had a map on his knee that he consulted when they had passed through the village and reached a fork.

"Right here," he said, surprising her.

The road climbed, dipped and ran through a patch of trees and ferns that brushed the roof of the car, and Kier muttered, "It's probably easier by boat." He took out a piece of notepaper with handwriting on it, and as they reached a farm gate he said, "Here."

"Here?" She braked.

The gate was open. "Down there."

There was a rough tanker track to a milking complex and he directed her past it and through more trees, until they came out on a wide flat paddock, empty of stock, and looked down on the harbor.

"This is it," Kier said.

"This is what?"

He opened his door and reached into the back for Samuel, then put the boy down.

Samuel trotted over to the grass, enjoying the space. Shahna left the car, brushing her hair from her eyes as a cool breeze whipped it across her forehead. Samuel had stopped, looking back at them, nervous of going farther on his own.

Shahna walked to him and as he toddled ahead let Kier take her hand and lead her to where the paddock ended in a steep, bush-covered slope.

Her eyes hurting, she gazed out at water diamond-sprinkled by the sun, the blue-shadowed hills lying gently on the farther shore.

Kier's arm came about her shoulders. "What do you think?" he asked.

Samuel turned to him and raised his arms. Kier bent to lift him, perching him on his hip.

"It's a wonderful view."

"A good site for a house? It's not far from the village. Or the ferry."

"A...house?"

"Not as close to the water as your cottage, but wouldn't that be safer for Samuel? We could have our own boat, though. And a studio with a view, for you. And lots of light.''

''We...?'' Her voice was husky, and when he turned her to him her throat felt tight and her eyes sparkled with tears.

''Shahna? What's the matter?''

''Nothing. The sun's dazzling, that's all.''

Samuel straightened his legs and wriggled, and Kier obeyed the signal to put him down. He immediately took off again over the grass.

''Plenty of space for him to run around.''

She lifted her face to him. ''I'm...not sure what the point is. You're surely not thinking of moving over here?''

''That's exactly what I'm thinking.''

She had to lift wind-whipped hair from her eyes again to stare at him. ''You're joking!''

''I can set up my office and communicate electronically and by phone with Sydney, or anywhere else for that matter. I've been exploring the idea of bringing the head office to Auckland. With a helicopter pilot's license I could fly down there anytime.'' He looked about them. ''There's enough space here for a landing pad, and then some.''

''Commuting?'' It seemed a fantastic idea, unreal. ''It will cost...'' She hated to think what it would cost, besides the purchase of the land and building a house. ''Have you bought this place? How did you find it?''

''Timoti found it for me. I told him what I wanted and asked him to look around. He knows every place along the harbor.''

''It's for sale?''

''If you like it, the farmer can name his price—for a subdivision of this site, or the whole farm. Whatever he wants.''

"That's…pretty reckless, isn't it?"

"What's the point of having money if you can't buy happiness with it?"

Shahna swallowed. "Is that what you're trying to do? Buy happiness?"

"Your happiness," he said. "And Samuel's." He glanced at the child, who had found something of interest in the grass and sat down to investigate it.

Following his gaze, she said, "I'd better see what he's got there, before he eats it."

She hurried over and scooped him up. A purple wild mint blossom was clutched in his chubby fist, and she admired his trophy, discouraging him from tasting it.

Kier said, "Shahna?"

She supposed at this point she was expected to fall into his arms and agree to his proposal. He had just outlined a total change of his lifestyle that he was apparently seriously prepared to undertake, all because she had refused to leave the Hokianga. What more could she ask?

But falling into his arms while Samuel had his around her neck wasn't possible anyway.

As if echoing the question in her mind, he said, "What more do I need to do to convince you?"

The inexplicable tears that had threatened when she looked out at the harbor prickled again behind her eyes.

She'd sensed a difference in Kier ever since he'd stepped off Timoti's boat this time. An air of almost angry determination, as if he would allow nothing to prevent him from getting what he wanted. She'd seen the determination before, but the anger was new, and with it an occasional disconcerting hint of ruthlessness that troubled her.

Surely if he was prepared to go to such lengths, his feelings ran deeper than she had ever suspected. Yet he

had never spoken the words that would reassure her.
"You could say you love me," she said, without even
meaning to voice the thought. It had come from her subconscious.

His expression was complicated, for a fleeting moment
almost antagonistic. Then he laughed. "All right," he
said, regarding her from disturbingly hooded, glittering
eyes. "I love you. How could you doubt it?"

Curiously, the flatly spoken avowal only increased her
nagging sense that something was wrong.

"You're supposed to reciprocate," he chided gently,
but with more than a hint of satire.

"What's the matter, Kier?" she asked him. "Something is bothering you."

He looked at her consideringly. "The only thing bothering me is that you haven't agreed to marry me." He
paused. "I've laid my heart at your feet, Shahna. If you
can't give me yours in return, I'll settle for the rest—your
company, your beautiful body—" he spared a long
glance, brooding and almost hungry, for Samuel "—your
son."

He looked back at her. She sensed he was still holding
something back, but she couldn't blame him for that.
Wasn't she doing the same? So much that she hadn't told
him, didn't know if she ever could. "Can you love him,"
she asked uncertainly, "as if he were your own?"

Something flared in his eyes, then died, leaving them
oddly lifeless. "I already do."

She was sure he was telling the truth. Common sense
told her there was no reason to maintain her opposition.
All her objections had been toppled, and her head was
telling her to go with her heart. Why hesitate?

There was only one thing to say. "I love you, Kier,"

she told him. "I'll marry you. But not because you've offered me a house."

He stared at her for a moment as though he thought he might not have heard right. Then he threw back his head and laughed. He looked at her with the laughter still in his eyes and said, "Why, then?"

"Because Samuel loves you already."

Samuel turned to look at him, and Kier held out his arms. The little boy shook his head and wriggled down, taking off again.

Kier laughed again, and Shahna couldn't help but join in.

He said, "Your cottage is a bit small for the three of us."

"I didn't say I didn't want you to build a house, just that it wasn't necessary to bribe me with it."

"I've never tried to bribe you, Shahna."

She bit her lip. "No, I'm sorry. It's just…is this what you really want?"

He took her face between his hands. "This is everything I want."

He kissed her and she returned the kiss, but then they both turned to see Samuel lurching back toward them.

Kier bent and held out his arms, letting the boy run into them, then swung him high, making him squeal with laughter, before settling him on his hip for the walk back to the car.

"I wish I'd known him earlier," Kier said as Shahna started the car. His look was penetrating.

"But you wouldn't have wanted to, would you?"

He frowned. "What do you mean by that?"

"Kier, you said quite clearly you had no time for children." She changed gear as they rattled over a cattle stop.

His eyes glazed and a frown appeared between his

brows as he made the effort to remember. He said slowly, "I was talking to Jill and Quentin while you were with someone else a few yards off. Then two other couples came along, and started swapping stories about being up all night with crying infants, and losing toddlers in supermarkets. And how when they were older there were music and dancing lessons and sports practices, and supervising teenage parties. They must have realized I was being left out of the conversation, and someone asked if I had children."

Shahna accelerated as the rough driveway gave way to the road. "And you said..."

"That obviously there was no room for children in my life. Or something like it. I couldn't imagine then that either of us was keen to disrupt our lives to that extent. And I hadn't even begun to think about having a family." He looked at her with a faint, bitter curve to his mouth, and said almost accusingly, "But you had."

She hadn't had any choice. And perhaps she had been wrong to deprive him of the chance to choose for himself. At the time she had thought she was doing the right thing—the only thing. "I just didn't think you'd be interested," she said.

For a moment she expected a biting reply. His expression when she glanced at him was cold, almost condemning. Then he seemed to make an effort to bring himself under control, forcing a smile. "It's no use going over old ground." He reached out a hand and took hers from the wheel, lifting it to his mouth. "You said you love me."

She said steadily, "I do."

He released her hand and sat still, watching her. Then he smiled. "Remember those words. You'll need them again in a few days' time."

"Days?" Her eyes widened, and she slid the car to a stop, turning to face him.

"We can get married over here three days after getting a license."

"You checked."

"Of course," he agreed calmly. "I don't see any reason to delay, do you? And I can't leave Quentin for too long. My time is limited."

"Three days is too short," she said. "Don't you know her wedding day is supposed to be the most important occasion of a woman's life?"

Kier looked confused, then almost embarrassed. "I'm sorry. It didn't occur to me you'd want all the trimmings, seeing you don't have a family."

"I don't want all the trimmings. But at least give me a chance to get used to the idea," Shahna hedged.

"Or to change your mind?" He looked at her searchingly.

Shahna hesitated. "I won't change my mind. I said yes and I meant it." He'd waited long enough for his answer, after all. "But are you sure this is what you really want?"

"You know I want you." He glanced again at the back seat, and his eyes softened. "And I want Samuel."

"And to disrupt your entire lifestyle?"

"It's a challenge. I like challenges."

Only this wasn't some tricky business maneuver, or a new daredevil sport. This was gambling his whole future. And hers. She too looked over at Samuel, obliviously asleep in his car seat. His future was tied up in this too. "I won't let you leave Samuel once he's accepted you as his father," she warned.

"I won't leave him," Kier promised, his hand capturing hers again and tightening. "Or you. Do I have to remind you, it wasn't me who left the first time?"

Shahna looked down at their joined hands, avoiding his eyes. "I know. I had my reasons."

Kier wished she'd tell him what they were. He knew, of course, but he'd hoped she'd let it out, and this seemed the right time. He curbed a savage desire to shake the truth out of her, and instead asked her, "How long do you need?"

She looked up. "Before the wedding? I don't know…a week or two."

"Ten days," he compromised. "Do you want it in a church?"

She shook her head, then said hopefully, "Alison might let us have her garden."

"Good idea. We'll ask her."

Samuel stirred and let out a peevish cry. Shahna turned the key in the ignition. "We'd better get back. He'll be hungry soon."

On the way they came to a country pub with wrought-iron tables on a terrace outside. "We could eat here," Kier suggested, "and have a drink to celebrate our engagement. Will they have anything suitable for Samuel?"

"I should think there'd be something." Shahna slowed and swung the car into the carpark.

She got a banana and an ice-cream sundae for Samuel, while she and Kier had a salad each. He ordered a bottle of sparkling wine and toasted her with his eyes, raising his glass. "Here's to our future," he said.

Samuel, attracted by the bubbles, stretched out an imperious hand from the high chair the waitress had provided, and demanded his share.

"It's not milk, mate," Kier said.

Samuel showed his displeasure, opening his mouth in an indignant howl.

Kier laughed. "You're spoiling our romantic moment."

"You wouldn't like it anyway," Shahna told the furious infant.

Relenting, Kier presented his untouched glass to Samuel, despite her laughing protest, and let the baby grab it with both hands, gulping down a sip.

Kier removed the glass immediately, and Samuel, suddenly quiet, sat with a stunned expression, then grimaced and sneezed, twice.

Shahna laughed again. "You shouldn't have done that!" she admonished Kier.

"It won't do him any harm, will it?" A hint of anxiety crossed his face.

"Just don't make a habit of it. At least you seem to have cured him of wanting it, for now." Samuel had returned to his ice cream and was digging his spoon into it. "But he can't always have what he wants, you know. You'll need to learn to say no."

Kier nodded. "You're a good mother," he said. "I hope I'll be as good a father."

"I wouldn't have agreed to marry you if I didn't think you would be."

"Thank you." He seemed quite serious. His glass touched hers and he drank some of his wine. "I appreciate your confidence."

When Shahna drove back through the farm gateway Kier said, "Shall we call in and tell them our news?"

She wondered if he was still afraid she might back out. The more people who knew about their engagement, the harder it would be to break it. "The men are probably out on the farm." But she drove up to the house and stopped in the driveway.

Alison came out onto the wide concrete terrace and

greeted Kier with a smile. "How nice to see you again, Kier!"

She insisted they come inside and bring Samuel. "Morrie's getting grumpy again. Ace and the new farmhand are doing some fencing, and his hand isn't up to it. Samuel will cheer him up."

Kier broke the news when they were all seated in the cool front room, where Morrie had discarded the farming magazine he was reading to take Samuel onto his lap.

"Oh, that's wonderful!" Alison jumped up and hugged Shahna while her husband held out his good hand to congratulate Kier. "I'm very happy for you both. Does this mean you'll be giving up the cottage, Shahna? We'll miss you."

"Not yet." Shahna exchanged a glance with Kier. "Is it okay with you if I stay in the cottage for a while?"

"Yes, of course. The lease hasn't nearly run out anyway. When are you thinking of getting married? And where?"

Alison was delighted with the prospect of having the wedding in her garden, although she immediately began worrying about errant weeds, and shrubs that needed pruning. "I'll have to work to make it look nice for the day."

"Leave that to me," Kier said firmly, even as Shahna was assuring her it always looked nice. "I'll do the work while you supervise."

"And you'll have the reception here, of course," Alison said.

"We weren't thinking of a reception," Shahna told her swiftly.

"Oh, but you must offer your guests something! I can get a couple of teenagers from the neighbors to help. And maybe Ginnie will come up for a day or two. It's time she visited again. You let me know how many people and we'll make the arrangements.''

"It's really going to be a very quiet affair," Shahna said, casting a glance at Kier's bemused expression.

After they got back to the car she said, "If you'd rather we went to the registry office and got it over and done without any fuss, we could quietly sneak off—"

"No," he said. "You deserve better than that. And Alison is in her element, haven't you noticed? She's really going to enjoy this."

When he took her in his arms that night, she went willingly, but was conscious of a restraint in him. She put it down to his being determined not to repeat the heedless passion of their previous encounter, and certainly this time he was meticulous about using protection.

He was equally meticulous about making sure she reached the heights of pleasure before he did. He had always been good at that, she recalled. Sometimes she had thought he was almost too clever at calculating her exact needs, meeting her moods and desires. He had applied himself to being an expert lover just as he did to any other skill he'd decided to master.

In the early days of their affair she had been afraid of his discovering how very limited her own experience was. Looking back, she laughed, remembering she had bought a book on sexual technique, hidden it in a drawer and referred to it occasionally in the hope of keeping Kier interested. She was sure his other girlfriends had been much more skilled and confident than she was.

Kier lifted his head from her breast, where he was doing delicious things with his tongue. "You're not supposed to laugh when I'm making love to you," he complained. "Don't you know it's bad for a man's ego?"

But they had sometimes laughed, and she laughed again now, feeling light and happy. "Your ego could do with some deflating," she retorted.

"Is that so? If my *ego* deflates, that might be disappointing for you."

She tugged at his hair in retaliation. It was thick and sleek between her fingers. "I know from experience it takes more than a small giggle to do *that!* Anyway, I was thinking of something else."

"I see." He leaned back on his elbow, regarding her with gleaming eyes from under his lids, and gently pinched her hip. "Is this what I can look forward to all my married life? A woman who loses no opportunity to put me down?"

"You still have time to reconsider."

"Not on your life. I know what I want. And if you back out now I may well drag you off by the hair into some cave in the bush. I'm sure there are a few around here."

He was much too civilized to do anything of the kind, she knew. But the underlying determination got through to her. She wondered what had made him so set on marrying her. He had shown no interest in matrimony when she'd known him before.

Perhaps neither of them had wanted to reveal their innermost heart to the other, so for a long time their relationship had remained static, because they wouldn't admit even to themselves that they were bound by anything but superficial compatibility and sexual need, unwilling to court the risk of anything more real and true.

Then she had changed, overnight. Not expecting Kier to be able to make the same transition. And yet, somewhere along the line, he had.

Maybe it was true that absence made the heart grow

fonder. He had told her he loved her, and surely she was being too imaginative in seeing some kind of hidden hazard behind the words.

Banishing the uncomfortable thought, she put a hand on his shoulder, and ran it down his chest. "I'll show you what you can look forward to for the rest of your married life," she offered. "If you're interested."

She peeked at him from under her lashes, and it was Kier's turn to laugh, even as his eyes kindled to flame, and he loomed over her. "Show me, then," he purred deeply. "I'm all yours."

She had thrown away the sex book after a couple of months. Discovering with Kier how her body responded to his touch, and what he liked her to do to him, was much more exciting and rewarding than studying pictures of people in what looked like impossible positions. She had soon learned that Kier seemed to instinctively know when she liked or disliked something, and she applied herself to developing the same kind of intuition about him.

And on the rare occasions when intuition failed, he encouraged her to talk. At first shy about that, she became increasingly able to tell him what she wanted, even as the need to do so decreased with their growing knowledge of each other.

He'd said on his last visit that he'd never had another lover like her. She had certainly never had one like him.

Intuition was with them tonight. Their lovemaking was leisurely and complete, and they hardly spoke until Kier rolled over on his side, still holding her tightly, and said quietly against her cheek, "This is what I've dreamed of ever since I left."

So had she. Too often for comfort. But now dreams were reality, and the reality was much better.

Outside, the morepork sounded as mournful as ever, but

now it had power to transfer its spurious melancholy to her. The wind stirred the trees, and the water rippled along the shore. A splash signaled a fish leaping in the moonlight. The scent of night stock in the garden under the window drifted into the room.

Kier padded to the bathroom, then returned and slipped under the covers, gathering her against him. His chest rose and fell beneath her cheek. His chin nuzzled her hair.

Shahna yawned, and curled against him, feeling like a cat enjoying the sun, although outside a sliver of moon rode bright and high against the black sky.

It blurred as she watched it, and she let her eyes close. There were questions in her mind, practicalities to be discussed, decisions to come to, but the major one had been made. However difficult it was going to be to adjust their different lives, she and Kier were committed to each other for life. And despite her misgivings, it felt utterly, blissfully right.

Chapter 13

They were married under a rose-covered archway in Alison's garden. Wearing a short cream chiffon dress that floated softly in a faint breeze, her hand tucked into Morrie's arm, Shahna walked steadily along a white shell path to Kier's side.

When he took her hand in his strong fingers her heart jumped. She hardly heard the celebrant's opening words until Samuel, held in Alison's arms, gave an excited little crow, and a ripple of laughter passed through the small crowd.

Kier turned his head and smiled at the boy, and in that moment Shahna knew she was doing the right thing. When it came time to make her responses she did so in a firm, clear voice, and then Kier slid a plain gold band onto her finger, and seconds later, to a round of quiet applause, he bent his head and kissed her.

As they turned for the short walk back to the house, Samuel wriggled from Alison's grasp and headed purposefully toward them. Kier swung him up and, holding the boy close, his other hand firmly clasping Shahna's, proceeded through the knot of well-wishers tossing rose petals in their path.

Despite the short notice, Quentin and Jill had flown over for the occasion. Jill hugged Shahna warmly and Quentin kissed her cheek. "Congratulations," he said to Kier. "We thought you'd never do it."

Kier, his arm around Shahna's waist now, laughed.

Ace slapped Kier on the back and boldly kissed Shahna on the mouth, giving Kier a cheeky grin and receiving a dry look in return. Ginnie, smart in cerise silk and high heels, said, "Watch out, little brother. Kier isn't the type to let you take liberties with his woman." She reached up to kiss Kier's cheek, then turned to do the same to Shahna. "Lucky girl," she murmured, but not so low that Kier couldn't hear. "If you hadn't had the sense to accept him I might have tried my luck myself." She cast a flirtatious look at Kier.

He smiled back her at her. "Thank you. And thanks for...everything."

"For what?" Shahna queried as the brother and sister moved away.

Kier gave her a bland look without answering, and then they were approached by one of the playgroup mothers, and the moment was lost.

They spent the night in the cottage while Samuel, at Alison's insistence, stayed at the farmhouse. "I promise if he's not happy I'll call you," she had assured Shahna. "But your wedding night should be spent alone with your husband."

Shahna's protest that Samuel normally slept all night fell on deaf ears, and finally she had given in.

Returning late in the afternoon, she changed out of the pretty cream dress into a brief white cropped top, with a flowered sarong tied about her waist, while Kier too put away his formal clothes and pulled on a T-shirt and cool cotton slacks.

"You made a beautiful bride," he told her, coming up behind her as she hung the dress in her wardrobe. He pulled her back against him and dropped a kiss on the curve between her neck and shoulder. "You smell of roses."

She'd carried a bouquet of them, and a few of the petals thrown by the guests had clung for a time to her hair and her dress.

She slipped out of his grasp. "What do you want to do until dinner?" Alison had provided a box of leftovers and a bottle of champagne, so there would be no need to cook.

Kier leaned against the wardrobe, his arms folded, a teasing grin on his mouth. "What do you think?"

She shook her head, laughing at him. "It's too early to go to bed."

Kier raised his brows. "That never bothered you before."

"I'm sure respectable married people don't make love in daylight," she said primly, her eyes dancing.

Kier gave a shout of laughter. "You have a lot to learn about marriage."

He advanced on her and she ran, a silly game that led them outside onto the lawn, ending with Kier catching her around the waist and swinging her off her feet, his arms around her while she laughed up into his face.

"Kiss me, wife," he ordered.

"I didn't promise to obey you," she reminded him, but she kissed him anyway, and he kissed her back, to her infinite satisfaction.

When their mouths parted, she said a little breathlessly, "Let's walk."

Kier made a small grimace but said, "If you like."

She was tempted to give in and go back into the cottage, but some part of her wanted to make the most of this day in every way, to spin out the anticipation as long as possible. They had made love many times before, yet in a strange way the exchanging of vows made it different, something to be approached more seriously now that they had made a solemn commitment. Tonight would not be like all the other times.

They strolled along the shore, arms around each other, stopping now and then to exchange kisses, seldom talking.

They went farther than usual, unencumbered by Samuel's presence. Part of her missed him, while another part reveled, a little guiltily, in being alone for once with Kier.

When they came back night was falling, the hills across the harbor disappearing into the gathering dark. They stood on the jetty watching the last faint glow of sunset fade and the first stars appear in the sky. Shahna lifted her hair from her nape with both hands, then stretched her arms above her head. She caught Kier's eyes on her, and smiled. "It's hot," she said.

He nodded, and looked at the water. "We could cool off with a swim."

They had swum sometimes, not often together. There was always Samuel to think of, to look after. But not tonight. She looked down at the rippling wavelets washing around the wooden piles. "Okay." Her fingers loosened the knot of her sarong and she let it drop to the wooden boards, revealing the briefest of undergarments, and slipped the canvas shoes from her feet.

Kier remained still, watching her. "Coming?" she

taunted him, slanting a challenging smile at him, and dived into the cool depths.

Within seconds he joined her, and stroked to her side. While she still wore her cropped top and the minuscule gesture to modesty, he was naked.

They played in the water, splashing and chasing each other, and occasionally snatching kisses, sometimes letting their lips cling together until they sank under the surface and came up spluttering and laughing.

When they climbed out it was fully dark. Shahna shivered and crossed her arms over the soaked and clinging white top, and Kier said, "Are you cold?"

"Not really." She bent over to squeeze water from her hair, her body forming a graceful bow, and when she straightened Kier was there, pulling her into his arms.

She met his kiss eagerly, their bodies straining together, slick and cool.

His hands pushed up the wet top and she raised her arms and let him haul it off. Then his arms were around her again and heat rose through her entire being as he lifted her and put his mouth to her breast.

She clung to his shoulders, her head thrown back, and let out a soft, gasping cry. And when he lowered her onto her discarded sarong, she didn't feel the hardness of the weathered wood under the thin material. Only Kier's warm body and magical, roving hands, and his mouth, weaving an erotic spell over her so that everything else in the world receded and she felt only him, wanted only him, gave herself up completely to the moment and the pleasure she could give him.

And that he gave her, turning so he was the one lying on the unyielding surface, while she was cushioned by his body. He was allowing her the freedom to control the pace and move as she wished, and even tease him a little before her own urgent need took over and she was flying with him into another dimension, his hands on her breasts, hers bracing herself on the firm, damp flesh of his shoulders, her glazed eyes meeting the blaze of passion in his.

Then she collapsed against him, their mouths colliding in a long, deeply satisfying kiss, passion draining into something less frenetic but perhaps even more profound. She dropped her head against his shoulder and gave a long sigh. His hand touched her hair and parted the wet strands, and his lips nudged her temple.

It was a long time before she stirred, and muttered against his cheek, "We should move. You must be uncomfortable."

His arms tightened. "This is the most comfortable I've been for a long time."

Her small laugh tickled his cheek. "Very macho, but I find that hard to believe." She moved aside. "You're lying on my sarong."

Kier caught her to him for one more kiss, then reluctantly rose, handing her the strip of material.

She tied it at her breasts and picked up the rest of her clothes. Kier didn't bother to dress, and back at the cottage he said, "Can we go to bed now?"

"Aren't you hungry?"

"Mmm-hmm." He nuzzled her neck, and she laughed and let him lead her to the bedroom.

It was nearly midnight when they finally left the bed and went to the kitchen in search of food.

Kier opened the champagne and they devoured chicken wings and pastries, and pieces of the wedding cake that Alison had insisted on making for them.

Then Shahna remembered something. "And just what were you thanking Ginnie for?" she asked him, licking icing from her fingers.

His eyes glinted at her. "Do I detect a note of jealousy?" he asked hopefully.

"Do I have any reason to be jealous?" Shahna kept her voice light, but she remembered him looking at the other young woman in much the same way, while they sat at this very table and she had tried to ignore the sparks flying between them.

He smiled, looking so pleased with himself she wanted to hit him. "She told me you were in love with me," he said. "I was grateful for the confirmation."

"*Ginnie* told you? I never said anything to her!"

"Woman's intuition, I guess. She said you wanted to scratch her eyes out."

Shahna's cheeks warmed. "Is that *all* you were grateful for?" Ginnie had obviously been available for consolation if he wanted it.

"She was good for my wounded ego," he confessed, his eyes teasing. When hers flashed at him, he reached out a hand and captured her fingers in his. "Virginia and I are friends," he said. "Do you know how jealous I was of Ace when I first came?"

"Ace?" Shahna laughed. She had never given Ace a second thought, except as a pleasant, helpful neighbor.

"He's a good-looking guy."

"Yes." She took her hand away and picked up her glass, regarding him over the rim. "And he's been good to me."

"Meaning?" Kier gave her a straight look.

She shook her head. "Just that. There's never been anything sexual between us."

"He seems a normal red-blooded male."

She laughed. "He's had girlfriends. But I'm not one of them." Ace might have been mildly interested at one stage, but she had been careful not to send out any signals that could be misinterpreted, and their relationship had remained strictly platonic.

Kier refilled their glasses, and Shahna yawned. "This is crazy, I'll never get up in the morning."

Shahna had agreed to accompany him back to Australia after the wedding. "If I'm going to move my headquarters to a different country," he'd told her, "there's a lot of reorganizing involved, and I don't want to leave you and Sam while I do it."

He was making massive changes in his life to accommodate her. Spending a few weeks in the city was a small thing in comparison.

They had to start early to make the airport and catch the plane that would take them on the first leg of their journey.

"We'll cancel everything," Kier suggested, "and stay in bed making love all day."

"No, we won't. Alison will be bringing Samuel over at eight."

"That's another thing those people at the christening were saying," he remembered. "Kids interfere with your love life."

"Will you mind?"

He must have noticed the anxiety in her voice. "There will be compensations, won't there?"

"Oh, there are!" she assured him. The stresses of parenthood were more than balanced by the delights, the unexpected moments of pure joy when Samuel climbed into her lap for a cuddle or bestowed a slobbery kiss on her cheek, or when he shared with her the wonder of discovering a buttercup in the lawn or gleefully tried to catch a darting butterfly. "Kier..."

"Yes?"

He looked up, his eyes so brilliant and expectant that

she hesitated before saying, "I'm very grateful that you've accepted Samuel. It can't be easy for you."

His expression changed, going blank. "It isn't hard at all," he said, but there was a harsh note underlying the even voice. "And gratitude isn't necessary."

"Still…" she raised the last of her wine. "Thank you."

He tossed off what remained in his glass and rather forcefully replaced it on the table. There was a sharp crack and the fragile stem broke in two. The bowl rolled to the floor and smashed.

"Sorry," he said. "Must have put it down the wrong way."

"It's all right." She gave him a puzzled, slightly shaky smile. "You're supposed to toss it in the fireplace, aren't you?"

He didn't smile back, busying himself picking up the fragments of glass.

Shahna fetched a brush and pan and swept up what remained, then wrapped it all in newspaper.

Kier rinsed out the plates they'd used and put them on the counter to drain. "You'd better go to bed," he said. "Get some sleep."

"Aren't you coming?" She paused on her way out of the room.

"I might go for another swim," he said. "It's still pretty warm."

"At this hour?"

He said lightly, "If I come to bed with you, you may not get any sleep at all tonight."

She made a face at him, relieved at his tone. "Promises, promises," she mocked. "Even you don't have that much stamina."

"Don't count on it," he warned, sauntering toward the outer door. "I won't be long."

Lying in the tumbled bed, she heard him enter the water, and then more splashing as he powered through it, not playing about as they had earlier, but rhythmically, and she guessed at a fast crawl. How did he have the energy? She was tired out, herself. Her lids drooped.

It seemed a long time before she half woke, sleepily conscious of his heavy body depressing the mattress beside her. She turned, smelled salty water and the outdoors on him, and snuggled close, her hand groping for his.

He took it in a cool clasp, and she felt the touch of his lips on her palm. Then he placed it flat on his chest, where she could feel the beating of his heart, the rise and fall of his breathing, and she went back to sleep.

Samuel had a wonderful time on the aircraft, spoiled by the cabin staff, and after falling asleep for a while woke to take in all the sights and sounds of the airport arrival hall.

They took a taxi straight to Kier's apartment, and by the time they got there Samuel was sleeping again.

Shahna held him in her arms while Kier carried the luggage. It was odd walking into his home again. Kier switched on a light, and she stepped into a room that was familiar and yet not the same.

There was a new picture on one of the cream walls, and the wide, soft-cushioned couch where she and Kier had sometimes made heart-stopping, torrid love had been replaced by a buttoned cream leather corner suite, and a couple of low, wide matching armchairs.

"We'd better put him down," Kier said, glancing at Samuel's oblivious face.

She followed him to the spare room, thinking they would have to arrange some makeshift sleeping accommodation for Samuel on the bed there, but when Kier turned on the light she stopped in the doorway, blinking in astonishment.

The austere, sparsely furnished guest room she remembered had been transformed. Pale-blue paper patterned with fluffy white clouds and flying birds covered the walls. Bright-yellow stars sprinkled darker blue cotton curtains. A yellow bookcase in one corner held a few board books, a brand-new fluffy koala and a plastic toy truck, and a corner cupboard matched the bookcase. Above a sturdy white cot hung a mobile of colored hoops and brightly dressed clowns.

Clouds similar to those on the wallpaper livened the blue ceiling, and peeking out from behind one of them were two dimpled baby angels.

"Kier!" She stepped into the room. "When did you…?"

"I got Jill to do it. She said she had a great time." He looked about critically. "Has she done a good job?"

"She's done a fantastic job! But we'll only be here a short while." Kier had estimated a month or two to set the reorganization of his business in train. "I thought we'd just buy a cot and make do."

He reached up and flicked the mobile with a finger, setting the clowns spinning inside the plastic hoops. "As long as he's here, he needs a decent room."

She walked over and laid Samuel down as Kier quickly folded back the covers. "It's a lovely room." She looked around it again, then began removing Samuel's shoes and socks.

"Nothing but the best for my son," Kier said, looking down at Samuel's sleeping face, the dark lashes lying against plump, slightly flushed cheeks.

He lingered while she tucked Samuel in, and then they left the door ajar.

In the master bedroom Kier pushed aside some clothes and made room in the big built-in wardrobe for Shahna's things as she began to unpack.

"You didn't bring much," he observed when she'd finished. The rest of her case was filled with Samuel's stuff.

"I didn't have much suitable for wearing in the city," she said.

"You used to have plenty of nice clothes."

"I gave most of them to a charity shop. Well—" she shrugged, catching his stare "—I didn't have any further use for them and they were taking up room."

"You can have fun shopping for new things, then."

She couldn't help a stirring of interest, even as she despised herself for it. "Why? I'll have to get rid of them once we go back home."

"We're bound to have invitations," he said. "You'll need some pretty dresses. You can use my credit card."

"Thank you, but no."

Kier considered her. "Why not? You're my wife."

"I'll buy my own clothes."

"You don't make much from your jewelry, yet."

"It's enough," she said briefly. She had managed, with the help of her savings. But she hoped there would soon be an end to dipping into her reserves.

"If you're afraid I'll think you married me for my money," Kier said, "don't concern yourself. I know you didn't."

She laughed. "The thought hadn't crossed my mind." She looked at him curiously, a little militant. "Had it entered yours?"

"No." He looked taken aback at the idea. "Money never interested you, did it?"

"I like what it can buy as much as anyone. But I don't need lots of it."

"What do you need, Shahna?" He sounded suddenly intense.

She treated the question seriously, giving it thought. "Security for Samuel," she said. 'Not so much in terms of money or material things, but emotional security. A happy childhood."

"And for yourself?"

"Enough money to give him that. The chance to perfect my craft and make beautiful things that will last until long after I'm gone." She hesitated briefly. "A good marriage."

His eyes flickered. "I'll try to give you all that."

"I don't need to rely on you for everything, Kier."

"An independent woman."

"You're an independent man," she retorted. "Why should it be different for a woman?"

"Because you are the ones who have babies," he pointed out. "It's harder for you."

She couldn't argue with that. Didn't her own life prove the point? "I didn't *need* to marry you," she said. "I could have done quite well on my own. I was."

"Okay." He held up his hands in surrender. "But I want to make it easier for you. Is that so hard to accept?"

She shook her head. "I don't mean to be difficult. I guess I'm not used to being...cared for."

"Didn't I care for you before?" A line appeared between his brows.

"Yes," she admitted. She remembered telling Ginnie that he cared for the woman he was with. "But it was different then."

There had been a subtle shift in the quality of his caring, and she wasn't sure when it had come about. Before, it had been part of his self-image, she thought. Kier had a standard of conduct that he'd imposed on himself. He recognized that he had an obligation to repay his partners for the pleasure they gave him, both in and out of bed, and he derived a certain amount of personal satisfaction from doing so.

But there had always been in the back of her mind the knowledge that she was not the first consideration in his life. That if ever she made demands, created difficulties for him, he would have almost certainly removed her from his world with scarcely a backward glance. Oh, he would have had regrets, but they would have lasted only as long as it took to find another woman to replace her.

Now there would be no other women, and he seemed willing to make real, almost unimaginable sacrifices to be with her. She couldn't help but love him for that. And for his obvious and growing love for Samuel.

Kier was right about the invitations. He asked Jill to recommend a good baby-sitting service, and fortunately Samuel seldom complained about being left with some bright, capable person trained to keep him happy while his parents were out. Once or twice Shahna put her foot down. "We can't go, we've left Samuel too often lately."

And Kier, bowing to her judgment, shrugged. "Okay. We'll tell them, another time."

Some invitations included Samuel, and she got to know a couple of families with babies of a similar age he could play with. Kier introduced him proudly as "our son," and none of them asked questions, although Shahna knew that some were rapidly calculating dates.

Shahna was surprised at the number of people who remembered her with pleasure and wanted to know what she'd been doing with herself. She looked up a few old friends and enjoyed catching up with them.

Often she wore pieces of her own jewelry, and several

women expressed interest in them, asking where they could buy something similar.

"You could have a whole new market here," Kier told her one night as they prepared for bed. "I'll introduce you to Harry Thurman. He owns a chain of boutique jewelry shops—"

"I know his name." Shahna carefully hung one of the three "pretty dresses" she'd invested in. "They specialize in opals and Australian work. I'd love to sell some of my pieces to him, but my jewelry is...it comes out of New Zealand, it's grounded in the Hokianga." Then, embarrassed, she asked, "Does that sound precious?"

"It sounds," Kier said, "as though you have tunnel vision. And that isn't like you. One of the things that impressed me when we first met was the way you could think outside the square."

Maybe he was right. Although her best pieces were inspired by the Hokianga, she'd done good work in Auckland before moving north.

Next day she put Samuel into his stroller and visited the harborside at Circular Quay, dominated by the famous opera house with its soaring white arches.

On returning home she pulled out her sketchbook, rather shocked that she'd let so much time elapse without working. Almost six weeks already. Between socializing and looking after Samuel she'd more than adequately filled the time when Kier wasn't there.

She was busy drawing when Kier arrived home. He looked a little strained, the skin over his cheekbones drawn tight, and his eyes less lustrous than usual, but a spark entered them when she smiled at him.

"What are you doing?"

She showed him what she'd done, inspired by the blue, busy harbors, the architectural lines of the surrounding buildings, the ships docked at the wharves, and the gulls circling against the sky.

While he studied them she poured his favorite drink, then settled beside him. "What do you think?"

"They're different from what you've done before, but just as unique and interesting. I phoned Harry today, and he'd like to meet you. I thought we might invite him and his wife to dinner." Finishing his drink, he pulled her into his arms, letting out a sigh against her hair.

"Bad day?" she asked.

"There are a few problems. We'll have to stay on in Sydney for a bit longer than I expected. Will you mind?"

"Of course not, if you need to be here." Looking down at the drawing before her, she felt an itch in her fingers, a desire to make the drawing a reality. "I miss my studio, though."

Harry was enthusiastic about her designs. "I'd like to see the final products," he said, studying the latest ones. "I could find a space for you in one of my workrooms."

"I have a year-old baby," she demurred, but he waved that difficulty away as of small account. "We can arrange something."

His wife said, "I look after my daughter's wee girl three times a week while she's at work. She wouldn't trust anyone else. I've been thinking Marianne could do with some company. Why don't we introduce her to your little one, and we'll see how they get along."

She was a doting grandmother with a practical outlook, and after spending an afternoon with her and her granddaughter Shahna had few qualms about leaving Samuel in her care for some hours several times a week, although she couldn't quite stifle a vague feeling of guilt.

It was stimulating working alongside other craftspeople, and the up-to-date equipment in the large workroom was an added pleasure. Harry was delighted with her work and suggested she spend more time designing pieces for his craftspeople to make.

"I'm not sure about that," she told Kier later that night as they were having coffee after dinner. "I'm used to doing the whole thing myself."

He took a thoughtful sip of his drink. "It's difficult to let someone else take over what you've always done on your own."

She supposed that was what he'd been doing, letting go of the reins he'd held firmly in his own hands. "Am I being selfish?" she asked abruptly. "Moving to New Zealand is a huge upheaval for you."

"You want it for Samuel's sake," he said. "That's not selfish."

"It's asking a lot of you, though."

"Are you having second thoughts about going back to the Hokianga?"

"I miss it." She got up and went to the window, looking out at the city lights, hearing the hum of the traffic, so different from the darkness and quiet about the cottage. "And I still think it's a better place for children."

He came and stood behind her, his arms looping about her waist. "I'm moving things along as fast as I can."

"Are you?" She turned to search his face. Occasionally she suspected he was deliberately dragging his feet, hoping she would change her mind and give up returning to her spiritual home.

Time to tell him something she'd been withholding for days, uncertain how he would react. "Kier...I think I'm pregnant."

For a long moment he said nothing and didn't move at

all. Then his eyes blazed, glowed, and his hands tightened on her. "Do you mind?"

Shahna shook her head. "No. I'm...surprised, though I suppose I shouldn't be." She asked tentatively, "Are you pleased?"

His wide smile said it all. "I'm ecstatic!" He lifted her off her feet and planted a long kiss on her mouth. "A sister for Samuel," he said, letting her down.

"Or a brother." Her heart melted with love for him. "It...it won't make any difference to how you feel about him, will it?"

He stared at her, seeming angry. "Of course not."

"I'm sorry. It's just that...knowing he isn't your biological child..."

"For God's sake, Shahna!" he snapped, shifting his hands to her shoulders, gripping them. "Why do you insist on pretending Samuel isn't mine?"

Chapter 14

Shahna's eyes widened. Something cold and fearful slithered through her, and her heart began to hammer. "P-pretending? What do you mean?"

"I know the truth," Kier said. "And I'm sick of waiting for you to say it! Why won't you just *tell* me?"

"No..." Shahna whispered. A dangerous, dark abyss seemed to have opened at her feet. Horrified, she shook her head in desperate negation. "Oh, no!"

"Shahna...!" His hold tightened, his eyes narrowed under frowning brows.

She felt the warm blood desert her face, leaving it icy, clammy at the temples. Her voice trembled with shock. "I told you the truth, Kier. That first day when you saw him and thought..." She swallowed hard, feeling sick. "You didn't believe me?" she whispered.

Was this why he'd proposed in that odd, abrupt fashion so soon afterward, and why he'd kept pressuring her to marry him?

His anger had turned to controlled fury. "You were pregnant when you left me," he accused her, and she discovered she was chilled all over, shivering. "Weren't you?" His eyes lasered her.

"You're putting two and two together and—"

"Weren't you?" he insisted.

"All right, I was! But you've got it all wrong." She cried out in anguish. "Oh, *why didn't you believe me?*"

Something changed in his expression, a dawning, reluctant comprehension overshadowing his frustration and fury. "Are you telling me," he said, his voice suddenly deadly quiet, "that it wasn't my baby?"

"No!" She wrenched out of his hold, putting her hands momentarily to her face, turning her shoulder to him, unable to look at him. "I mean, yes. It was yours."

"Then—"

"But Samuel isn't!" Surely soon she'd wake and find this was unreal, a horrible dream.

"What the hell do you—"

She dropped her hands and whirled to face him, crying, with all the remembered pain and desolation that had overwhelmed her at the time, "I lost it!"

There was a long, tense silence. "Lost it?" Kier repeated, sounding dazed. "The way you 'lost' your parents?" He shook his head. "Samuel was born nine months after you left!"

"But not nine months after he was conceived! He was seven weeks premature."

Kier looked dumbstruck. "Seven weeks...?" he repeated. His eyes glazed. She could see him readjusting his knowledge, making the calculations.

She said, "If I'd been pregnant with him when I left, how could I possibly have known so soon?"

"Jill said…" He shook his head again, impatiently. "It doesn't matter. Is this true?"

"Why would I lie to you now?"

He ran a hand over his face, looking haggard. "No reason," he mumbled, and drew in a breath. "I suppose I *wanted* it to be possible. Enough to talk myself into it."

Shahna bit down hard on her trembling lip. "You could have asked for tests," she said, desolate at the enormity of his misconceptions, the implications of it. "Why didn't you, if you thought Samuel was yours?"

"I thought I knew. I was so sure of it, but I wanted you to tell me. And you wouldn't." He paused, and blinked like a man waking from sleep to a bleak, unfriendly day. "Couldn't," he amended.

"I'm sorry." Shahna felt tears prick at her eyes. "I miscarried," she explained, reliving her grief for the tiny human being who had never breathed, "almost as soon as I landed in New Zealand. I wondered if the plane journey…but the doctors said there was no predicting. Just bad luck, and maybe stress. They said I could try again as soon as I felt up to it. I was crying all the time, you see." Crying for her baby, and for the lover she'd left, and the whole sorry mess she'd made of things. "I suppose they thought if I'd wanted a baby that much…"

"Did you?"

She slanted him a swift glance. He looked stunned, and very grim. "I hadn't thought so, at first. When I began to suspect, I tried to pretend I was mistaken. I couldn't think of any reason…didn't remember slipping up with my pills, but in the end I had to find out. And once I knew, everything changed. I couldn't…just get rid of it."

"You didn't say anything to me. How far…?"

"Three months when I left. I was lucky, it hadn't begun

to show. Even you hadn't noticed. But if I stayed, I knew I'd have to tell you.''

"But you *didn't* tell me!''

"After hearing what you had to say about children, that day at the christening, I couldn't.''

"I had a right to know!'' He was pale, his eyes seeming sunken. "It wasn't your decision to make, on your own.''

"I know, and I knew you'd insist on doing your part, maybe even suggest we get married.'' She couldn't help a small shudder, making a quick frown appear between his brows. "Or you'd try to talk me into an abortion.''

"I wouldn't have done that,'' Kier contradicted her.

She flicked a glance at him. "Either way, we'd have quarreled, and I didn't want us to part in anger.''

"So you up and left without a word—acting on a throwaway remark overheard at a party!'' His angry skepticism showed.

"It only confirmed what I already knew. You'd never mentioned anything about children, and you were dead set on taking precautions.''

"For your sake as much as mine. More! It would make a whole lot more difference to your career than mine.''

Stubbornly she said, "All I knew was you'd said you definitely didn't want a family.''

So she'd burned her boats. Cast herself adrift on a dark sea.

"You didn't think of coming back afterward?''

"No.'' How could she, when that lay between them? "There was no way we could take up where we'd—*I'd*— left off. Nothing would ever be the same. My life had changed. And there was this great aching void inside me. I missed the baby, every moment. I never believed that something so tiny, a child I'd never seen…could have created so much…love. I was still grieving for him when I met…Samuel's father.''

Kier's chin jerked as if an invisible fist had connected with it. "Tell me about him."

Did he really want to know? She stared at him for a second or two.

She'd told him so much, he might as well know the rest. "He reminded me of you," she said, her voice dropping. "His looks, the way he held his head, at an almost arrogant angle, even his smile, sometimes. I think that's why…"

"Why you slept with him?" Kier asked harshly.

Her eyelids flickered. She looked down at her hands and deliberately loosened their tight clasp. "He worked in the firm where I got a job soon after coming out of hospital. The first day at lunchtime, when I was standing on the street, trying to persuade myself I had to eat, he asked me if I was well. I guess I still looked pretty shattered and a bit lost. He carried me off to a restaurant and bought me lunch, made sure I had something. Kindness is a great aphrodisiac," she added, with irony. "And I wasn't feeling strong enough to assert myself."

Kier's lips compressed. "And then he carried you off to his bed."

"Mine, actually. Not immediately." Her mouth curved momentarily, bitterly. "I said he was like you. A campaigner."

Kier's jaw looked tight, as if he was clamping his teeth together, and his eyes burned, but he said nothing.

"We met several times out of office hours. Casually, for a drink after work, then for a meal. He made me laugh. Sometimes for a little while I could forget…everything. And like you, he didn't probe when I avoided personal questions." She paused, and said reflectively, "I guess he didn't care."

Kier moved slightly, clenched a fist and shoved it into his pocket. "Go on."

She looked at him. "Do you remember the date when you and I first made love?" When he didn't answer she laughed, but it caught in her throat. "I do. I tried to forget, but the calendar was there, and it wouldn't let me. That night I worked late because I needed to occupy my mind, and he…he said he had stuff to catch up on. Anyway, we were the only two left in the office, and when I was packing up he came in and suggested we have a nightcap in a bar. It seemed a good idea. To put off the time when I had to be alone again."

Kier rocked on his heels, regarding her with half-closed lids over glittering eyes.

"I drank too much," Shahna said baldly. "Not enough to make me incapacitated, but more than I should have." Enough to cross the line of sobriety. "He saw me home, he was very…solicitous. I can't say it was his idea. He kissed me good-night. And I believe he would have gone home then, only I…didn't want him to leave."

"You *asked* him to sleep with you?"

Shahna flinched. "Not in words." She remembered only hazily lifting her arms to the shadowy man standing in her hallway, darkened because they hadn't switched on the light. Looking so much like Kier. Oh, she knew it wasn't him, she hadn't drunk so much that she was unable to distinguish them. But she could pretend… "I didn't want to be alone that night," she said simply. The loneliness, the overwhelming loneliness had been too much.

She did remember making a decision, then. Her brain miraculously clearing, she'd recalled looking at the calendar and knowing not only that it was a kind of anniversary, but, her body having quickly returned to normal after the miscarriage, she had reached the most fertile time of her cycle, confirmed by the symptoms she recognized. It had seemed such a waste, intensifying her grief for the baby she had lost.

"I wouldn't let him use anything," she said. He hadn't protested much, surprised but easily persuaded in the heat of the moment. She couldn't blame him for repudiating any responsibility, later.

"You said you *planned* to have Samuel," Kier reminded her.

"It was a conscious decision."

"Hardly a rational one!"

She didn't dispute that. It had been selfish and unwise, even dangerous. But that night it seemed right. "I guess I wasn't thinking straight."

"You took an enormous risk with a man you hardly knew!"

"I know." Never before and never again. "I had tests to make sure I hadn't picked up anything I could pass to the baby." It had been a huge relief to find they all came up negative.

"You told him you were pregnant?"

"Yes."

Kier's eyes were stormy. "He was better informed than I was."

Shahna bit her lip. "I was never more glad than when he said it was my problem, he wanted nothing to do with it." She gave a short laugh. "He also told me he was married."

Kier gave a short, sharp exclamation. "You didn't know?"

Her gaze was shocked. "Of course not! I would never have—"

"You were working together—"

"No one had mentioned it. Even if they suspected we were seeing each other, I guess the other staff thought it wasn't their business."

"How long did you stay there?"

"Not for long. It was awkward after that. And I had to

look at making a good home for my baby. I thought I'd
done rather well, taken charge of my life, found a new
career that allowed for Samuel's needs. And then you
came along and..."

And asked her to marry him.

He was gray-faced and haggard, and he closed his eyes
momentarily, lifting his head, his mouth a tight-drawn
line. When he looked at her again his eyes held pain. "I
thought he was mine. I was so sure..."

Oh, God, she thought. *What have I done?* Nausea rose
in her throat. "Excuse me!" she gasped, and raced to the
bathroom.

A few minutes later when she lifted her head from the
basin after rinsing the sour taste from her mouth, Kier
was standing in the doorway.

"Can I do anything?" he asked quietly.

"No." She took a facecloth and wet it with cold water,
wiped her face. "I'm all right now."

"You don't look all right. You'd better lie down."

She glimpsed herself in the mirror, deathly white and
dull-eyed. No wonder—her world had just shattered into
myriad, irretrievable pieces.

He insisted on holding her arm, helping her onto the
bed, taking off her shoes. "If you can sit up for a minute
I'll help you with your dress," he said. "You might as
well get into bed properly."

His touch was chillingly impersonal. Stripped to her
underwear, she said, "I'll manage now."

"Sure?"

He looked doubtful, and she said, "Yes."

Kier stood gazing down at her for seconds. "All right.
Will you promise to stay in bed? I'd like to go for a
walk."

She guessed he needed to think, or to work off some

residual anger. "I promise," she said. And as he walked to the door she said his name. "Kier?"

It was a moment before he turned, his face closed, remote. Frighteningly controlled.

"I never meant to deceive you. About Samuel."

He glanced upward as if searching for something to say. Then his eyes returned to her, somber and unreadable. "There's no going back now, is there?"

Then he was gone.

She lay staring at the darkened ceiling, not expecting to sleep. So it was something of a small shock to wake to daylight and the sound of Samuel burbling gently in the next room. And find Kier sleeping beside her.

She hadn't heard him come in.

Slipping out of the bed, she hurried to Samuel and picked him up, changed him and turned to carry him to the kitchen.

Kier stood in the doorway, naked to the waist, his hair still tousled and his cheeks shadowed with unshaven beard.

She started, her heart jumping, and he said, "Sorry, I didn't mean to give you a fright."

She clutched Samuel closer. "I thought you were asleep."

He stood watching them. "Are you all right?"

"Yes. I'll get myself some toast while I feed Samuel."

His gaze was concentrated on her face, ignoring Samuel even when the little boy said his name in a pleased tone. "Let me know if you need help," Kier said. "I'll have a quick shower and get dressed."

She watched him turn away, her heart sinking like a hard stone. Samuel bounced in her arms, making little morning noises, and she smiled at him through stiff lips.

"Okay," she said, trying to make her voice sound normal. "Breakfast coming up."

Samuel was in his high chair, messily spooning up cereal, and Shahna at the table forcing down a piece of dry toast when Kier appeared in the doorway, dressed for the office except for his jacket.

"Coffee's made," she said. "And bread's in the toaster."

He nodded and pushed down the toast, poured himself a coffee and sat opposite her. "How sure are you about being pregnant?" he asked.

"I'll get a test done, but I know the pattern now."

"I suppose so." His gaze turned to Samuel, broodingly.

"It isn't his fault," she said desperately.

"I know that!" His eyes returned to her, and she wondered if it was shock she saw in their depths. "You don't think I—"

The telephone shrilled, and he swore quietly, then got up to answer it. "Yes, Quentin," she heard him say. "Yes, of course. Good luck."

He put down the receiver. "Jill's gone into labor. Quentin won't be in today." He ran a hand over his hair, regarding Shahna with a slightly harassed air. "We're in the middle of a tricky negotiation and Quentin and I can't both miss today's meeting. Are you sure you're all right?"

"Perfectly." Physically, at least. As far she knew there was no reason for concern.

Samuel decided he'd had enough to eat and began pounding his spoon into the remaining cereal, spattering milk across the table and around his high chair. Shahna jumped up to take the spoon and plate from him over his objection. "No, Scamp," she said firmly. "Food is for eating, not playing with." She took a cloth and wiped his face and hands, then started cleaning the mess while he objected vigorously.

Kier finished his coffee and toast standing up, then headed for the bedroom. When he returned, wearing his jacket and with his hair neatly recombed, Shahna had pacified Samuel and he was still sitting in his high chair, trying to fit three plastic beakers inside each other while she cleared the table.

"I'm off," Kier said and bent to kiss her, lifting her chin with his hand. His eyes searched hers briefly, perhaps detecting the anxiety in them, and then his mouth was on her lips, in a kiss that was anything but perfunctory. So fierce it almost hurt.

He turned away from her and paused by the high chair.

Shahna held her breath. She couldn't see his face but his shoulders were tense. Then he reached out a hand and touched Samuel's hair.

The little boy looked up and smiled. Kier hesitated a moment longer, then bent and kissed the petal cheek.

Without looking at Shahna again, he strode out of the room. Moments later she heard the front door close.

He was too decent to suddenly repudiate Samuel. But it was all too obvious that he felt differently now. He would go through the motions, pretend nothing had changed, while she knew in her heart that everything had.

"Oh, Sam," she said, lifting him out of the chair and holding him close, more to comfort herself than him. "I'm so sorry. I thought I was doing the right thing."

But what she had done was trap Kier, herself and Samuel, and the new baby as well, in a situation she'd sworn never to accept.

Kier had been too clever for his own good. Why hadn't he told her he didn't believe her story about Samuel's conception? She could have produced proof if he'd asked, and that would have been the end of it. Instead he'd schemed and manipulated, and let her think he was in love with her.

Her heart momentarily stopped. Just like the first time he'd maneuvered her into his bed, he'd played her like a helpless fish on a line. Why hadn't she realized what he was up to?

He'd enlisted Ginnie's help, and Ginnie with her woman's intuition, heightened by her own undisguised interest in Kier, had told him Shahna loved him. From then on it must have been easy.

She recalled how he'd made her confess to loving him. And only when she'd challenged him, forced him into a corner, had he finally said, "I love you," with that disconcertingly cynical expression, and claimed to have laid his heart at her feet.

Lying. Because he'd convinced himself that Samuel was his son and had discovered he wanted to claim his child. It had taken him a very short time to figure out that Shahna wouldn't marry him only to give him his paternal rights.

Kier would do anything, say anything, to get what he wanted. Motivated by the ingrained, primeval desire to perpetuate himself, and to watch his son grow in his own likeness. A desire he hadn't even known he had.

Only Samuel wasn't his son, had none of his genes. And the knowledge would always be there, poisoning the relationship between them.

She was carrying his own child now. Unless she lost it, as she had the first...

That didn't bear thinking of. Already she was experiencing the same all-encompassing, protective love she'd felt for Samuel as soon as she knew he was present in her womb.

No matter how hard Kier tried to hide it, Samuel would sense that his love had been withdrawn. And how successfully could Kier conceal his feelings when he had his own child?

She popped Samuel into his stroller, spent a couple of hours aimlessly pretending to shop for things she didn't need, and came home with a pregnancy testing kit that confirmed what she already knew.

Ceaselessly in her mind the same question repeated itself over and over. What was she going to do?

It was the longest day of her life.

Kier's secretary phoned to tell Shahna he wouldn't be home for dinner. She wondered if he was deliberately staying away until after Samuel was asleep, so that he wouldn't have to take part in the bedtime ritual. He was probably thinking as furiously as she was. And she doubted he'd come up with any kind of solution. There was none, she thought despairingly.

When he arrived Shahna was sketching at the kitchen table, trying to concentrate.

She heard Kier enter, and a few minutes later he was standing in the kitchen doorway, but she didn't look up.

"Busy?" he queried.

"A new design." She put down the dark-green pencil she'd been using and sat back to examine the sketch, still not looking at him.

Kier strolled across and looked over her shoulder. "The Hokianga again."

"Yes." She'd recalled how the harbor looked in a storm, pewter-gray and foamy, with rain hiding the hills and spurting into the water, the wind whipping the trees back and forth, making a world of confusion and turmoil.

The picture matched her mood and she was trying to translate it to beaten pewter and polished jade. "I've been thinking…maybe Samuel and I should go home."

She thought he stopped breathing for an instant. When he spoke his voice was quiet and very even. "Why?"

"I don't like leaving him while I work. And it's taking longer than you expected to tie up things here."

"Do you really think this is a good time to be flying? Did you get that test?"

"Yes. It's positive."

The silence stretched. He said, "You don't seem exactly thrilled."

"Well, it's no surprise."

"I don't want you going back to that isolated cottage alone," he said decisively.

"I'll be all right."

"No. You already lost one baby—"

"You're not giving me orders, are you, Kier?" She looked at him at last, shocked to see that his cheeks were gaunt, his eyes bloodshot.

"What are you running from this time?" he asked.

"I'm not running—"

"That place is your bolthole, your refuge. You were afraid to leave it, and now you want to scurry back to it. Why?" he reiterated. "Does the thought of another baby frighten you?"

Everything frightened her…most of all the prospect of their future, and what she might unwittingly have done to Samuel. "I do my best work there."

"You've done some fine work for Harry. He told me he can scarcely keep up with the demand. You'd do a lot better here."

"That's what you hope, isn't it?" she challenged. "That I'll give up the idea of going back and settle here instead?"

He looked incredulous. "For God's sake, Shahna! I've been moving heaven and earth to get this change through. And at the same time trying to make sure Quentin isn't overworked, breaking in a new manager, and juggling a dozen projects already in progress. I promised I'd do this, and I will. All I need is a bit more time. Did you really think I'd double-cross you like that?"

Ashamed, she shook her head wearily. All this seemed irrelevant now. "I don't know. You've always been so…"

"So what?" he demanded.

"So good at getting what you want," she said. "Somehow you manage to arrange everyone's lives to fit in with it."

"That's unfair," he said flatly. "But I'm not in the mood for an argument. I'm going to pour myself a stiff drink and go to bed."

Shahna sat staring at the design until it blurred before her eyes. Kier was right, she had been unfair. She should have trusted his word.

Everything was going wrong, just when they should be at their happiest, with a new baby on the way.

But she always came back to the sickening, irrefutable fact: he had married her under a misapprehension. Whoever was to blame—himself, Shahna, fate—nothing could change that.

She got up, feeling stiff like an old woman, and went to find him.

Samuel's door was ajar. The room was in darkness, but she could see the shadowy outline of Kier's figure, standing over the cot. He didn't move, and she knew he hadn't noticed her presence. His hands rested on the cot sides; she could see the rise of his knuckles in the light from the passageway, as if he were clutching hard at the wood.

Chapter 15

Shahna quickly banished a spasm of primeval, instinctive fear. Kier wouldn't harm Samuel. He would never hurt a helpless child.

What was he thinking, standing there in the dark?

She watched him a little longer, then quietly moved away, feeling she was intruding.

Coming into their bedroom, he seemed surprised to see her already there, but otherwise his expression gave her no clue to his feelings. He asked her if she'd finished with the bathroom and vanished in there himself.

When he came out she was in bed, watching him warily as he switched off the light and came to join her. He lay back on the pillows, an arm propping his head, and closed his eyes.

She knew he wasn't asleep, but it was a long time before he moved. And then it was to turn and gather her into his arms.

His mouth found hers in a fierce, almost desperate kiss, and his hands were impatient, tugging at her gown.

He made love to her with heat and excitement but curiously little joy, ruthless in his passion, pausing only once to ask, "Will this do the baby any harm?"

Shahna shook her head. "No." And he didn't wait any more, for once taking his pleasure first, but she was not far behind. Despite her troubled mind, her body, always attuned to his, took over and for a few seconds she forgot everything except the ecstasy he could give her. That he had never failed to give her.

Unusually, he fell asleep immediately, seemingly exhausted.

As soon as she heard Samuel stir in the morning she crept out of the bedroom and closed the door, guessing that Kier desperately needed sleep.

Samuel played happily in the sitting room while she put some washing through the machine in the laundry corner off the kitchen and cleared up their breakfast, peeking at him now and then. She and Kier had childproofed the apartment as far as possible and Samuel enjoyed having the run of it, but he still liked to know they weren't too far away.

The machine filled and began swishing the clothes back and forth, and Shahna checked on Samuel, who was climbing onto one of the big, buttoned cream leather armchairs, a board book clutched in one hand.

She smiled. Lately he had taken to imitating her and Kier while they sat reading a book or the paper, sitting importantly in a chair and solemnly turning pages.

It wouldn't last long; soon he'd probably be toddling in, demanding some attention from her. Meantime she picked up her sketchbook and pencils that she'd left in the kitchen last night.

In the other room Samuel was quiet. Then he coughed, and her head lifted momentarily, but the cough wasn't repeated. She picked up a pencil.

She heard the sitting room door open, then Kier saying something explosive, and yelling, *"Shahna!"*

Dropping the pencil, she ran into the other room. Kier, wearing jeans and nothing else, was holding Samuel who was limp in his arms. "Call an ambulance!" he said, hardly glancing at Shahna. "He's not breathing."

She went cold even as she reached for Samuel, saying, "You call them. Give him to me." Because it was obvious Kier had no idea what to do.

Samuel's eyes were staring, his face was a frightening gray, going blue. He must have swallowed something. Why hadn't she checked when she heard that little cough?

Dimly she heard Kier barking their address into the phone. She sat down and peered into Samuel's throat but could see nothing. Carefully she hooked a finger into his throat, but whatever it was she couldn't feel it. Turning him over on her knee, his head dangling, she smartly thumped his back.

"They're on their way," Kier said, leaving the phone. His face was gray, too. Knowing they had only minutes, Shahna kept working on Samuel, trying not to let panic take over.

Kier squatted beside them. "Come on Sam," he urged, his hand on the baby's head. "Cough it up, *please!*" His eyes when he raised them to Shahna's were anguished. "Isn't there anything I can do?"

It seemed ages since he'd called the emergency number. "Hold him up by his feet," she urged, letting him take the boy as they stood up.

Again she thumped Samuel's back, and at last he coughed up a cream leather-covered button, took a wheezing breath and coughed again, vomited a little and burst into loud sobs. He had somehow pulled one of the buttons from the upholstery and eaten it.

"Thank God!" Kier said as Shahna gathered the baby into her arms. "Where's the bloody ambulance!"

Then they heard the siren and Shahna said, "Go and meet them. He'll need to be checked over anyway."

The medics were calm and competent and congratulated Shahna on her first aid before taking her and Samuel to the hospital while Kier followed in the car.

It was hours before Samuel was released, neither of them leaving his side until the doctors cleared him to go home.

They both hung over his cot minutes after tucking him in, anxiously watching for any signs of his ordeal until he was fast asleep, and when finally they returned to the sitting room, Kier looked at the leather suite with its buttoned upholstery and said with loathing, "This suite goes, tomorrow!"

He collapsed onto the sofa, his head in his hands, sawing several deep breaths into his lungs.

Shahna, still inwardly shaking and sick, herself, looked down at him. "It's all right," she said. "It's over."

Kier lifted his head and she saw with shock that his eyes were wet. He brushed the back of one hand across them. "I thought we were going to lose him," he said unsteadily. "Oh, God, Shahna. If it was anything like this for you when you lost our baby…"

She went down on her knees, taking his hands in hers. "It was bad," she said. "But losing Samuel would be even worse. Thank you, Kier."

"For what?" he said impatiently. "He's our son. Oh,

I know he's not flesh of my flesh, but I'm more his father than his biological father will ever be. I love him...*so much!*"

She couldn't doubt it now. "I was afraid you didn't," she said in a low voice, "after you found out he wasn't yours. You seemed so...withdrawn, I thought everything had changed."

Kier looked appalled. "That didn't change! Love can't disappear overnight. But I'd been so certain, and to discover I was wrong...it was a hell of a shock, a crashing disappointment. I *wanted* Samuel to be mine in every way, just as much as he was yours." He ran a hand over his hair, frowning. "It made me sick to my soul that he wasn't. In a way it was like today when I found him and he wasn't breathing—only this was ten times worse."

His hands tightened painfully on hers and she knew he didn't realize it. His eyes burned. "I needed a little time to come to terms with the reality, and get over it," he said. "I was...grieving. But nothing could stop me loving Sam! Just as nothing could stop me loving you. You're both a part of me, like two halves of my heart. Take that away and I'll die."

Shaken by the raw emotion in his voice, his eyes, Shahna said, "I thought, maybe it was Samuel you wanted most, with me just part of the deal."

He frowned. "Why would you think that?"

"When you said you loved me, you didn't seem...loving. You were angry."

"Because you wouldn't tell me that Samuel was mine. I kept waiting for it, couldn't understand why you were withholding that from me."

"I would never have married you if I'd guessed you believed he was yours."

"You think I don't know that? It's why I didn't dare

challenge your story right after Jill said you were pregnant before you left me. Then I put two and two together and made what I thought was four."

"Jill said…?" Shahna queried in bewilderment. "When?"

"After Quentin's heart attack, when I came racing back."

"But…" How did that make any sense? "That was long after you proposed to me!"

His brows rose. "Yes."

"So it wasn't just because you thought Samuel was yours?"

"I hardly even thought about Samuel, then!" he said, confirming her original thought at the time. "I'd only just met him. But I was willing to take on another man's child if I could have you."

"Oh, Kier!" She blinked away a rush of tears. "I've misjudged you so badly. I'm so sorry I've been such an idiot."

"Yes, you have." His hands were gentle as they drew her up and pulled her across his lap. He scowled. "I can't believe that a chance remark at a party sent you packing. It was an excuse. You grabbed the first one that presented itself."

"That's not true!" How could he think she'd wanted to leave him? She remembered all too vividly the torment of being caught between equally impossible choices.

He arched a skeptical eyebrow. "You ran out on me without even asking me to explain. Without according me the same rights you gave to that bastard who didn't want Samuel. It won't wash, Shahna," he said sternly. "Unless his reaction didn't matter to you, and mine did."

She opened her mouth to argue with that, then stopped. Maybe there was truth there. It hadn't mattered that

Samuel's father didn't want him—she'd known he had a right to be told but when he refused to acknowledge his child she'd felt nothing but relief.

With Kier much more had been at stake. She hadn't wanted to hear him repudiate their child, because that would have been unbearable, and even less she'd wanted an offer of marriage made under duress.

She said slowly, "My parents got married because of me. Every time they quarreled, my father accused my mother of trapping him. I knew somehow it was all my fault. And after he left and my mother disintegrated before my eyes, I felt that was all my fault too."

"You weren't to blame."

"I know…here." She touched her forehead. "But in my heart, that guilt and shame never went away. I'd die rather than have a child of mine feel like that."

His arms tightened around her, and he kissed her fiercely. "That won't happen to us. I could never reject Samuel, he's a part of you. And you're a part of myself. I think I've always loved you, but I only knew it when I saw you with Sam, and began to realize what I'd missed."

"You didn't want to say it, did you? That you loved me."

"I couldn't forgive you for not telling me Sam was mine…as I thought. And I was trying in my pathetic way to protect myself."

"Pathetic?" She smiled, giving him a skeptical look.

"I guess it goes back to when my mother was dying, there was nothing we could do, and I felt so helpless."

He'd been only fourteen, she recalled. "It must have been awful."

He didn't argue. "For months before her death, years after it, I walked around with this huge lump of pain and sadness inside that I couldn't share with anyone."

"Not even your father?"

He shook his head. "We didn't talk about it. And then he died too. I made up my mind never to give anyone the power to hurt me again. But you did it anyway, and it took me a long time to admit that, even longer to realize that love always entails the risk of pain. And that it's worth it."

"I didn't mean to hurt you. I had no idea it would go so deep."

He kissed her temple. "You said once we never talked enough. You were right. I want to know everything about you. Your thoughts, your feelings, your insecurities."

She gave him a long look. "If I show you mine, will you show me yours?"

He laughed, throwing back his head. "Deal."

They checked on Samuel one more time, reassuring themselves he was peacefully sleeping and breathing softly, regularly.

They kissed right there, and then Kier picked her up in his arms and carried her to their bedroom. They made love joyously, openly, giving all to each other, keeping nothing back.

Afterward Shahna lay contentedly in his arms, and came to a startling conclusion. "Kier?"

"Yes." He turned his head, his hand idly stroking her hip. His lips nuzzled her temple.

"You were right. I went to the Hokianga...not exactly to hide, but to try to recover some kind of security. Partly for Samuel, but really because I remembered being happy there when *I* was a child. An illusion that I wanted to recapture. I know I've left it very late, but if you don't want to move there..."

"I never want to end up having a heart attack before I'm forty, like Quentin. I won't wait until something like that happens to me before I make time to be with my family.''

"So…?"

"We'll build our retreat on the Hokianga," he said, "just as we planned. But if you could think about having another home nearer Auckland, I'd have a shorter commute. We could spend weekends and holidays in the north."

"It sounds…it sounds ideal," she decided. "We don't need to be right in the city, do we? We want room for the children to play. A garden…"

"And a studio. Anything you want."

"I want you. To be with you, wherever you are."

He kissed her lips, long and sweet. "I love you. Forever. I'll never leave you, never. Or Samuel. I couldn't live without you both."

"And the new baby?"

He put a hand on her still flat stomach, looking down. "I can't quite believe in it as yet. It seems unimaginable that I could love another child as much as I do Sam."

"Even though this one's really yours?"

"It can't be more really mine than Samuel is," he said. "I want to adopt him legally, then there'll be no question about that."

She put her arms about his neck and drew his head to hers. "I love you," she said. "I love you so much!"

"Do you believe in it now?" she asked him, months later, holding their new baby in her arms and smiling up at Kier and Samuel from her hospital bed.

Samuel, perched on Kier's hip, pointed. "Baby!"

"That's right." Kier sat down on the edge of the bed. "Your new brother."

"B'other," Samuel repeated, pleased. He eyed the sleeping baby with interest.

"Do you want to hold him?" Shahna asked Kier.

Samuel held out his arms. "Me."

"We'll both hold him," Kier told him, and held out his arms too. With Samuel securely cradled against his body, he supported the little boy's hold as Shahna transferred the tiny bundle.

Watching their absorbed faces as they studied the baby with identical expressions, Shahna thought no one would ever guess Kier wasn't Samuel's natural father. They looked so alike.

Then the baby yawned, making Samuel giggle delightedly, and opened his eyes. Kier smiled down at him, and Shahna saw love in his face. He looked up and caught her gaze. "The first time he looked at me," he said, "when they handed him to me in the birthing room, I fell in love. I was so afraid I wouldn't feel the same about this one as I do about Sam, but it's okay. Everything's all right."

"Yes," she said, as he leaned awkwardly across their two children to kiss her, their lips meeting in unspoken promise.

Everything was.

* * * * *

Don't miss Laurey Bright's
next romantic tale,

LIFE WITH RILEY,

coming next month to
Silhouette Romance (SR#1617).

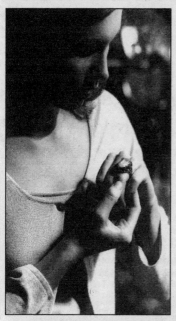

If you enjoyed what you just read,
then we've got an offer you can't resist!

Take 2 bestselling
love stories FREE!
Plus get a FREE surprise gift!